THE TROUBLE WITH CAKE

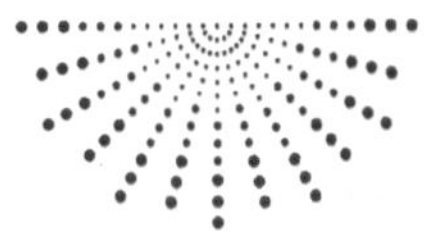

MAJELLA JAMES

First published in Great Britain in 2019 by
Lily Wychwold Books

First published in paperback in 2019

A CIP catalogue record for this title is available from the British Library.

ISBN-13: 978-1-9160105-0-5 (paperback edition)
ISBN-13: 978-1-9160105-1-2 (e-book edition)

Cover design by
The Dutch Guy

For Rick. My Heart.
Thank you for being there.

CHAPTER ONE

Plucking up the courage to follow Andrew may have been one of the hardest things I've ever had to do, but my concerns about the ethics of it sailed out of the window last Tuesday afternoon.

Perhaps I should take this up as an alternative occupation – private investigator or even secret agent – as I've managed to keep three cars in between us for the last five miles.

A quick glance at my speedometer tells me I'm travelling at a steady sixty miles per hour. Thank goodness Andrew is staying under the speed limit.

A white van comes up from nowhere at yet another roundabout and tries to squeeze into a tiny gap in front of me. 'Don't even think of cutting me up,' I screech.

Car number one indicates right, eek! Well, even if we get down to two cars, I still have the advantage as my car is the invisible type. The old, trusty, dark-blue Honda blends in well with other traffic while his shiny new, black Range Rover Sport stands out like a peacock in a flock of sparrows. He wouldn't risk or put it in danger, hence why he's trundling along. Following him is so easy.

'Nooo, spoke too soon,' I screech as Andrew pulls into a lay-by to answer a call no doubt. I can hardly stop behind him, so continue past, staring straight ahead, praying he hasn't spotted me.

The nearest turn off is a little way ahead, my sat nav tells me. Indicating left, I turn into it and quickly find it's a narrow farm lane. But with nowhere to turn around I have to keep going. It goes on and on, and anxiety creeps in when grass appears in the middle of the already narrow track. This can't lead to anywhere. How long can it be? Andrew is hardly going to hang around waiting for me to catch up.

My question is answered after a quarter of a mile when I finally reach a farmyard, and with a shrug and a smile I do a not-so-nifty seven-point turn while a man wearing blue overalls, his hand on a cow, stands watching me, scowling. But I'm too relieved to care. A quick wave and I bump my way back down to the end of the lane at hair-raising speed, hoping Andrew hasn't already passed. Luckily, he hasn't and I only have to wait two minutes before he appears, and I nip out onto the main road between two passing cars, one beeping loudly as I re-join the queue of traffic.

I wonder if he was phoning *her*. How can he do that when before leaving he spouted the usual words of love? 'Hate working Friday night and Saturdays,' he had added. 'Perhaps you should have arranged to go to your mum's. Maybe you should phone her.'

'Mum's in Italy, remember?' I had replied.

'Oh yeah, I forgot. Jo then.'

Jo's my best friend who lives in Chester some distance away. 'I might,' I had answered, knowing my only real intention was to find out exactly what he was up to.

Only two cars now separate me from Andrew's. He won't see me, he hasn't seen me for a while. I might as well be invisible. So, he's unlikely to suspect anything. He views me as being level-headed, which is true, I suppose, to most people anyway though perhaps not to my best friend Joanne or, okay, Mum. I imagine if someone were to describe me that wasn't Jo or Mum, they would say something like 'work-from-home book-keeper of small businesses: mobile hairdressers, plumbers, copywriters, dog clippers, and other such exceptional occupations.' However, my work is far from boring. Owing to my amazing entrepreneurship, my life is fabulous with lunches out with clients in three-star Michelin restaurants, candlelit dinners by the ocean, weekend parties in the country, and trips on a whim to Paris or New York, it's one big exhilarating social whirl.

Well, maybe not. What really happens is I sit in my attic office, totting up columns upon columns of figures that seldom tally, and with many a day wasted searching for that elusive missing amount – generally about two pounds fifty. My life is less *Sex and the City* and more crying into a disappointing salad at lunchtime while I search for the two pounds fifty.

Only a month ago I thought my life was perfect, presuming once the renovations of Holly Cottage were complete, everything was in place ready for the next phase in our lives. That was until I rather belatedly realised there was one thing not in place – Andrew. And without him there could be no next phase.

The extra time I gained with not having to work seven days a week to earn extra money, enabled my extra-sensory perception to kick in, and my suspicions rose. I began to notice little things. And the resultant clues led me to going with my gut feeling, well, 'kicked-in-the-gut' feeling. Reality surely can't be any worse than my imaginings, so following him is the next step. That's normal, surely, if your significant other is seeing someone else. Well, not normal if he's seeing someone else, but normal to want to know. And as there's no piggybank labelled 'in case of needing private detective, please break open' it's up to me to do those investigations myself.

But it could be worse (or better, depending on which way I look at it), I could still be stuck in my office and books in blissful ignorance instead of risking everything.

'Whoops, pay attention, Miranda.' Andrew has turned into a gateway, but a snail-like oil tanker is partially blocking my view. With a violent wrench of the wheel, I turn sharply, causing an alarming spin on the tyres and an ear-splitting screech. The stench of burnt rubber fills the car though a deft manoeuvre means I barely clip the edge of the kerb.

Andrew's car has disappeared around a bend, so I reduce my speed. I know where I am now as a large welcome sign indicates that this is the entrance to North-wood Park, a country-house hotel. Business must be going well for him. Funny, that's not what he's been telling me. Trivial clues such as this would be an insignif-icant nothing to anyone else, but to someone who believes they are being cheated on they mount up and come together to form a huge, substantial something.

With determination, I continue along the sweeping driveway edged by majestic beech trees. As I swing around the corner Andrew's car is turning into the parking area.

The hotel is a huge Georgian mansion house with extensive parkland. On any other day the gardener in me would be itching to explore the beautiful grounds and woodland. Instead, I find a space on the opposite side of the car park to where Andrew has turned in and observe him in my wing mirror. He steps out, and striding to the back of the car, lifts his suitcase from the boot and his suit from the passenger side. My stomach plummets. Earlier he told me he was staying in the usual budget hotel.

When he leaves the car, I turn to watch him. There's a jauntiness to his manner, a swagger almost, as he strolls towards the entrance.

As soon as he disappears through the doors, to kill time, I root out my phone and scroll through my social media.

•   •   •

The longest hour ever later, in disguise as warrants the occasion and befits any good detective, I glance in the mirror to check my red wig. I bought it for a fancy-dress party Jo and I went to a few years ago. Andrew hates red hair so shouldn't give me a second glance. Jo is a redhead and he hates her too though I'm sure the feeling is mutual.

Andrew sees Jo as scatty, shallow (he uses that word frequently when describing her), desperate, disorganised, pretentious (he likens her to a health-conscious film star), and a man hunter who never gets her man. Jo, in turn, sees Andrew as being spoilt and entitled, and far too good-looking for his own good. But would be wholly flattered by Andrew comparing her to a film star, health conscious or not.

Jo is, in fact, unlucky in love, too trusting, yes disorganised (but not in her work, she's good at that and successful, so it's only in a domesticated way), exasperating, and her many food intolerances cause a penchant for quinoa and pomegranate and not much else. However, she is sweet, loyal, and as close as it comes to having a sister.

I step out of the car and immediately feel self-conscious in my long, loose, black shirt and skinny, cut-off jeans, but then I didn't know Andrew was heading somewhere posh. I thought I'd be sitting in my car like a PI on stakeout, outside a restaurant or someone's home. I've even brought snacks and drinks. But here I'll be more exposed. Hopefully, my large sunglasses, trilby, and OTT makeup job should help disguise me.

A deep breath in, puffs out my chest and adds Amazonian woman to my slim physique, providing me with strength and courage before I breathe it back out and tread with purpose through the stone-flagged entrance. I emerge into a vast neoclassical reception hall buzzing with a hum of lively voices.

Ahead of me is a superb curving staircase. The vestiges of grandeur remaining in this hotel reflect a past filled with romance that is at odds with my own situation though it might well fit in with Andrew's right now, depending on his intentions.

People spill out of the bar opposite and into the foyer, mostly one party as they are similarly dressed: the women swanning around with their champagne, glammed up; the men in black-tie – one or two looking uncomfortable in their formal dress; but all in high spirits.

The bar would be my best bet to spot Andrew, so I head that way. My smooth-soled ballerina pumps slip and slide along the marble-tiled floor and I take baby steps, hoping I don't land on my bum. As I glide past a man in black tie, he pretends to whip an imaginary gun from under his jacket, using two hands to fire it at me. I can't honestly blame him for choosing me to shoot the way I'm dressed.

'Fancy-dress party,' he asks. 'Who are you going as?'

'Ziggy Stardust,' I reply, feigning laughter and hurry past, not wanting his shenanigans to draw attention to me.

My watch reads seven fifteen, so Andrew should be

down for drinks or dinner shortly. Unless he's going out to eat.

I squeeze through the crowd into the bar, keeping to the edges of the room. There's no sign of Andrew. I'm a proper Inspector Gadget, sneaking behind groups of people, peeping out and moving onto to the next lot. This is nerve-racking.

The far end of the bar seems the best choice, and I make my way over and perch on a stool with a reasonable view of the room and the restaurant entrance. Somewhat preoccupied, I hear a loud cough and realise the barman is waiting for my order.

'Large glass of Merlot, please,' I say, on auto. 'Wait! I meant—' It's too late, the barman has gone off to pour it. Well, it'll help me blend in better. I just won't drink it.

A group of men in business suits gather at the other end of the bar, but Andrew isn't among them. God, I'll feel such an idiot if it's only a business meeting or conference he's attending and I'm mistaken he has a rendezvous with another woman, but at least I'll know and can stop fretting. Recent events play out in my head like binge racing through an entire series of *The Good Wife*. A snowball's chance in hell – that's the odds of something not going on even if it's not tonight. And Friday evening is a strange time for a conference. Get real, Miranda.

When the voice of a woman with a Spanish accent comes from my right, I glance over and my heart bangs so much it's in danger of exploding. But it's not her – Leticia Fuentes. The chief suspect.

A middle-aged man in a suit who has been standing nearby alone, approaches me.

'Working tonight?'

'Sorry?'

'You know – *working*? He winks and gives me a knowing look.'

'Excuuse me! Harass me again, sleazebag, and I'm calling management,' I growl, horrified.

'Sorry, my mistake,' he says, and hurries away.

Oh my God, what am I doing here?

I'm considering leaving when a few moments later a waiter herds the suits off to another room, revealing Andrew, gorgeous as usual – tall, dark, suave, granite jawline, immaculate grooming – and my stomach leaps at the sight of him, causing me to almost fall off my stool. He's standing near the restaurant door. How odd it is studying him unobserved, like watching a different person – a stranger. His stylish grey suit must be new as I don't recognise it. My heart hammers in my chest.

Then it jumps out at me – no briefcase or laptop. Surely, he should have one if this is a business meeting, and he definitely told me he was going to an important meeting.

Someone is with him. I missed her at first as she was facing the restaurant. My whole body begins to shake as the woman looks up into Andrew's face adoringly and possessively places her hand on his arm. I have a powerful urge to run over, drag her off, and demand to know what's going on, but that would be stupid. Instead,

I grip the bar to keep myself on my stool, fighting the rising tide of panic.

The woman says something and laughs. Andrew leans down to answer her, puts his hand over hers, pats it and smiles. My mouth goes dry. Although it's not Leticia Fuentes, my instincts are only slightly askew. There is a woman and that's why I'm here. It hardly matters who she is.

This woman is older than Leticia, and Andrew for that matter, short, far smaller than my own five feet eight, is blonde and voluptuous, and squashed inside an emerald-green dress. Smart cream-coloured shoes with feet-killing heels and a matching designer clutch finish her ensemble. Her frequent smiles show ultra-white perfect teeth.

Spots begin to cross my line of vision. I'm hyperventilating. After taking deep breaths in and out with my hands cupped over my mouth, I'm relieved when a couple of minutes later my brain behaves normally again. It would be so embarrassing to have to ask for a brown paper bag to breathe into.

The woman stares into the restaurant again. They're waiting for someone to take them to a table. The waiter duly appears and directs them inside.

Rationalising was a waste of time as there's nothing rational about this situation. My instinct is to flee as I can't bear watching them together, but I did that last time I was in this position and I'm determined not to make the same mistake twice and spend another three years wondering.

I strengthen my resolve by drumming up my Amazonian woman again, grab my drink, and I'm off my stool and walking towards the restaurant before I have time to think too hard. The bar remains busy and a group of people are standing near the restaurant chatting and drinking. Too much distance away from the double doors forces me to take a gamble and step behind them.

Glass of Merlot in my hand and trying to act natural, I peer out, again regretting my choice of wig colour, but I can't take it off as Andrew might recognise me.

Andrew and the woman with the dazzling smile have stopped by a small table, and once she finds a place for her handbag, he deftly pulls out a chair for her. Using his considerable charm as usual. No one else is there on their table set for two.

A few minutes later my doubts disappear into the ether. This is no business meeting; a woman in love knows these things. The couple sit relaxed like good friends or even lovers and it's not helping that they're showing at least eight of the 'Ten Body Language Signs of Attraction' (according to the list in *Women in the Know* magazine, which I read yesterday).

Eventually it comes, I recognise the motion, number three on the list from what I remember. The one where he slides his hand forward and casually slips it over hers. Andrew withdraws it but I'm sure the woman has received the message. Her head bobs shyly and she smiles, her own hands straying onto his side of the table (number four I think).

My anxiety levels shoot up and my glass vibrates in

my hand, and I grab it with the other to steady it. How can he blatantly flirt like that? As if he's heard me, he looks directly my way. In a flash I've joined the group I was hiding behind, turning my head so he can't see my whole face, and laugh heartily in a deep voice even though I've no clue what they're discussing.

When I sneak a glance at Andrew, he has leaned back from the table, and my sigh of relief is so audible, the woman standing closest to me turns around and stares before catching sight of my wig under my hat and sneering. I stick my tongue out at her and she spins back. Phew, that was close.

Back at the table and a main course and a bottle of white wine later, apart from chatting, there's been a surplus of coy glances and fluttering of eyelashes and that's just on Andrew's part.

A quick glance at my glass of wine tell me I've drunk most of it and I wince in dismay. Shoot, how will I get home now? With this place being out in the countryside, the station can't be too handy. I'll have to work it out later. I take another sip.

My focus is back on Andrew as his hand slips into his inside pocket and he pulls out a roll of papers followed by a pen. The woman takes them from him, and after flicking through the pages, signs each one. I wasn't expecting that. Could this be a business meeting after all? Andrew folds and slips the documents back into his pocket, then leans in towards her, smiling.

It's just my luck that an elderly couple are threading their way between tables and blocking my line of vision. Willing them to get out of my way doesn't work as they insist on chatting to a waiter who is carrying an ice bucket containing what looks like a bottle of bubbly. The woman holds her hand out in the manner of someone showing an engagement ring and the waiter makes a great pretence of being interested.

Two minutes later, they at last stroll on and Andrew is leaning back in his chair again while the woman playfully bites her bottom lip and twiddles with a strand of hair. Whatever happened just now, I missed it, but a satisfied smile begins to spread across the woman's face, her teeth sparkling, obviating the need for a candle.

They both look at the waiter who moves forward and places the ice bucket on their table. He opens the champagne with a flourish and a pop and pours it before heading back my way. Andrew chinks glasses with the woman and moves to a chair next to her. Then he touches her fingers, this time more deliberately, and strokes them, overstepping the boundaries of the 'Ten Body Language Signs of Attraction'. Dread bubbles up inside me as he turns her hand over and kisses her palm. She smiles and her fingers brush his cheek. His hand moves to the back of her head and their lips lock onto each other.

I gasp and my stomach lurches, grief rushing up, threatening to choke me, a well of emotion hurting my throat and jaw. I can't watch. I turn on my heel and come to a dead stop as I collide with someone – someone huge – and my glass flies out of my hand and with a deafening noise crashes on to the tiled floor, the stem spinning into the centre of the room. The paltry amount of wine remaining, spreads out like a litre of blood. People stare at me and check their clothes for wine splatters.

'Oops. So sorry,' says the man even though it's my fault. 'Are you all right?' I'm desperate to get away. He seizes my arms, which are flailing in distress, but I keep my head bent, struggling to conceal my face. 'Let me fetch you another drink.'

I can't see his expression as my forehead is resting on his chest. Tears blind me and I want to sweep them away, so attempt to push past him. His hands are firm though on my upper arms and I'm unable to free myself. The barman arrives with a dustpan and brush accompanied by a woman in a suit holding a mop. I lift my head. The woman appraises me, and I can read in her eyes – lush.

My murmur of apologies to them are barely audible, and I whimper to the man, 'N-noo, it's fine, my fault. I'm not well. Need to go home.'

'You're not in any fit state to go anywhere.' It's a brook-no-argument kind of voice and he frees one of my arms. Defeated, I allow him to steer me towards the bar, away from the vicinity of the restaurant.

A stool is free and I plonk myself on it.

'A large brandy, please,' the giant says to the barman. He turns. 'Just a guess, but you've had a shock?'

Why protest? The grief is crushing me. My voice catches as I manage to croak, 'Yes, yes, a shock.' I want to go but don't know how to get to the station or how far it is. Removing my sun glasses, I dab at my eyes with a tissue from my pocket, a big blob of mascara coming off onto it. All my assumptions concerning Leticia were wrong, but there *is* someone else, someone with hair faker than my red wig. And those teeth! But that doesn't stop him from smooching with her as if I don't exist – don't love him.

The brandy arrives and the giant passes it to me. Snatching it up, I swallow it in one and slam the empty glass on the bar. The brandy burns my throat and I wheeze, 'Another,' I say to the astounded barman like a cowboy in a saloon. 'Er, please.'

'Steady now.' With a grimace, the giant holds out his hand. 'Jack Langford, by the way.'

I shake it. His grip is not limp, not crush-your-fingers hard either for the size of him, but firm, and that grabs my attention. Blinking away more tears I inspect him more closely.

Though not handsome like Andrew, his face is strong and his mouth sensual. His olive-green eyes show no emotion although there's evidence of a few crinkly laughter lines which help to soften them. Thick blond hair curls onto his collar and he has a short, trendy moustache and beard. He's well over six feet tall with herculean shoulders and the broadest chest I've ever seen on a man. Dressed in a black jacket, black t-shirt, and blue jeans, he has an easy, confident appearance. He's early forties, I guess, and looks vaguely familiar, but I can't place him.

Why am I thinking this? Why does it matter? I can't deny though that his sheer size is like a protective cloak.

That feeling doesn't remain as his gaze roams over me in return, his brow furrowing. Raising his eyebrows, he asks, 'And you are?'

'Oh, sorry, Miranda Stone,' I reply, blushing at my rudeness. My smile, I hope, is making me look saner although I doubt it if Jack Langford's expression is anything to go by.

'Private detective?'

'W-what?'

'The disguise. Not totally a fail, the hat works but your wig has slipped.' He lifts my hat and with a tug, straightens my red mop. 'Other clues – dark glasses even though we're inside and have had no sun since – Tuesday? Hiding behind people while spying on a particular, amorous couple…'

Cringing, I shake my head.

He steps back in mock fright, hands up in defence, eyebrows knitting. 'Stalker?'

I give a rueful grimace.

'Wife.'

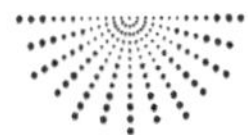

'Wife?' says Jack Langford, astounded. 'Sorry to hear that. Do you want to talk about it?'

I look up into the face of this man that came to my rescue and see only kindness and sincerity there. I nod.

'Take your time.'

I wonder where to start that won't have me opening the flood gates of tears, and my thoughts carry me back to earlier in the week.

Tuesday

Andrew's mobile phone calls to me from the bathroom window ledge, a beam of sunlight shining on the screen, lighting it up as though someone has teleported it there, surely a message from the cosmos. As I reach out for it, a text message briefly flashes up and the words 'darling' and 'love you' jump out. A woman's name 'Leticia' is the only other word I catch before the screen goes dark.

Heart thumping fast and hard, I whisk it up. Andrew is relaxing in the garden, taking advantage of the last of the summer sun, but will search for his phone the moment he misses it. He's possessive of it, obsessively so, and takes it everywhere: when he has a bath, to bed, whenever he leaves the room, and yes, even to the loo. Whenever he loses sight of it the panic registers in his body language. First, he'll pat his pockets, then he'll frantically glance around until his gaze finally lands on where he was sitting last, say the sofa, and when he spots it, the look of relief on his face is disturbingly obvious.

A spouse or partner doesn't feel the need to do that unless they have something to hide, and he doesn't want me anywhere near it. I mean, in the minute it takes him to go and pour a whiskey, it's hardly going to disappear into oblivion, like bloody Shergar, is it?

After a moment of hesitation, I click on the side button, but the blasted thing fails to come to life. I keep trying, every movement causing anguish and nausea to rise, blood rushing to my cheeks. Jabbing at the buttons again, my hands trembling, the screen finally lights up.

The pin is his year of birth, easy, but navigating this damn phone is like navigating the centre of London. The call log reveals nothing, mostly numbers, no names, so that's not helpful. Messaging apps then. On my phone I have the icons on three pages, simple, but not Andrew. Folders cover his home page, each with grouped items, and one is hiding the social media. There are loads. How many apps does one person need?

I glance behind me, half-expecting him to appear. Okay, I'm invading his privacy, but something is off the way he's been acting lately, and it's not just his love affair with this phone.

Locking the door first, I close the toilet seat and drop onto it, fingers fumbling as my investigations continue. The first folder I open has Currency, Bank, Calculator, How Rich You Look (what the hell?), Bitcoin Checker. *Bitcoin!*

Why does this phone make so much noise? Doesn't he silence the keyboard sounds? It's so annoying for other people on public transport or sitting quietly in a park. For God's sake, what's wrong with texting quietly?

The second folder has EasyJet, Trip Advisor, Uber, Maps, Weather, Trip to Mars (who is this man?). Stupid me – in my hurry I missed the folder has a name, 'Travel'. The first folder is called 'Moneybags'.

Finally, listed under 'Communication' – no fewer than seven messaging apps.

One by one I flick through them and at last find something from someone I've never heard of – a message from a Leticia Fuentes.

I miss u too, Andrew darling. Sorry for not being in touch. Cannot speak now. Phone when I get out from my work, 5.15 or so. Love you. Besos

Love you! And there's a heart emoji. There is no return text and no previous text. What's 'besos' mean? There are no messages on the other apps, but he must have contacted her somehow. Then it dawns on me, he might have used his laptop, email or office landline.

There's one more text from yesterday, time 5.20 pm with three heart emojis and a pair of lips.

Out from work now if u can talk, my love, my heart. Cannot wait. Phone me. Besos.

And lastly, the text that just came in with accompanying sad face and heart emoji.

Darling, why did u not answer my call today? U OK? You still at work? Love you. Besos. Leticia.

Nausea rises, and lifting the toilet seat lid, I fall to my knees and throw up.

A well of emotion pulsates through my body and I drag myself up wanting to cry, but knowing that can't happen as it will give me away. A glance in the mirror shows my flushed cheeks, eyes shiny with unshed tears, and a splash of cold water on my face does little to cool down the blush, especially as a vigorous rub with the towel puts it straight back again. After brushing my teeth, I decide it'll have to do as my ablutions are taking too long.

With gritted teeth, I march outside to the patio and into Andrew's view. 'You left this in the bathroom.' I hold out the phone. He's in shorts, reclining on a sun lounger, his trim, bronzed body more muscular than usual, six pack defined. He stretches out his long legs, and I scrutinise his handsome features as he glances up to see what I'm on about.

His sleepy brown eyes open wide with shock when his gaze alights on the phone in my hand – caught! The book falls to the ground and he fumbles for it, but can't find it. 'Oh, right. Yes.' With an anxious stare at the phone, he smiles with tight lips and tries to grab it from me. 'I wondered where that had got to.' My grip is strong and he has to tug it several times. One final tug and it lands on his stomach. He snatches it up. 'Er, thanks.'

My smile is sweet as I say, 'Is it your turn to cook or mine?' It's actually my turn.

He's relieved and jumps to his feet. 'Mine I believe. Glass of wine?'

Yes, a whole bottle, thanks, I think, but say, 'Yeah, sure.' *Bastard!*

He disappears into the kitchen, and quickly I move to the window and peer through. His thumbs tap the phone frantically, deleting stuff no doubt. Jo would think I'm mad not confronting him right away while the texts still exist as evidence, but I know Andrew all too well, and he would deny they were anything incriminating, the conversation soon escalating into a row with me not getting anywhere and him deleting the texts without showing me.

Retreating to the lounger he's vacated, I lie on it and feign sleep.

What do I do now? There has to be a next step, not like last time. Three years ago it might have been, but like elephant-brained women everywhere when it comes to their partners, I remember it like yesterday. It was back in Chester and Jo had turned up unexpectedly on my day off to drag me out to lunch at a new trendy place called The March Hare and Dormouse.

Jo drove as she had an appointment with a client at three and I could have a glass of wine, which under the circumstances, I discovered later, was just as well. There was a second reason in that Jo hated being a passenger believing she was the only safe driver on the road. Strange that while I always strive for perfection, I am the impatient and, at times, aggressive driver while Jo, the untidiest and most unpunctual person I have ever known, never drives one mile over the speed limit and prides herself in sticking to every letter of the Highway Code.

'Come on then, it's almost one o'clock,' I said as having negotiated the ring road (twice) and finding a parking spot at the second car park we tried, we ambled through Chester city centre as if we had all the time in the world.

Jo stopped to stare at a red flared coat in the window of an exclusive fashion shop, so exclusive there was only one rack of clothes and two assistants (she has a thing about coats in the way other people collect handbags or shoes).

I strolled on to drop a hint for her to hurry up and passed a wine bar, which was reasonably busy considering it was a Wednesday. Someone familiar had caught my eye, causing me to back up slowly. On the other side of the room sat Andrew, and sharing an alcove with him was a woman.

I stood there, open-mouthed, staring. She was about forty, dark-haired and voluptuous, and his arm was draped along the back of her seat. Like an idiot, I froze, mesmerised, and watched as he leaned in and kissed the tip of her nose. She laughed and he moved towards her again. He was going to kiss her on the lips. The shock dragged me kicking and screaming to my senses, and running to Jo, I grabbed her, hoping she hadn't noticed my humiliation, and pulled her behind me across the road to the other side

'What's the matter?' Jo asked, panting as we hurried through the restaurant door.

'Large…glass of wine…please.' The words were an effort, my wretchedness mounting with every sputtered word.

As soon as the waiter had pointed out our table, Jo headed to the bar while I threw myself down into a seat. No way could I wait for menus, then for the waiter to ask us about drinks, then another ten minutes until someone brought them.

When Jo returned, I was unable to speak, my head refusing to get around the fact that Andrew could risk me like that. Wasn't I good enough? Was she better? Was he having an affair? Surely, if so, he wouldn't conduct it in public.

After a few gulps of wine, I plucked up the courage to explain to Jo what I'd seen even though I was mortified and embarrassed. She wanted to go back and confront him, but I wouldn't let her; Andrew had humiliated me enough.

The following evening when I was still trying to figure out how to approach him, I found an email. He'd left his laptop open after he had gone to take a phone call and the word 'love' jumped out at the bottom of the email – *'love Claire'*. It was to his work email address. Angry, I confronted him.

'What's this? Who's Claire? The same woman you were cosying up to in the wine bar yesterday?'

'Yesterday?' His eyes widened with shock and his skin tinged pink.

'In that wine bar near Watergate Street. I was in town with Jo.' I looked sideways, trying to read more of the email, wishing I had before I'd blown my top.

'Don't be daft, Miranda. I don't know what you *think* you saw but you're imagining it. Claire's a friend. A client – who's a friend too.' He glanced to his right, which anyone who read *Women in the Know* magazine knew, meant he was lying. 'And you shouldn't be reading my emails. Ever heard of privacy?' He deleted the email and snapped the laptop lid closed.

'I'm not being daft. You left it open and why have you deleted it if it was so innocent? Who says, "love" at the end of a work email?'

'You do. That old guy, you know, the builder. The one you do the books for occasionally.'

'He's seventy for God's sake and Claire looked more than just a friend and she's young-ish.'

He folded his arms, his expression hardening. 'Here we go. Time of the month is it?' I felt like slapping him and my expression must have indicated as much as his voice softened. 'Didn't mean that. It's just that you're raising your voice and getting things out of proportion. Calm down, nothing's going on.'

'That's not what I saw. You had your arm around her…and were about to kiss her. You did kiss her nose.'

He threw out his hands and rolled his eyes. '*For God's sake*, now you're exaggerating. Can't I have an innocent lunch with clients now?' His arms shot back into a folded position. 'Jo put this into your head because she's jealous she can't find a man. Are we having dinner or what?'

And that was that. Yet the woman in the wine bar with whom he was intimate and the woman who used the word 'love' in the email were the same person and there was not a thing I could do.

'There's a dinner meeting in Bath, a conference of sorts, Friday, so I'll be gone overnight and until late Saturday evening,' Andrew says, and helps himself to salad. We're eating outside as he's forced me off the lounger to eat the carbonara he's cooked, but wasps buzzing around the food are enjoying it more than I am. 'Can't get out of it. The client's too important.'

Suspicion launches a second offensive. How could he do this so blithely, so calmly? But at least he doesn't suspect I've read his texts. 'I'll take time off and come with you, darling. No more working at weekends for me. Bath is lovely and I can take Friday off too, especially now I don't have to work such long hours.'

He swats away a wasp. 'Damn things. No, it'll bore you stiff. The meeting isn't in the centre of Bath, and you'd be sitting outside a concrete building in the car park for hours.'

I don't give in that easily. 'That's okay, we can leave early, and you can drop me off in town first – meet up later.'

'Er, no, that won't work either. I'll probably be taking colleagues with me and they wouldn't appreciate taking detours. We're not going until late afternoon anyway, and I'll be back Saturday evening after working most of the day, so hardly worth it. We can go next week – make a day of it.' He smiles but concentrates on spearing an olive.

'Then I'll take the train and meet—'

'Don't know about you but I'm eating this in the kitchen, these wasps are a bloody nuisance.' He picks up his plate and wine glass and disappears inside.

Outwitted. But it hasn't gone unnoticed that he would normally suggest we both go in and carry my plate for me. The bottle of wine remains on the table and I waste no time pouring another glass, abandoning all attempts to eat. The wasps are welcome to it.

Later, when he's in bed, I search his LinkedIn for Leticia Fuentes, my heart pounds, afraid of what I'll find. Scrolling through hundreds of contacts takes forever.

When I find her profile it reveals she is a photographer, and Spanish speaking. Worse still, she's based in Bath where he's going on Friday. My stomach does a somersault as panic surges; he's planning to meet her. In the texts she'd said sorry for not being in touch, which means they've been in touch before, and he's been to

Bath on business several times. She called him 'darling' and 'my love', and said, 'love you'. Her photo is probably years old though, or filters have been used because she's so young and pretty. Well, she is in the photography business.

This can't be happening, this is my husband, my love. There must be a rational explanation for the texts. Perhaps this woman takes photos for the business, was theatrical in her speech, and Bath is a coincidence.

How immediately my excuses on his behalf bubble up, no doubt as they would have done for him had I confronted him. Pigs fly off into the distance as rationality laughs hysterically at my naivety. 'You're such an idiot,' I say to myself, knowing I'll fret the whole weekend. But what can I do? What do other women do?

A web search throws up articles with comments for victims of cheating, all resulting in the same advice – leave. One on serial cheats discusses how some men and women thrive on having their cake and eating it, and how they bloody enjoy it too. Again, it advises victims to do a sprint to the door.

Despair surges. There was that Claire incident. The texts have brought that memory back when I'd almost let it go. Is having two women serial cheating? Whatever, my newfound intuition tells me, Leticia is a danger and our marriage is in danger. How much is another matter and will depend on what's going on.

A Facebook search, now that I know her location, soon reveals her business page. She's done work at Andrew's company. As I flick through her photos, pain grips my chest and my throat dries so much I can't swallow. She's not just pretty but stunning, there's something else oozing from her, a certain sexiness, the screaming of fertility that a curvaceous mid-twenties evokes. Pictures of them together loom up in my head and hurt like hell and an awful trembling takes over my body.

Is it 'cake' then with Andrew? The trouble with cake is that it's so bloody delicious – hard to refuse and even harder to put down once you start nibbling.

Wednesday

At seven o'clock Andrew gets up. He leaves for work, kissing my cheek first, to which I mumble a 'bye, darling' as if drowsy, not wanting to speak to him.

Sleep does get the better of me for a while and it's lunchtime before I grab a coffee and phone Jo, intending to ask her for advice. She's the nearest I have to a sister, being an only child, and with Mum away on holiday with her boyfriend, Steve, there's no one else right now. How much sympathy I'll get from Jo is impossible to determine as she's been a trifle smug about how happy she is with her new boyfriend after being single for two years, but still.

'Hi, Jo.' My voice sounds distraught as it breaks.

'Hi, you,' she says. 'What's up?'

She sounds concerned enough for me to venture, 'It's Andrew. He's, well…I found messages from a woman *again*. Love messages. And she's stunning.' I pause and can't help adding, 'Okay, a bit chubby, but yep, beautiful and she's at least ten years younger than I am.' My patheticness spews out across the radio waves and I sniff and wipe my eyes on my sleeve.

Jo thinks my words are pathetic too as she offers, 'Could it be innocent flirting? You know how he can flirt.'

'Don't think so.'

'Is he getting enough sex? Phil and I have loads of sex and he never flirts with anyone else – too occupied.'

Her lack of sympathy has chased away my remaining tears. 'You've been together three months. Yes, of course he gets enough sex and, anyway, even if he didn't, he should talk to me and not go out looking for extra.'

'Yes,' she answers, ignoring me, 'but is the sex exciting enough? Quality and quantity?'

The drawer in my dresser full of sexy underwear proves quality. 'Well, yes, save jumping off the wardrobe naked it's still pretty exciting.' I pause. 'Perhaps not five times a day, like you and Phil, or a week, well maybe three times a week…most of the time, but good, yes.' My brows knit.

'Are you nagging him about picking up his socks and all that? You're such a clean freak. Takes the joy out of a relationship, domestic stuff.'

What is it that if your husband cheats it must somehow be *your* fault in the eyes of others when he is just a cheating arsehole? 'No, I did not! And I pick his socks up without complaint.'

'And his undies?'

'Jo—'

She laughs. 'Sorry, Randa, that was a poor attempt at making light of the situation. You sounded close to the edge. Anger is better, isn't it? What you should do is re-evaluate your own life, it revolves too much around his, and it could turn out to be nothing and you've wasted your energy worrying. Take up a hobby, do a course, be adventurous, let up on work a bit, get out and about. Be you.'

I bite my tongue as she's right, but she's hypocritical too as she's doing exactly the same thing herself – her life revolving around all things Phil. I change the subject before I'm tempted to tell her as much.

Jo works in PR – marketing with frills – she's creative and a bit wacky and people love her mad ideas. She tells me about her new Alexander McQueen coat she's bought at a great discount (still costing a grand). In return, she listens patiently to my chat about the company I'm doing the books for. My bookkeeping job is boring even to me. Jo's right, I need to get out more, join groups, take a class, and concentrate on me for a while.

Gardening and housework occupy me for the rest of the afternoon. My idea of therapy involves mowing an already pristine lawn and tidying an already tidy house.

Two hours later I send a text to Mum to ask if we can chat. Not that I intend to tell her what's happened but hearing her voice I am sure will be comforting.

My phone rings. 'Everything all right?' Mum asks before I have time to greet her.

'Yes, fine.' I close one eye as I cringe at my words. 'All's well. How's the holiday going?'

She ignores me. 'You don't sound as if "all's well". You sound sad, upset. Have you and Andrew had a row?'

She's astute my mum. 'Nope, no row.' At least I'm telling the truth. 'A difficult account and didn't sleep well after counting columns of figures half the night. I'm tired, that's all.'

'Hmm, forget the account for today. Take some me time. Do something nice, a walk in the fresh air.'

An emphasis on 'account' indicates she doesn't believe me. But she's right, people go stir-crazy working from home and start hallucinating. Promising her I'll do something nice at the weekend, we chat about where she and Steve have travelled and what attractions they've visited until we eventually lose connection.

Mum is an interesting person, has plenty to talk about, is always on the go, and loves to travel, and she's sixty-three. All I seem to talk about is work, the cottage, and Andrew. Mum sensed there was something wrong even with her preoccupation with her travels and Steve. There is something wrong and I hate it.

By the time Andrew arrives home from work, I'm back on the offensive as soon as he's changed out of his suit and has come back down to the sitting room, plonked himself down on the sofa, and opened his laptop.

'So where will you be staying in Bath on Friday night,' I ask nonchalantly while pretending to busy myself tidying up – straightening one magazine over and over and moving a plant as if I were seeking a better place for it.

'Oh, the usual budget hotel.'

'Which one?' I shift the plant to the window ledge and step back to view it from a distance, at the same time, sneaking a glance at Andrew's expression reflecting back at me in the glass.

He's glaring at me, scowling. 'How the hell do I know? Stop with the third degree. Someone else in the company is booking it and they'll tell me in due time.' He closes the laptop and shoots off upstairs without giving me any more details.

Does he always do this, be defensive, not telling me where he's staying? For the last few months he's certainly been cagey about it. And lately, he's been telling me not to contact him at work and yet he has no problem with Leticia Fuentes doing it.

What's happened to me? Jo's right. Why does my life revolve around his, grasping at, and being grateful for, the tiniest amount of attention he deigns to pay to me? Effectively, I've come to realise, the cake crumbs. Regardless of any other factors, my life must change. And how can I make changes and work on improvements to my life if I don't know whether Andrew is cheating or not? I need to become devious, find out the facts, and make decisions after that one way or another.

CHAPTER THREE

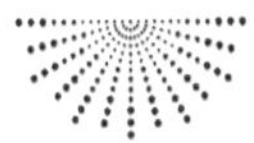

'Tough for you.' A man's voice jerks me back to the present – Jack Langford.

'Yes.' I take a huge gulp of my brandy.

'Take it easy now,' he says, sipping his own glass of sparkling water.

'My husband's conducting an affair right in front of me and you're asking me to take it easy?' I snap. I'm immediately contrite. 'Sorry, it's hardly your fault.' I relate the highlights of the past few days and even mention the Claire incident.

'What will you do now,' asks Jack after I've finished.

'Go home.' I take the last gulp of comforting fluid while calculating how much a taxi will cost. A fortune, no doubt, so it will have to be the train. Then there's the car to collect tomorrow. I can't stay over and risk running into Andrew and, indeed, even if they have a free room it will be too expensive. How Andrew can afford it, I don't know. Actually, how can we afford it? Spending money on that woman – dinner, champagne, and after… Freddie, his boss, can't possibly be funding such extravagance. He's a skinflint according to Andrew.

My imagination goes into overdrive.

He strips off by the huge four-poster bed in the honeymoon suite. He spins the blonde around, unzipping her dress and kissing her neck as he slips it down and over her hips, revealing her sexy black-lace underwear. His hands slide over her body and she turns, dazzling him with her brilliant white teeth. He picks her up and throws her on the bed, and dives on top of her. They roll around in a passionate clinch. I'm in the economy room below them (if there is such a thing in this hotel) *listening to every sound of pleasure, mumblings of love, and banging of the headboard.*

A groan escapes. 'Why am I sitting here…?' Not caring about Jack's reaction, I slam my glass down. My stool tips as I quickly slide off, and I feel the fleeting touch of Jack's hand on my arm as I march away. When I reach the restaurant, I go inside and frantically search the room, but Andrew and the woman have left, the waiter still clearing the dishes from the table they shared. The champagne, along with ice bucket, has also gone. Jack appears beside me.

I give a cry of anguish and vexation. 'They're not here.'

My imaginings are probably reality right now. I head to the entrance hall, shuffling swiftly over the polished floor, managing not to slip. Jack tags along rather than trying to prevent me again. It's like having a bodyguard and my resolve strengthens.

When they're not there, I turn to Jack, wanting to scream in frustration, wishing I could magic myself home to weep in peace. Through sniffs I say, 'I need a taxi to the station. Have to leave the car. Can't drive like this.'

'Come on,' Jack orders. 'Let's get you out of here. Stay right here while I'll pay the bill.'

Jack hurries to the bar while I, ignoring his request, head held high, slip and slide to the door. But when I get outside and run down the steps, it's quiet. No taxis, just a few people about. Tentatively, I turn to wait for Jack not knowing what to do next.

After a minute or two, he comes through the door and strolls towards where I'm standing in the road. When he catches up, his hand grips mine as a car approaches and he pulls me out of the way. Glancing back towards the hotel I regret not going to the reception desk to ask what room Andrew has booked. There's still time. I could say I'm his wife, show them ID, and stop him doing whatever it is he's doing with that woman. Still I hesitate, mulling over whether or not the woman is a client regardless of if he's having sex with her right now. Andrew's job could be at risk. He might even have left the hotel for all I know.

Jack frowns, following my gaze. 'Not wise. Anyway, the receptionist will phone first so that'll put him on his guard. If you want to risk a scene we can go back in, but I'd wait until you're er…calmer.'

He means sober. Glancing at him in disgust as if it

would never have crossed my mind to make a scene, I turn back.

Jack, still holding my hand, guides me through the car park. Andrew's car is in the same place, so he hasn't left the hotel and my hand flies to my mouth to stifle a cry at the implication of that.

Jack lets go of my hand and manoeuvres me around by the shoulders to face a van with 'Langford Gallery' printed on the side. 'Let's get you home. Where to?'

'The station if there's one nearby.'

'Really?' His voice is laden with incredulity. 'Where do you live?'

'It's too far… I don't expect…'

He raises his eyebrows in a better-not-challenge-me kind of way.

'Just outside Ashford.'

'Great, I pass it on the way home. I live in Netherbury.'

Thank bloody goodness. But still with stranger-danger warnings going through my head, I check again what's written on the van. 'Langford Gallery, High Street, Netherbury.' Could that be where I've seen him? I popped in there a couple of weeks ago looking for a suitable sculpture for the snug. A pretty, auburn-haired girl of perhaps sixteen was in charge there and was helpful. I mention it.

'That would be Sophie, my daughter,' he says, pride evident in his voice. With a glint in his eyes and a roguish grin, he adds, 'She's eighteen. Yeah, I know, I don't look old enough – but I never leave her on her own in the gallery for long.'

Hmm, defending his parenting skills. I sum it up. Jack Langford, friendly (ish) giant and five-star-hotel visitor, is an art dealer, sensible drinker, mind reader extraordinaire, has a sense of humour, and is father of Sophie a teenage daughter, all of which indicates a safe person, hopefully.

'Do you have any ID?'

He laughs. 'Do you? Only joking.' Rooting in a back pocket, he pulls out his wallet and removes his driving licence.

Sure enough, it reads Jack Langford. His picture is dreadful though. Just in case, I whip my phone from my handbag and snap a photo of him. He blinks, startled. I send it to Jo for security. *This is Jack Langford from Langford Gallery in Netherbury. He's giving me a lift home. Usual drill.'*

Jack opens the van door for me and helps me clamber in. As he drives away, I peek at his large capable-looking hands gripping the steering wheel. No wedding band, so not married.

Why am I thinking this? I have to glance away as he catches me staring at his jeans stretched tight across his strong muscular thighs. Gulping, I rummage in my handbag for a tissue, pull down the visor and examine myself in the mirror. What a fright I look. My eyebrows are bleeding and my waterproof mascara has run and is now waterproof again and won't rub off my skin. Even worse, my wig is skewed under my hat. A sharp tug and they're both off, revealing messy brown hair roughly tied in a bun. Jack is probably not surprised Andrew is playing around. This brings up images of smart Miss Blonde Husband-stealer again, a sob breaks free and I try to disguise it as a hiccup. Worse, I need the loo and am not sure I can make it home.

'Would you mind stopping on the way back? A pub will do. Erm, need to freshen up.'

'The next place we pass.'

I sniff again. 'Thanks.'

We travel for a few minutes in silence while I compose myself. When I finally let out a long sigh at the hopelessness of my plight, Jack clears his throat and says, 'Look, I haven't eaten. I was on my way to the hotel restaurant when you – when we met. Have you eaten? Hungry? You can freshen up then too.'

I'm not hungry. I'm too upset to eat. But he's good enough to take me home and, considering his size, I can't prevent this giant from eating, he must need fuel, and he did extricate me from a sticky spot. Anyway, I'm dying for the loo.

'Sorry I interrupted your meal, especially as it was so good of you to come to my aid. I might manage a cup of tea.'

'There's a decent little pub in Westbridge that serves great food until late, if that's suits you. We're almost at the turn off.'

I murmur agreement and he turns off the main road while I have another go at the mascara and wipe off the over-pencilled eyebrows, part of my disguise.

My hair's a mess, so I pull out several hairgrips and let my hair drop loose. A quick root in my bag reveals a small hairbrush. I drag it through the tangles and drape hair over my face as much as possible, for once glad it's so thick. My eyes have disappeared into two marshmallow puffs of unshed tears, but I manage to disguise my red nose with a dab of green eyeshadow. Apart from a piece of fringe sticking up – and I'm tempted to lick my hand to smooth it but after glancing at my companion decide against it – I'm looking half-decent by the time we arrive there.

It's dusk when we pull into the sheltered courtyard of the quaint inn called The Three Horseshoes, its walls crisscrossed with black painted timber, part of its low roof thatched. Window boxes filled with gold and purple pansies sit on ledges, while on a wall, baskets hang, dripping with trailing begonias and petunias. Beside a gate with a sign saying, 'beer garden' stands a huge but old, brightly painted blue cart, brimming with cheerful geraniums and busy Lizzies, the Indian summer keeping them well in bloom. There are several cars and it looks busy.

We park up and walk across the cobbled yard towards the entrance. A skinny, doll-like, attractive woman with glossy chestnut hair is on her way out of the door with a menu in her hand. She stops and her mouth opens in surprise. She must know Jack as I'm sure she mouths the word, 'great'.

'Jack! You should have told me you were coming.' She hurries over and, reaching up, plants a kiss on one of his cheeks.

Jack bends to receive it. 'Stephanie, this is—'

'Come in, come in. I'll find you a table. Chef is still here if you want to eat. I was about to change the menu but it can wait.' Stephanie bustles through the door. I'm the invisible woman obviously and I get a familiar feeling of being beneath someone's notice.

Inside, it's warm and welcoming. Most of the tables are occupied and there's an atmospheric buzz of voices. Stephanie shows us to a corner table. Automatically, I choose a chair so my back is to the wall and give an involuntary sniff as I sit.

Stephanie fixes her gaze on me. I've become visible again, and her raised eyebrows inform me my teary eyes and swollen nose remain significantly noticeable. 'And this is…?' she asks, but she's not addressing me.

'Miranda Stone,' Jack replies, and throws me an apologetic glance.

'Friend?' asks Stephanie, still staring at me. She's definitely snooping and doesn't care.

'We've just met as it happens. I'm giving Miranda a lift home from Bath. She found herself in somewhat of a pickle.'

Stephanie's cackle makes the Wicked Witch of the West sound like Snow White as she works out that 'in a pickle' means 'being pickled'.

'Rescuing women again, Jack.' She laughs and addresses me finally. 'Well, pleased to meet you, Miranda.' She excuses herself.

'Old friend?' I ask, curious now myself.

'Ex-wife,' he states. 'Sorry about that. I thought she no longer worked weekends. Obviously didn't take my advice to have time off.'

Brilliant, it's directly from one stressful situation into another. The so-called 'ex' seems friendly. As friendly as Cruella de Vil can get, I suppose.

He reads my mind. 'We've remained friends for Sophie's sake.' There's slight emphasis on 'friends'. 'But it can still be awkward at times.' He grimaces but there's laughter in his eyes.

Of course, Stephanie is the mother of the auburn-haired daughter who works in the gallery.

A young man brings the menus and I pretend to peruse mine to avoid small talk as my thoughts have drifted back to the hotel. Where is Andrew now and what is he doing? Abandoning the menu, I excuse myself before tripping off to the loo.

Once I get there, I phone him. The palpitations begin again and the phone tap-taps against my ear as I struggle to keep it still. The call goes straight to the answering machine. He must have it switched off, or he switched me off. I break out in a cold sweat but keep my voice normal while I leave a message saying I miss him and to phone me soon. I send him a text for good measure to remind him I exist, and hopefully make him think twice about taking things further with Miss Luminous Smile.

After visiting a cubicle, the mirror shows my clean-up job in the car didn't go as well as I'd hoped as my eyes are smudged and my fringe is still sticking up. So, after wiping under my eyes, I throw water on my fringe and try to flatten it. It doesn't work and I end up with something that resembles a cow's lick.

As I trundle back to the table, Stephanie is in deep conversation with Jack. I guess he's told her my sorry story because once I'm in hearing, she throws me a glance of sympathy and babbles with a false tone about how good business has been with the lovely summer.

He receives one of the looks I reserve for people who upset me. He ignores it and orders wild salmon and lemon risotto while I ask for soup and a glass of house red. Jack raises his eyebrows and pointedly requests an orange juice for himself. Judgemental much. Stephanie trots off, menus in hand.

'I'm not...I don't usually...' I stammer, knowing what he must be thinking. A drop of water drips from my fringe, dribbles along my nose and splashes onto the table. We both stare at it.

'Don't worry. Understandable in the circumstances, you're still reeling from the shock. Still you'll want to be strong tomorrow with so much to face.' He's frowning, thinks I'm a lush no doubt, another one of his rescued women. I haven't forgotten his ex's remark about him being some kind of superhero. How often does he do this? And what type of women are they? Just my luck that even my hero is a womaniser. Perhaps it's better not to ask as it might make me feel worse.

I examine my surroundings. Tasteful, traditional, and popular country pub-with-grub. Stephanie is rushing around, directing staff and clearing tables. It must be why she's so slim, bordering on skinny.

'So, what does Miranda Stone do in Ashford,' Jack asks me.

'Bookkeeping.' It sounds inconsequential so I add, 'I've had my own business now for three years since we – we moved from Chester as there was no job for me at that point. But now I prefer being my own boss, working from home.'

'Ah, you have children?'

'No.' I purse my lips.

There's an awkward silence.

'So, you came into my gallery.'

He's really grasping at straws now. 'Yes, a couple of weeks ago. I love your jewellery section and spotted a gorgeous, antique, emerald pendant you have there. Nice collection.' He doesn't react apart from a barely perceptible raising of an eyebrow and a wry smile. 'But jewellery wasn't what I was looking for, just a sculpture for my snug, art deco or something of a similar design, but I couldn't find one within my budget.' I pause. 'But the pendant was pretty.' His pretend grimace prompts me to ask, 'The jewellery section isn't yours, is it?'

He grins, bringing the attractive man in him back. 'Ha, no, but that's all right. A friend owns the building and sells the jewellery. He rents most of the place to me and only retains a small part as most of his business is online. However, today I sold a pair of large urns to the Northwood Park Hotel. Just as well as they were taking up precious space in the storeroom. A left over from my parents' business. They're not exactly the type of thing you have out in the gallery. More for outdoors.' He chuckles.

'It must be so interesting the art business.'

'Yes, it is. I not only get to indulge in my favourite hobby but earn a living from it too. If I spot a sculpture I could let you know. Contemporary okay?'

I nod. 'Yes, contemporary's fine as long as it has that art deco look.'

'If I come across one, I'll keep it for you. You'll have to let me know your details. Do you have a particular style in mind and approximate budget?'

'Tall, elegant, a naked female figure. I'd love bronze but that might be difficult within the budget of say five hundred pounds. A green patina would be nice, regardless.'

'I'll keep an eye out.' He smiles at me, a genuine twinkly, kind smile.

I smile back, wondering what I'm doing, mentioning buying a sculpture as if nothing has happened, but it was more to avoid awkward talk. We continue to chat, avoiding any mention of spouses, ex-spouses or children although Stephanie continually interrupts us with little mentions of Sophie and her studies. The message they have a daughter together is hard to miss. And that she started university in Bath a week ago studying the History of Art and Design and how proud they are as parents, makes me want to stick my fingers down my throat. But only because I'm jealous they have that rapport even though divorced.

Stephanie scurries away for the umpteenth time. 'Sophie takes after you with the art interest?' I say, deciding to be more civil in my thoughts.

'Yes—' He grimaces. 'Yes, she does, in the main.'

Aha, a clue that his marriage wasn't exactly a bed of roses then. I warm towards him more and we continue chatting with me telling him about the businesses I keep the books for, boring him to death, I'm sure, until we finish eating. I insist on paying but he refuses. After he says goodbye to Stephanie with another kiss, she turns and shakes my hand, giving me a look of sympathy because she senses I'm upset or for being with Jack. I'm not sure which.

We're both quiet the rest of the way to Ashford. I close my eyes and periodically open them to check my phone, always resulting in the same thing, no message from Andrew. There's still nothing as we arrive at the cottage.

'Holly Cottage. Sweet place.'

'It was called *Dunroamin* before we moved in and changed it,' I say. 'Now there's irony for you.'

Jack throws me a look of sympathy and jumps out of the van, coming around to open my door. I grab my bag and hat and slip out as gracefully as possible, which is challenging with being a touch squiffy after yet another glass of wine, and I'm bloody sure it's a ten-foot drop to the ground. He catches my arms for a moment as I land, to ensure I don't stumble.

The security light is on, providing illumination.

Jack leans against the van admiring the façade of my

pretty home and its pink roses winding around the doorframe.

'Wasn't always like this,' I say. 'We've been renovating for three years. It's finished now, hence the search for decorative art. My office is up there.' I point to the attic window.

'While we're on the subject of your office, my book-keeping skills are sadly lacking and my assistant got married and emigrated to Australia. Would you be able to take on my accounts? Bit of a nightmare keeping everything up to date, so I was considering getting someone.'

I'm astounded he wants to trust me, as I can't have made much of an impression so far. Serendipity? 'Um, yes…happy to, if that's okay.'

'Pop into the gallery sometime and we can discuss it.' He pauses. 'Hang on – you'll need to pick up your car tomorrow, won't you?'

'Shoot, yes. I'll take the train in the morning. Hopefully Andrew will have left.'

'Actually, I'll be delivering the urns to the hotel tomorrow so I could collect you en route and you could drive yourself back. How would that suit?' His expression is unfathomable.

Thinking it would suit very well, I say, 'It's very kind of you, thanks.' Emotions start taking hold again. 'And thanks also for dinner and taking my mind off…you know. '

'No problem.' A sincere smile crosses his face.

After an awkward pause, we shake hands and I'm

conscious of how my own hand is lost within his and I'm overcome by the strangest urge to kiss his cheek or hug him with gratitude. Alcohol effects of course, so I resist.

He waits while I unlock the front door, and in turn, I stand on the doorstep to watch him walk back to the van.

Before climbing in, he says, 'Goodnight then. I'll pick you up in the morning around ten o'clock.'

He slowly manoeuvres the van out of the driveway, and I wave even though he probably can't see me. When I turn to walk into the dark hallway, I suddenly feel bereft and abandoned. Not knowing what the future will hold.

CHAPTER FOUR

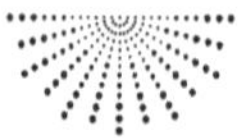

In the hallway, the mirror shows me a stranger: on the outside a scarecrow, on the inside a shadow. The feeling of isolation remains and I want to retreat to bed so the morning can quickly arrive. After a shower and more comfortable in my bathrobe, my reflection looks more like me. Me with a swollen face.

Once in bed, I check my phone again, but my screen indicates no messages. There's little point in checking anymore as it's late. I try to sleep, but the night is long and dark, last evening's events playing annoyingly over and over in my brain like a child singing a favourite song and only knowing the chorus. Mostly there's Andrew and that kiss, along with me being too late to confront him, and then imagining him in bed with that horrible woman.

Then there's the imaginary conversations with him when he returns, always ending in me triumphant at having caught him out, rapidly followed by the realisation of the consequences of that. Being right is only satisfying for a short time.

I open my eyes and sit up. The curtains are open. Light from the moon shines in through the window casting eerie shadows from the tree outside onto my duvet cover. I switch on my lamp and get up to draw them closed. A creak from outside the room spooks me. Cracks and groans are normal for this cottage as it settles, but the big empty bed, the isolation of being in the countryside, and the overall feeling of loneliness are suddenly too much with the accompanying unhappiness. The security light comes on outside. I tell myself it's probably a fox on the driveway and not to be stupid. It's not as if this is the first night I've been alone in the cottage.

A herbal sleep aid might be helpful, but after getting up to check a drawer, I don't find any. My childhood teddy bear, Big Ted, sits on a chair in the corner of the room. 'Come on, Big Ted,' I say. 'You can keep me company.' I take him into bed with me.

After reading the same page of my book several times, I abandon it. Maybe I should try to sleep. And maybe not, for after turning off the lamp, I toss and turn for another hour. Other pictures and conversations soon tick over in my head, with me envisioning myself storming across the restaurant (having removed the wig of course), interrupting Andrew and the woman mid-kiss, pulling them apart, demanding an explanation. In some scenarios (they change by the second), I remove the champagne bottle from the ice bucket and tip the contents over Andrew's head. This one works for me. Better still, following it up with the champagne, saving the last bit to tip down my throat.

At three thirty I get up again and venture downstairs to the kitchen, taking Big Ted with me, and putting on every light in the house on the way. After making myself cocoa, Big Ted and I retreat to the sitting room intent on watching a film together to pass the lonely night away. I rummage in a cupboard and pick up an old black and white one that belongs to my mother, *Now Voyager.* An ugly duckling tale that results in an affair but at least they fight against it eventually. Instead I try Netflix and my list comes up with rom-com after rom-com – best to avoid as most are about betrayals. I give up and choose *Love Actually* as at least it ends well or, at least, satisfactorily for most of the characters, and I could do with a happy ending.

I try to focus and fast-forward the bit where Alan Rickman's character cheats with that sexy girl from work. What does Emma Thompson do when she finds out? She tells him in a most dignified way that she knows about the affair, and he acknowledges it, something Andrew would never do. Has Andrew bought that woman a gift? Jewellery? Urgh? My thoughts are shooting out into the cosmos and probably zooming in on him like a missile, giving him ideas. I can't find the stop button quick enough and switch films to *Labyrinth.*

I'm running through the hotel but can't find my way to

Andrew. Every door leads to a corridor, then another, all exactly the same and going nowhere except more corridors. I jerk awake and find myself still on the couch, neck aching, and with the lamp on. It's daylight and the TV has long gone into standby, but music is playing, and it seeps into my foggy brain that my mobile is ringing. It's Andrew. I check the time – eight thirty.

'Morning. Sorry, darling, couldn't phone back, got caught up in a meeting.' He lies without effort. 'You know how it is when you're out in the sticks and the signal disappears and then the battery runs out.'

Gosh, he isn't even putting any effort into the lies now. What happened to hotel Wi-Fi? And I'm sure he didn't leave without a spare battery. Come to think of it, he said the meeting would be in a building surrounded by concrete the other day? And he mentioned a budget hotel, which is at odds with 'the sticks'. That's a slip-up too.'

'That's okay,' I find myself saying and cringe. Any confrontations are not going to happen on the phone. 'So, was the hotel comfortable?' This is my feeble attempt at fishing. I'm no Emma Thompson.

'Not even reasonable. Crap place. Bloody hard bed. Freddie's such a cheapskate.' The lies slide off his tongue like honey from a dripper. Perhaps he should have gone on the stage. If I hadn't seen what he was up to myself, I'd be believing all this bull. 'How was your evening?' he adds.

'Oh, the usual. Watched a film. Early night.' There's

a hard edge to my voice. 'I didn't sleep well though, so just woke up.' *Chicken.*

'Ahh, right, not good. Sorry, I have to go – breakfast meeting with Freddie in a couple of minutes. Boring. See you tonight, darling. Love you. And go back to bed for a while. Orders from me. Speak later.'

'Breakfast meeting? Wait—'

The phone goes off before I finish. Big Ted flicks me a glance of sympathy. 'Thanks for the support last night,' I say, and take him upstairs back to his chair.

After a shower, I sit at my mirror and stare at my reflection with dismay, I only have an hour to make myself back into a human being before Jack arrives. It's too late for cold teabags or sliced cucumber and even though the makeup covers up the dark shadows, I can't get rid of the bags, which are still hanging like marshmallows, now melting, under my eyes forcing me to start at my chin to cover them up with concealer, in the process adding approximately two pounds to my weight. I press one marshmallow and it's firm – not deflating anytime soon. At least my hair is now more its usual glossy bouncy self and falls over my shoulders in soft waves.

I choose my clothes carefully, deciding on a tight, black top tucked into a Prince of Wales-checked mini skirt. My strappy, chunky-heeled shoes, never yet worn, and leather jacket should go perfectly. I'm aiming for a completely contrasting look to last night, and what I've managed when I finish dressing is rock-chick rather than my usual girl-next-door retro woman. I check the clock.

There's just time for a coffee to help wake up my tired brain.

Jack arrives punctually at ten. When I walk out to the van he jumps out to open the door for me and I catch him glancing at my legs, his eyes telling me my complete change of style hasn't gone unnoticed. He looks hunky in a white long-sleeved top and jeans. His biceps showing he's used to lifting heavy frames. I almost remember where I've seen him before, then, in a flash, it's gone again. Should have had more coffee.

I heave myself up into the van, aware of Jack behind me and conscious of my short skirt. Jack slams the door after me and walks around to the other side. I sit in the seat next to the door, leaving the seat empty between us.

'You left this behind,' he says as I'm fastening my seat belt. He waves something furry at me and, for a second, I think he's handing me a guinea pig before recognising my wig. 'In case you want to put it on again though I suppose it would have been better to put it on your car last night instead.'

It takes me a moment to comprehend. 'Oh, a car disguise, gosh, yes. Say Andrew has spotted it?' I begin to concoct excuses to why my car is sitting there outside the hotel. *I was checking the place out for a weekend away; I followed you to surprise you and changed my mind as I realised you'd be busy* (yeah, that sounds natural). *A coincidence but my car broke down while I was passing by* (big coincidence). Pathetic. I'll have to come clean if Andrew's spotted it.

'I parked it out the way, under a tree. Fingers crossed the car park hasn't emptied,' I reply.

In the bottom of my shoulder bag I find a hair bobble and pull the visor down to reveal the mirror. With a heavy sigh I drag my newly coiffured hair back into a ponytail and shove the wig on my head. After a fair bit of adjusting, I give up trying to make it look cool in the harsh daylight. The ginger tone doesn't suit my olive complexion and accentuates my pallidness after another sleepless night. With nothing I can do, I push the visor back up.

The idea of the wig was so I would bear no resemblance to the usual well-dressed me. I've achieved it and more, now looking like a lady of the night, and in the process, annihilating my cool, rock-chick self-confidence. No wonder a man approached me in the hotel. Now, revisiting what happened last night, including my appearance and emotional behaviour, I'm filled with mortification. I must never do that again: act hysterical, weep like a baby, get drunk, follow Andrew again.

One yank and the wig is free from my head. I shove it in my handbag. If Andrew sees me, then he does, I don't give a damn. After what he did last night he can hardly reproach me. I tear the bobble out and shake my hair loose without explaining myself.

In my peripheral vision I see a slow smile curve Jack's lips. 'Better,' he says.

The ensuing silence makes me aware of the male

presence beside me and the atmosphere in the car heats up. I surreptitiously glance at Jack's strong hands resting on the wheel as he stops at a junction and turns the car onto the A350.

A frisson of danger runs through me. Why did I agree to be alone with Jack? But I shouldn't have to ask myself as I know why. The same as when I accepted his help last night, because he makes me feel safe and I like him. He may not be handsome in the same way as Andrew, but his sheer masculinity makes Andrew with his symmetrical features, perfect model height, and well-proportioned body look like a pretty boy.

I wince as a picture of my errant husband pops into my head, his lips curling into a slow sensual smile. My camera eyes pan out and I see the smile is for that woman at the hotel. I blink in an attempt to cut out the image, but it won't budge. My gaze drifts back to the strong hands and stranger-danger.

Small talk might be distracting.

'Nice weather, isn't it.' Is that the best I can do? 'I – I mean we've been lucky this year with the Indian summer. I thought, well, that was it after the last lot of sun earlier this week. But yes, today it's – it's well, nice…again, sort of.' For God's sake.

'Just in time for the weekend,' Jack contributes, purely to be kind to me, I bet. 'So, how are you this morning?'

'Fine. Looking forward to my time off, to relax – first weekend off for a while.' Why did he ask me such a stupid question?

Jack glances at me apologetically. 'Look, I know it's no business of mine, and I know everyone starts with that when they're going to give someone unwanted advice, but might it not be easier to talk to your husband?'

'Easier than what?'

'Following him wearing a hat, wig, and erm gallons of silly makeup. Then there's the general subterfuge… that must have been stressful.'

The heat rises to my face and I clench my teeth. I'm seething. When did it become his business what I do? Oh God, I know the answer – when I involved him. Actually, that's unfair as he involved himself.

The view out of the window becomes interesting. Okay, what did I do that wasn't warranted? Let's recap: followed my husband of seven years because another woman sent him texts asking him to phone, and called him 'darling' and 'my love'. That's a good enough reason on its own right there, and even worse when I couple it with Andrew avoiding me at every turn. Not answering my calls and texts, not telling me where he's staying, I can add to that. And lastly, his antics with Miss Bleach Junkie. The two of them sitting there like the perfect celeb couple while I stand watching, face like a clown, weeping – mascara running down my cheeks. Silly makeup is accurate but justified, I think.

Humiliation gradually takes the place of anger. Perhaps Jack is right and I should have confronted Andrew on the phone, demanded he return to explain himself, but my thoughts are still that it would have been futile, putting him on his guard instead. But Jack did come to my rescue, and I shouldn't be directing my anger at him.

'Absolutely no point,' I manage to say, knowing he's waiting for a response. 'Not yet anyway.'

We drive in silence for a while, the trees flashing by, keeping my attention focussed, but they soon dissolve into a blur of stinging tears. In the end it's no use and I have to fumble in my bag for a tissue.

'Sorry,' said Jack. 'It must be difficult for you and I really have no idea of your situation, or the state of your marriage.' He sighs. 'Too opinionated, Stephanie used to say. Should have kept my big mouth shut. You've shown great courage.'

'It's – it's okay.' My voice catches as I ponder over when it was exactly that communication broke down between Andrew and me. The fact that I can't remember, making it so much worse.

Jack slows the van, pulls into a passing lay-by and parks as deftly as a van will allow. He watches me carefully, giving me a chance to compose myself, and then puts his hand briefly over mine as it rests on my knee while managing not to touch my leg. 'Hey, if you ever need to talk…'

Looking up into his sincere, sympathy-filled green eyes, I nod, knowing it'll never happen. Jack is being polite, saying helpful things like a knight in shining armour automatically does. He drives off again.

My phone buzzes and my stomach sinks in case it's Andrew. The ringtone follows, it's 'Help' by the Beatles.

Jo. I answer only to find the loudspeaker is on and struggle to turn it off, madly stabbing the screen, but it won't work and I give up. Bloody screen cover. 'Won't know it's on there,' the bloke on the market stall said.

'Randa, are you at home?'

'No, not at the moment. Why?'

'I'm on my way to your house for the rest of the weekend. Just left. Tell Andrew he can bog off if he doesn't like it.' She sniffs.

'He's away until tonight. What's up?' It must be something traumatic because she lives more than four hours away and generally needs an operation to prise her from Phil's side. Now she has him, she'll hang on to him like a child clutching a comfort blanket.

'Phil dumped me.'

Or Phil does emergency surgery.

'I'm so sorry. What a bastard. I'll be back by the time you get here.'

'Great, thanks. You've no idea how this feels. It's horrible.'

'No, indeed, I wouldn't, would I? Speak soon, I have to go I've pulled into a lay-by, busy road.' Well, I can hardly tell her I'm in a van with a strange man again, can I?

'You need someone to examine your engine,' she says. 'Sounds noisy.'

Jack raises his eyebrows and grimaces as I stare at the phone, then put it away in my bag. I've just zipped it back up when Take That's 'Everything Changes' blasts out. My face prickles with heat as I unzip the bag again and root for my phone. Must change that ringtone.

This time it is Andrew. 'Hi, darling,' he says. The phone is still on loudspeaker.

I manage a feeble 'hi' back.

'Sorry, been held up and have to stay another night. Freddie. You know how he is, lots of discussion to get through. I'll be back tomorrow evening.'

The shock of this renders me speechless.

He coughs when I don't answer. 'This contract could mean a future partnership, and I can't pass up such a good opportunity.'

My stomach plummets. 'Oh…right…no. Where are you staying?' I ask innocently, but can hardly hear my own voice over my hammering heart.

'Sorry, didn't catch that. You're cutting out—'

We're disconnected, and when I try to phone back, it goes straight to the answering machine and I'm left staring at my screen. What a wimp I am just accepting what he said. I know where Andrew is now, and I have the ammunition that he lied and is not at a budget hotel, and that he dined with and kissed another woman. There's a witness too. Well, I'm not sure if Jack saw the kiss, though he did see something. Still, it wouldn't be fair to drag him into it. My own eyes witnessed it and that's enough.

A few minutes later we're driving into the hotel car park and I scour around for Andrew's SUV, but can't see it. I ask Jack to drive up and down the lanes and he does that while frowning, realising my intent. I mentally slap my wrist and again tell myself it's not fair to drag him into this mess. With a sigh I point out my car and he parks in the space next to it.

Confused and defeated, I'm unsure what to do for the best.

'Do you want to get a tea or coffee before driving home?'

'Sorry? Er, no thanks. I don't want to see the interior of that hotel ever again and I don't want to come to Bath ever again.' I sound petulant, but my grief is immeasurable, imagining Andrew spending a romantic weekend in the city with that woman hanging onto his arm, clinging to his every word.

We step out of the van and I retreat to my own little car. Jack's expression is filled with concern and I try a smile before saying, 'Thanks so much for stepping in. You must think… I'm sorry for dragging you into this.'

His expression softens, his hair flopping over one of his intense sea-green eyes. He brushes it away and says, 'No problem. Beautiful damsels in distress are my forte according to my ex.' He laughs.

Beautiful! What a hero being able to see beauty through my distress. I blush as it has been a while since anyone has said that to me. For a moment the thought of revenge flashes through my tortured brain and I see myself walking through Bath, holding Jack's hand, bumping into that pair of deceivers.

'Two wrongs don't make a right,' I hear my mother shout down my ear as if I've suddenly developed clairaudience, bringing me to my senses. This is not the way to go on, and revenge is not the answer. If I see Jack again, it'll be on a business footing that's if he is serious about his accounts, which he probably isn't, otherwise even I will doubt his sanity.

I thank him again. Do I shake hands with him? Hug? He decides for me. When he puts one hand on my shoulder and leans down to kiss my cheek, it takes me by surprise. His lips only brush my skin, but in my panic I move my head and his second kiss lands precariously near my mouth instead of the other cheek. I barely have time to register that butterflies are whizzing around my stomach before Jack swings open my car door and says, 'Take care. See you soon.'

Soon! I jump into the car, cheeks flaming, wondering what it means. Does he think because my husband's cheating I'm up for grabs? Even if a moment ago I was envisioning us together in Bath, that is not the point.

'The accounts – I can drop in to you if you prefer. You said you have an office? Phone me – my number's on the website.'

Come to the cottage! 'I'll drop into the gallery when I have time,' I say curtly, and slam the door. As I drive off, I check in my rear-view mirror to find he's watching me quizzically and can't help wishing I could read his mind.

CHAPTER FIVE

Jo's here and she looks worse than I do, not that she's noticed how I look even with my rock-chick gear. Her normally straightened titian hair is wiry and wild, skin pale, freckles standing out, and her big blue eyes rather resemble my own – puffy. Phil dumped her with no explanation. Said it wasn't working for him but not why. But she can guess.

'I'm gutted,' Jo says as we sit in the snug on my plush cream-coloured sofa with our glasses of red wine. 'He must have been seeing someone else. At a guess, his ex. A couple of times lately he's cried off a date or dashed off home earlier than normal. I ignored it, made excuses, like you do. In denial.' She waves her glass around and my hand follows hers as I poise to pounce should she get careless.

I'm tempted to tell her that perhaps it was the sex, not exciting enough, or ask does she ignore his sweaty socks or undies, but refrain as she's so miserable and would not be in the mood for jokes.

Taking her glass from her, I place it on a coaster to protect my solid-oak coffee table and lean over and give her a hug instead. Telling her there are plenty more fish in the sea and time will heal, I'm sure is the wrong thing to say. She fancied herself in love with Phil for a year before their first date. 'I'm here for you,' I say instead, meaning it. 'And I do know how you feel.'

'I hate men. They're all pigs.'

Jack looms up in my mind. Not all men perhaps, but then I don't know really know him. 'They are.'

Jo throws her head against the back of the sofa and screw up her eyes. 'God, I'm so sorry. I'm all about me and I forgot about you. I was so mean winding you up on the phone. Wasn't thinking. Now I have a taste of my own bloody medicine. If it's any consolation, my punishment was harsh.'

'Don't be daft, Jo. We're sisters in arms now.'

'Okay, tell me what happened, it'll help me take my mind off Phil.'

I wrinkle my nose and close one eye, reluctant to admit what I did. 'After those texts I was suspicious and followed Andrew to a hotel in Bath. Found him with another woman, and it isn't even the same one who sent the texts.' The rest of my sorry tale follows but I'm reluctant to mention Jack although I'm not sure why. In the end I do because I did send her his photo but don't reveal too much; not that it works as she senses something, her eyes are narrowing.

'So, so sorry. Didn't realise it was as bad as that. Please forgive me for making light of it. Thought it was his usual flirting. I had a feeling about Andrew, you know, he always was a slick bastard. Handsome but no depth. Likes to have a beautiful woman on his arm. And that's all you are to him, Randa, you're better off without him.'

Beautiful! That's twice in one day. 'Any beautiful woman will do though,' I say, thinking back to the hotel and again to Chester and Claire. 'Or just any woman.'

'Very good-looking men like him probably develop some resentment at missing out on other opportunities, and there must be plenty of them coming his way. Too much temptation. With Phil, he never got over the split with his ex, though I thought we were getting there.'

I mull her comments over. 'I thought Andrew was immune to come-ons – happy with me. He always seemed to take them in his stride. How deluded can you get?'

We sit in silence for a while lost in our own thoughts with mine drifting to such mundane things as what time to cook dinner and back to bracing myself for Andrew coming home tomorrow, glad that Jo is with me. My phone bleeps. A text message flashes on screen from Andrew: *Talks going slow. More delay. Looking forward to being back home Monday morning though. Love you XXX.*

Monday! Hysteria rises as my fingers get to work and I type four messages back in quick succession.

Why Monday?

Where are you?
Where are you staying?
What's going on?

They send but are not received. With a sinking heart I phone him and it goes straight to the answering machine. I shake with rage. No one can tell me now that he isn't up to something. He is and it hurts like hell. When he gets back, we are over. But I know that's just anger talking.

Jo has been observing the latest episode in the soap called 'Cake'.

'Hmm,' she says, and after patting my back, tops up our wine glasses. Drips fall onto the table but I'm past caring. 'You might have to bide your time for a while to get revenge. No one will ever believe he's fallen down the stairs at his age.' She sighs heavily. 'Well, there's nothing either of us can do about it, so let's wallow tonight, watch a film, and tomorrow we'll have a day out together.'

All I want to do is go to bed, stick my head under the pillow and hide there for the foreseeable future. Reading my expression, Jo does a puppy face, and forming her hands into paws, begs and whimpers. I cuff her across the top of her head and can't help smiling. 'Suppose we could as long as it's not a romcom.'

Jo laughs, not a 'ha ha' laugh, more like a bizarre, desperate laugh. She halts. 'Maybe we *should* watch a romcom, it'll give us faith that there's still, well, hope for us. And tomorrow we can go sightseeing.'

I agree to a day out in Netherbury, but say a firm 'no' to the romcom, especially after last night.

'Great, you can show me around town,' Jo suggests. 'We can visit the cathedral, I always wanted to see the crooked spire. Then we'll do a bit of shopping therapy and find a cosy pub for lunch.'

I sigh. 'The *twisted* spire's in Chesterfield and it's a church. This spire's the tallest— Never mind. Sounds like a plan.'

<hr>

When I wake, I have a headache even though I thought I was being careful with the wine. I slept better but did load myself down with herbal sleep meds picked up after a quick trip to the local health shop yesterday, and sniffed heavily at a bottle of lavender oil before pouring half of it on my pillow. For a while I lie still, trying to spur myself into facing the day, pondering on events.

Last evening went as reasonably as could be expected for two women whose men seemingly enjoy cake.

There were bouts of uncontrollable sobbing – Jo.

Rabid ranting – me.

And hysterical laughter – both of us.

But having Jo here, the empathy that's between us, and being able to share our emotions, is comforting. If only she lived closer by.

There is a strange whining noise emanating from downstairs; it's Jo with an off-key rendition of a Maroon 5 song, 'Sunday Morning'. I jump out of bed and run to the window. Rain is indeed falling. I should have known. All our plans for today are ruined.

The smell of burning and a lot of clanging and clattering, prompts me to grab a bathrobe and hurry downstairs.

Jo is busy making pancakes and the gloopy mixture is spread over my granite worktops and flour ground into my Tuscan limestone floor.

'Making breakfast.' She wipes a streak of flour across her face and grins. Her eyelids are more swollen and redder than they were last night and I melt.

'Love pancakes. You're a darling.' Tearing my eyes away from the anti-bacterial spray, I take the plate of blackened offerings Jo hands to me. 'You have some first,' I say.

'They're all for you, I can't eat them – gluten.'

A lump forms in my throat and I gulp. Finding the maple syrup, I smother the pancakes, hoping to disguise the taste while Jo takes two eggs off the boil that I eye with longing.

After eating enough pancakes to be polite, one and a half to be precise, which takes forever, I mutter something about having no appetite and tip the remainder in the bin. Jo, meanwhile, prattles on. 'Tried to contact him this morning, but his phone's switched off,' she twitters. 'What have I done to deserve this? It can't be the sex, he got loads.'

'Quality?' I can't help asking, only to receive a floury thump on the arm.

'He's just a pig,' she says. 'Wait until he has the same

problems with his ex again or she goes off with someone else, then he'll come running back to find it's too late.'

I agree but my eyes keep drifting towards the cleaning spray as I continue to gawp at the sticky floury mess. Just to add to my concern, Jo whips her arm across the worktop to grab her phone, swiping more flour to the floor in the process, making me cringe as her flip-flops grind it in.

'Anyway,' she continues, 'I'm switching my phone off, so there!' With a dramatic gesture and holding her finger aloft, she brings it down onto the button. 'Ha, now he can't get hold of me.' She wipes her phone on her bathrobe. 'Why don't you switch yours off, Randa? Let's stage a protest and not be at their beck and call.'

It's not a bad idea, so I switch off my own phone, though I bet neither man is trying to contact us. I'm about to put it on the greasy worktop but snatch it back. 'Er, why don't you go and get ready and we can get off to Netherbury – sod the rain. Forget those two, find a good pub and enjoy ourselves.'

'Yes, and we'll have a bloody good time,' she says, laughing. Who needs men?

As soon as she's left the room, I dive for the spray and start work putting my kitchen back to rights. The floor is horrendous and bits of flour remain in the grooves, even after I've mopped it twice. It takes ages and it's a good hour until the last dish is safely stacked in the dishwasher and I'm able to dash upstairs to shower.

. . .

I'm still ready before Jo, who is straightening her hair but still has half of it to do. I tell her to speed it up or the day will be gone.

'Well, with you cleaning, I thought I had a lot more time,' she quips.

We take the train, so we can both have a drink, and Jo insists on paying. Once out of the station we head straight for the cathedral, and braving the rain we do a ladylike trot together down the High Street, reminding me of when we were teenagers. Determined to put Andrew out of my head, I enjoy the moment.

A stiff breeze blows the mizzle in every direction, rendering our umbrellas useless. Rain sprays on my face and I laugh.

'Nooo, that's all I need,' shouts Jo, over the sound of traffic. 'All that straightening my hair for nothing.' A quick glance sideways tells me her curls are all back with an added frizz.

Jo comes to a sudden halt by a row of shops and our umbrellas crash. 'Hey, Langford Gallery. Isn't this the place that belongs to the guy who gave you a lift home?' She presses her nose up against the window. 'Is that him? Looks like the pic you sent.'

'Jooo, nooo!' Grabbing her arm, I pull her away. 'He'll see you if you're not careful.'

'What's wrong with that? Aren't you going to say hello?'

Still holding her sleeve I accelerate towards the cathedral.

Jo scurries behind me, having no choice. 'Oi! I'm wearing heels! Not so fast. Anyway, what's the rush, it wouldn't hurt to thank the guy.'

'No need, I've already said it a million times.'

'You don't want me to see him,' she says accusingly. 'Is he fit as well as single, is that it? Are you hiding him from me?'

Blood courses into my face and neck giving me away. Jo grins. One big tug and she turns and pretends to go back. 'What aren't you telling me? Right, I'm going to find out for myself.' She starts to walk backwards along the road.

I grab her sleeve again. 'For goodness sake, Jo. Okay, okay, I'll tell you. I had a fair amount to drink the other night and well—'

'You kissed him!'

I'm horrified. 'No, no, nothing like that. A bit tipsy that's all and I wept a lot and he looked after me. Nothing untoward.'

'Hmm, nice excuse but won't wash. He has you in a tizzy and I need to see why. You're holding back on me.'

'No, I'm not holding anything back. Come on, the cathedral awaits.' Jo stares at my hand where it's clutching her grand's worth of coat and raises her eyebrows. I release her. 'Up to you, I'm going.' And with that I carry on down the road, crossing my fingers and screwing up my face, one eye open while listening for her clip-clopping. After a pause, she comes. Moment of crisis successfully diverted, I relax and smile in victory. It's not often that happens.

Thankfully, the rain has stopped by the time we enter the cathedral grounds. 'Wow it's magnificent,' Jo says as we approach the perfect example of Early English Gothic architecture. She stops to stare up at the spire. 'Doesn't seem that crooked to me.'

'Right at the top just a teensy bit twisty.'

Jo pretends to examine it for a while. 'Nope, can't see it.'

We both giggle like schoolgirls and I shake my head.

I point out the famous flying buttresses for which I receive a deliberately blank look as my knowledge of architecture does not easily impress her. Inside I show her the features she's more likely to be interested in.

Luckily, Sunday services are over, but still, Jo's clip-clopping heels echo off the walls and the remaining people turn and frown, resulting in an apologetic grimace from Jo and an attempt to tiptoe.

After a few minutes, two tombs grab her interest and she studies the Tudor lovers lying side by side. 'So beautiful. Now, I bet their relationship lasted,' she says. 'True love. Together in life and death.'

'Not really, she died before reaching her thirties. Here's some information if you want to read it.' I point to a card on a stand. 'Probably died of the plague or in childbirth, so no opportunity to cheat. If I were to die now, Andrew could say he had a successful relationship with me until death did us part.' Hurt makes you cynical.

'Yep. My relationship ended a touch too early for that. In fact, in reality, it was pretty short.'

Moving on we visit the cloisters, smaller dedicated chapels, and examine the colourful stained-glass windows depicting various biblical scenes. Lastly, getting bored, we try to spot the green men hidden on the ceiling and tombs.

'That's it,' Jo declares after an hour of searching. 'Must have found them all now. Let's go and eat, those eggs weren't that filling.'

A lot more filling than burnt pancakes, but I say, 'Come on then, you've seen most of the highlights, we'll find a pub and then shop. Wouldn't mind a large glass of wine too.'

'And me.' She pulls her phone out of her pocket and stares at it. 'Is it the same for you? I mean, are you finding it hard not to switch it back on? Say they're trying to get in touch?'

'It was your idea to switch the phones off, you mad woman, and it was a good one. We shouldn't be so available, remember? Anyway, if they want to contact us that desperately, they can call again. For now, they can stew.' I'm acting more determined than I feel. Of course, I wonder if Andrew has tried to call, but there's no way I'll check. And Jo might be bothered now, but if she learns Phil was using her to fill time and to make his ex jealous, she should rally.

'Okay,' she says, 'but mine's going back on at seven. That's long enough.'

We head back up High Street and I'm pleased that Jo strolls straight past the gallery, which isn't hard to miss as it's situated in an impressive Tudor building. But the moment I'm breathing a sigh of relief, she does an about-turn and disappears inside.

'Jo! Don't!'

CHAPTER SIX

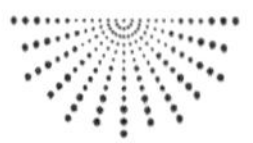

What to do now? Walk, or better still, run on? How can I face him? This is so embarrassing.

Jo pops her head back out and shouts, 'Miranda, aren't you coming in?'

How can she do this to me? With my eyes closed and fists clenched by my sides, I count to three. I'll kill her for this.

'Give me a chance, Jo,' I shout back, and follow her in, while praying she's joking and Jack's not there.

He's there, along with a slim, eccentric-looking man with a crazy mop of white hair. They're staring into the jewellery cabinet at the back. As we move forward, Jo glances from one to the other, screws up her eyes, and focusses on Jack. Almost as if he can sense her interest, he looks up and, after briefly acknowledging her presence, switches his gaze to me. 'Oh, hello. Thought I heard the name Miranda.'

'Hi, yes, just popping in for a quick gander. My

friend wanted a quick gander that is,' I gabble. This is so embarrassing.

Jo weaves her way through the fixtures and tables with their paintings and sculptures, hand held out. 'Joanne Costelloe, Miranda's *best* friend. Very, *very* pleased to meet the man who came to her rescue.' She shakes his hand vigorously while gazing up to his great height from her five feet three and a bit. Brazenly looking him over, she half-turns, nods, and smiling says, 'Randa, you didn't tell me he was so handsome.' Her eyes open wide. 'And a celebrity too.'

Celebrity? I wander over with certain dread.

Jack laughs. 'That's because I'm not particularly.'

'Which, handsome or a celebrity?'

He shakes his head and grins while I try to figure out why Jo thinks he's famous.

'Oh, but you are both,' Jo continues, emphasising each word. 'You're a presenter on that programme *Hidden Treasures*.' She wheels around and winks as she taps my arm. 'The photo Miranda sent me was rather dark and she was comparing you to her husband when she described you. And I have to say he is ab-so-lute-ly gorgeous.'

She's doing this deliberately to wind me up. I did compare him rather unfavourably with Andrew when describing him, but that was to stop Jo from forming unnecessary suspicions. How did I not recognise him? Too caught up in my own wine drinking, wine spilling, panicky melodramatics, that's how. Art gallery – art expert. Dr Jack Langford, of course. I mentally slap my forehead. He pops up from time to time in different art and antique shows and co-presented one a few months back. Here's me thinking I must know him in some other capacity.

Jack raises his eyebrows at Jo, but his eyes sparkle, and heat creeps up my neck. I can't believe he's fallen for her pretend, over-the-top gushing.

'Oh, Jo,' I say, 'can't you be more original.' I turn what must be my tomato-red face to Jack, roll my eyes and tap him on the chest with my fingertips. 'She says that to all the handsome guys. I mean all the, um, guys. Even the – the –' I scour around my befuddled head for the words – 'ugly ones. Likes to flatter.'

Jack lowers his head towards me, and frowns. 'Ugly?'

'Yep, like – like giant ogres for instance…even.' What the hell is a giant ogre when it's at home? 'She says that even to giant types…of men, I mean. Or any types…of men.' For God's sake! How can I be jealous? I'm married!

Jo grins.

Jack grimaces. 'Right, I'll take giant for myself, if that's okay.' Jo giggles. 'And this giant needs to woo two princesses to stop him from turning into a total giant ogre, so how about lunch?'

If looks could kill. I direct mine at Jo, but she lives on.

'Great! We were just on our way to find a cosy pub. Randa needs a large glass of wine. Don't you, Randa?'

Jack's gaze drifts to me then back to Jo and his eyebrows raise just the slightest.

'Er, yes, we're famished, so pub for lunch, but it – it doesn't have to be a pub,' I stammer, 'any reputable café will do. It's not as if I'm reliant on alcohol.' I put my fingers to my lips and make a noise that I hope sounds like a carefree laugh but sounds remarkably like a titter. 'You know me, Jo, I can take it or leave it.'

'Mostly take it though.' She winks at me. 'So, pub it is.'

White-haired man comes forward. 'I'm quite jealous, Jack, but unfortunately it's my turn to hold the fort,' he says. 'Do introduce me to the lovely ladies.' He's staring directly at Jo and she responds with a beaming smile.

Jack turns. 'Oh, sorry. This is Hector Thackeray. Does jewellery. Owns the place. And this is Miranda Stone whom I met in Bath on Friday, and her delightful friend Joanne.' He gives no further explanation and I breathe a sigh of relief. I shake hands with Hector who has what I'd call an agreeable face, but also has incredible, almost turquoise, eyes.

'You're not on TV, are you, Hector?' asks Jo, nudging me out of the way and taking his hand. 'I'm sure I wouldn't forget you.' There's no shaking involved, and they stand holding hands wearing big smiles.

'Not expert enough,' replies Hector. My own expert eyes detect him giving Jo's hand a slight squeeze before he lets go.

'That can't be true,' Jo spouts, moving to the jewellery cabinet where she quickly examines each shelf of items. 'Special collection you have here. There must be skill involved in choosing these pieces.'

'Love one of your pendants,' I add. 'Saw it a couple of weeks ago, don't know if it's still here. The moonstone, Arts and Crafts, one.'

Hector nods, delighted. 'Ahh, the gold one with the moonstones and a pearl. Pretty and eminently wearable. Yes, I still have it.'

'Which one?' asks Jo. 'I owe you a birthday gift.'

Hector strolls over, takes a key from his pocket, and unlocks the cabinet, removing both the pendant and what I know is the accompanying price tag of three hundred pounds.

'Eek!' says Jo, laughing. 'Well, perhaps on your sixtieth.'

We all laugh, and I say, 'I'll keep you to that.'

'Deal. I agree though, it is gorgeous and right up your street.'

'I'll fetch my jacket then.' Jack directs this at me. And deep inside me, a strange fluttering begins at the prospect of spending more time with him.

The pub is a short stroll away and Jo and I find ourselves on either side of Jack. The weather has improved, and more people mill about the historical town. Walking next to him is awkward as I'm still conscious of his giant presence, so let Jo prattle on about Hector's collection. She describes several pieces in detail, saying what style of outfit each would suit, her sudden enthusiasm for jewellery thankfully diverting her focus from Jack and me. Jack listens with interest, feigned or real it's hard to tell.

When we reach our destination, a cosy pub I've never been in before, it's with much relief. The restaurant side is busy and a server tells us it'll be a few minutes until a table is available, suggesting we wait at the bar and have a drink. Jo requests a glass of Pinot Grigio saying she needs to track down the ladies to freshen up. Before Jack has a chance, I move forward to the bar and ask him what he would like and place the order, pointedly requesting a mineral water to give a better impression of myself.

Once the drinks arrive the atmosphere becomes awkward. Wine would be handy now, and if Jo isn't back soon, I vow to drink hers. People in the pub become interesting but are a sea of strange faces. A woman from Ashford, or someone who looks like her, comes through the door, but people get into my line of vision and then she's gone, probably left again on seeing the crush. Shame, being alone with Jack again is disconcerting, it's not as if he blends into the background easily. Where could Jo be? She's taking ages. There must be a queue.

If Andrew phoned me now with all the background noise, would he be surprised that I'm not sitting at home waiting like a good little wife? That's not particularly fair as he would never expect me to sit at home, and would only be surprised if I ventured out instead of hanging around the cottage or working. Besides, the deal was to keep the phones switched off until this evening.

'So how are you today?' Jack says, interrupting my thoughts.

I glare perplexedly at him. Like hell, how else would

I feel? Why does he do that? But his expression shows the atmosphere between us has become uncomfortable for him too. 'Overall I'm fine. But I'm glad Jo's here,' I reply.

'Fine enough to attempt to reconcile my messy accounts sometime this week?'

I'd forgotten about that. There's one problem though, I've no idea what will happen regarding Andrew when he gets home. Still, a girl must earn her living. More so with all this uncertainty. 'Would Wednesday afternoon suit? Say two?'

'Fine,' he says.

I stare at him, but he looks innocent enough and takes a sip of his real ale. (I know. He does actually drink, it turns out.)

'Your table is ready,' says a man behind the bar. 'Kim, will show you.'

Kim duly arrives, picks up Jo's wine, and leads us to a table in the centre of the room.

When I attempt to pull out my chair, Jack is there in a flash doing it for me. An eerie sensation of déjà vu strikes me. It takes me a moment to work out it's a flash-back of Andrew and that woman at the hotel. Not that I intend to kiss Jack. Still, here I am, sitting alone, about to have lunch with a virtual stranger, a single man in my age group. Jo had better not have disappeared.

Kim hands me the wine list. I drop it as if it's one of Jo's dodgy burnt pancakes. 'Perhaps a tad early for me.'

Jack retrieves it. 'Red or white?'

'White.'

He orders two glasses of Pinot. 'Joanne?'

'Still has this one.' I point to the wine, frowning. 'Where has she got to?'

'At a guess I'd say she's slipped out. Shopping perhaps.' Jack swigs the last of his beer. He isn't holding back on alcohol today.

'So, you live around here, you said?' I sound nosey but curiosity has the better of me.

'Yes, in Netherbury, above the gallery in the flat. For now, anyway. Handy, but I'm in the middle of house-hunting as I could do with a bigger place for Sophie and her friends to stay over – and a second bathroom.' He grins. 'And a home away from work would be nice. When you live where you work, there's a tendency to work more hours than you intend or should.'

'Tell me about it.' Some of us indeed have no choice if we can't afford a separate office, or even an office space in the garden. I recall the tiny, diamond windowpanes in the old Tudor building and I'm gratified that at least Holly Cottage, although old, is surprisingly light. The attic is one of the darker rooms admittedly, but down-stairs the kitchen-dining room, part of a newer extension, has bigger windows and a sunny aspect. I wouldn't want to live anywhere too dark and claustrophobic no matter how historical and quaint.

Why would this concern me anyway? What's it matter if his home is dark, light, or sky-blue-bloody-pink with polka dots? I'm never going to live in it.

Jo at last appears at Jack's side looking far from as if she's fresh from the loo. Well, maybe fresh out of the loo. She's windswept and a bit wet as it's raining again. 'Here you are. Happy belated Birthday!' She slides a gift box across the table to me.

My birthday was almost a month ago. 'Oh, Jo, you shouldn't have. I wondered what was taking you so long.'

'Open it then.' She takes off her coat and Jack pulls out a chair for her.

I open the box and there, lying on velvet as I suspect, is the moonstone and pearl pendant.

'Oh my God,' I squeal, and heads turn towards me. Lowering my voice I say, 'You can't do this, Jo, you really can't. What are you playing at?'

'A simple thanks would be good, considering I've sold my soul to the devil to get it.'

I frown at her. 'What does that mean?'

'Hector's the devil.' She laughs. 'In return for it I promised to help him bring his website and marketing into the twenty-first century. Before I travel home tomorrow I'm going back to discuss it with him. Nice guy. Really nice in fact.'

'Oh, right.' Still thinking she must be mad committing herself to all that work, I get up to give her a kiss. 'Thank you, it's beautiful. You shouldn't have though.'

'You deserve it.'

I sit back in my seat and try to fasten the pendant around my neck but struggle as my hair soon tangles in the fastener. Jack is on his feet in a jiffy and comes around to the back of my chair. 'Allow me.' As his fingers lift my hair, I recoil as if I've had a static shock. Certain it was noticeable I pretend to cough to cover my reaction. My shoulders rise as he touches my neck while fiddling with the old catch, and I try to stop the quiver that's travelling straight down my spine and throughout my pelvic area, prompting me to cross my legs. I cough again. How can this be? Only Andrew has been able to provoke this response in me before.

'Thanks,' I croak when he drops my hair back in place. 'Think I'm going down with a cold.'

Jo regards me with narrowed eyes, and I know she knows, and that she also knows that I know she knows. I think he's hot that is. Not that I'd ever do anything about it. Best to ignore her and concentrate on the menu.

Kim arrives back with the wine and pulls a notebook from her apron pocket, so I order a sensible Caesar salad.

'Do you have a gluten-free menu?' Jo asks. Kim shakes her head. Then we wait several minutes while she goes through each item with Jo, telling her all the ingredients. Jack smiles, the twinkle back in his eyes. He has the patience of a saint. Jo eventually sighs. 'So, it's just the steak, salmon, or chicken I can eat then? Bit much for me at this time of day.'

Kim is desperate. 'We can do the Caesar salad without croutons,' she suggests.

Jo smiles at her. 'As long as it doesn't have lactose.'

There's a sigh. 'It has parmigiano reggiano.'

'Low in lactose,' I say helpfully.

Jo slams the menu shut. 'I'm off dairy. I'll have whatever's left, please.' As soon as Jack tells Kim he'll have the salad too, Jo turns to me. 'Randa, be a darling and show me where the ladies' is.'

My eyes close. She can't be serious. I glare at her. I

don't even know where they are myself. Jo throws me an 'are-you-coming-or-what' look and walks away while glancing over her shoulder to ensure I'm behind her, and seeing I'm not, waits. I don't need to look at Jack to sense he's watching the scene unfold, knowing he'll be the topic of conversation. Feeling I have no choice, I shrug, grab my bag, and throw him an apologetic half-smile before sheepishly following Jo who now knows exactly in which direction to go.

The moment we're though the door of the ladies' she squeals, 'Randa! You do fancy him. And don't tell me you don't, I saw you. He turns you on. You were fluttering like a trapped butterfly, not knowing what to do.'

'Jo-anne!' I reply crossly, and roll my eyes. 'Yes, okay, he's nice, but I'm a married woman and it's immaterial what I think of him.'

'Yes, married to a cheater.'

'And that makes it right? I'm not even one hundred per cent sure Andrew did have sex with that woman.'

'Because you're in denial. He cheated. And a bird in hand is worth two in the bush.'

I puzzle over that. 'Wouldn't Andrew be the bird in hand and Jack be in the bush with say a second man?'

Jo scowls at me. 'Whatever. Jack seems a good guy. And he's famous. Strike while the iron's hot.'

'They're two contradictory sayings, Jo.'

'Oh, bloody hell. You know what I'm saying, so don't pretend you don't. Look after yourself instead of pleasing Andrew all the time. That's all you've ever done. And he certainly isn't holding back. Do what *you* want for a change.'

'I can't, I – am – married. You're a fine one to talk. You worship Phil for months, a year even! You wait for him and reject lesser mortal beings.' I'm exaggerating but my mouth keeps going. 'Then you fawn all over him only to be dumped after a few weeks!'

'Well, if you're not interested, I'm free to pursue Jack, yes, seeing as I'm single now?' she bats back.

'No! I mean, yes, fine.' She may as well have slapped me as I'm quite stung.

She grins. 'Aha, now we're getting somewhere. I rest my case. Think about it. There will be life after Andrew. And you're hardly going to stay with him now, are you?' She disappears into a cubicle.

I have thought about it, that's the problem. I spin around and find myself gazing straight into the mirror. There's a warm glow to my cheeks, partly from embarrassment and partly from indignation. It suits me. I'm pleased with the effect and suddenly see an attractive and alluring woman reflecting. My hands stray to my hair and running my fingers through I fluff it up a bit. I check my profile in a long mirror. If I'd known I was going to lunch with Jack, I'd have worn a dress, but the short, black skirt shows off my long legs and my ivory silk blouse is loose fitting and the tiniest bit sheer with a sexy hang. Damn it. What does it matter? I have a husband I love, no matter what. I turn away and sigh.

'Heard that,' comes from the cubicle.

'See you back there,' I say before slamming out the

door and strolling purposefully back to the table, determined to become immune to all men except my husband, and maybe him too, but especially one particular man. I have to sort out my marriage and distractions are a definite no-no. Jack is attractive to me because my self-esteem has taken a hit. Two wrongs don't make a right. Gosh, I sound like Jo now. But then she'd retort *'and don't put all your eggs in one basket.'* It's no use, I must see Andrew. Talk to him. Sort things out.

Jack throws me a quizzical look when I sit and I'm aware my lips are set in a tight line. Launching straight into a description of our day out, I avoid catching his eye while discussing the merits of the cathedral. I'm grateful for all the knowledge I have and harp on about pointed arches and Purbeck marble while preying Jo hurries up.

She promptly returns and throws me a conciliatory smile, and I smile back suddenly amused, and shake my head almost imperceptibly. We are both grouchy and inwardly struggling, with men being the cause. She's right, I am always trying to please Andrew, knowing he would have many choices if he were single. And, yes, having suspicions for the past three years hasn't helped. He's used to having females running around after him, and he takes my sycophancy for granted. But then Jo did the same with Phil. I mean sex five times a day, honestly. No wonder she never found time to clean. We both need a personal overhaul.

I glance up and catch Jack staring at me in a puzzled way. Our gazes lock onto each other for longer than they should and my stomach leaps and churns. He glances away first, casting his eyes downwards to reveal eyelashes that are thick and long. If I had a fan right now, I'd be attempting to cool myself.

I imagine us together. *We're lying on the floor on my Persian rug in front of my double-fronted wood burner, which throws out a fierce heat. Jack unbuttons my blouse and slips my skirt down over my hips. I wriggle out of it. His soft lips kiss the tops of my breasts and he pulls down one cup of my lacy, white see-through bra...*

The cosmos vibrates as my thoughts disseminate throughout the atmosphere, trying to find a landing point.

'What's your take on this, Miranda?' Jack says, bringing me back to earth with a thump. His gaze is penetrating and reminds me he has the ability to read me. I glow like a beacon at the thought.

'Er, think?'

'About me?'

The lump in my throat makes my voice croaky. 'About you...'

'About me revamping the gallery website too,' Jo says, coming swiftly to my rescue with a huge grin on her face. 'I have to come back soon anyway, so can kill two birds with one whatsit and so on.'

'Sounds good.'

The food arrives and Jo stares at her plate of lettuce and plain grilled chicken. She glares at Kim.

Kim ignores it. 'We're not sure if the dressing has gluten, so we left it off.' The girl with her puts down a plate of cardboard-looking white bread and a small pot of butter. 'We found some gluten-free bread and defrosted it,' adds Kim. 'It's real butter.'

'Er, thanks,' Jo grumbles as Kim glides away. She removes the pot and pushes it out of the way. 'Good job I'm watching my weight.'

Jo spends the remainder of lunch discussing her ideas for the website while munching on her lettuce leaves. I'm surprised she doesn't use the business chat as an excuse to use her phone, but it stays in her handbag as she fires off suggestions. Jack using his phone instead to make brief notes.

Jo asks for Jack's phone number and he hands her a business card, then peels off another and gives it to me. Jo hands him one of hers in return. This prompts a scavenging in my handbag for a rather dog-tailed business card. I pass it to Jack. He glances at one side then turns it over to reveal an imprint of my lips where I've used it to blot my lipstick. If Jack's surprised, his face doesn't show it. Instead he takes out his wallet, slips the card in and is now in possession of my permanent kiss.

Jo doesn't notice any of this but continues her chatter, mostly about Hector and his business, seeing all sorts of possibilities, making me worry she's getting carried away with both.

Eventually I relax and contribute an idea or two of my own for both websites. Not that I'm that good at marketing with having no experience, but I am creative. Jack joins in with gusto, but lets Jo lead the discussion. He's so dashing, a perfect gent.

• • •

'Until Wednesday then,' Jack says as we stand outside the pub ready to say our goodbyes. We move towards each other and I try to avoid what happened last time and head for his right cheek first and he goes to my left and then switches, and we do that awkward hesitant nose-bump thing. The skin-to-skin contact causes another shiver to nudge its way down my spine. And as if sensing it, Jack steals a glance at me. It isn't just me that feels an attraction, it's written in his eyes. A lump forms in my throat. Pull yourself together, I tell myself. Attraction between two people can happen, even when one or the other is married. Though, admittedly, this is the first time in seven years. The trick is to ignore it.

Jo coughs to attract our attention and I realise I'm still standing in front of Jack, so move aside. We both thank him for lunch.

'Please tell Hector I'll speak to him in the morning,' Jo says to Jack, leaning in for a kiss but getting it right. 'Friendly, isn't he? Married, single?'

I cringe, but Jack laughs at her frankness. 'Single and free.'

'I'm so looking forward to seeing him again. He's such a lovely man.'

'He's a great man,' Jack returns. 'One of the best.'

As is Jack. No matter how hard I deny it, he is a presence in my life that's hard to ignore. And worse, I don't know if I want to.

CHAPTER SEVEN

Monday morning I'm pacing the kitchen floor while going over what I'll say to Andrew. In fact, I'm having a full-blown argument with him even though he isn't participating in any way. Eventually, I come up with a questionnaire worthy of *Women in the Know* magazine.

The questions range from *Who was she that pint-sized blonde with the teeth? I followed you and saw everything,* to the multiple choice – *What have you been up to this weekend? Explain in detail any of the following:*

1. *You spent it in a five-star, not budget hotel, with…?* (Fill in female name.)
2. *Is it love or sex or both?*
3. *Necklace or not?*
4. *Do you still love me? As in – are you in love with me?*
5. *What now?* (Especially if the answer to

question four is the usual 'love you but not in love with you' cop out.)

NB: Actually, question five is for me to decide.

Jo left for home this morning, intending to pop in to meet Hector first, but at least I had her company last night to help distract me. We hunkered down under a duvet with chocolate, wine, and a Netflix binge. Not romance but horror, and we enjoyed scaring ourselves to death.

By six o'clock Jo had given in and checked her phone. Phil had not contacted her, so she chanced phoning him only to be told that he refused to discuss things further and he had nothing else to say on the subject as he was in company. 'Company' being loaded with meaning. This sparked a few tears from Jo followed by an angry determination that he clearly wasn't worth fretting over.

My phone, however, was another matter. It was ten before I switched it on. There were seven missed calls and several text messages over two messaging apps:

Trying to call you.
Why aren't you picking up?
Still not answering.
Is your phone switched off?
Been trying for eight hours now!
What's going on?
Call me as soon as you get this.

Reading the messages brought great satisfaction to

both Jo and me, though she pointed out that it also meant that while Phil and her were over, Andrew and I were not. That remained to be seen, but thinking up answers to the questions was easy. I used all his favourites in one text.

Was out for the day with Jo. Sorry no signal and forgot to charge my phone last night so it conked out. Was such a busy weekend for you, and with limited contact, didn't think it mattered. Xxx

Consequently, he wasn't happy and I received a curt, *See you in the morning.* Not even the usual three kisses.

Blasé as I was last night, this morning I'm nervy and can't keep still. My talk with Andrew can only go one of two ways. The first one is rather negative, but the lesser of two evils.

He comes in the door with a huge bunch of roses that have guilt written all over them. I drop them straight into the kitchen bin.

'Why the hell did you do that?' he asks indignantly. 'I should be angry with you for not answering your phone. I missed you and just wanted to chat.' (Okay 'chat' is stretching it.)

'Don't, Andrew, just don't. I know about you and that woman. You lied to me.'

'What woman? What the hell are you on about?'

'Don't act the innocent with me. The woman at the Northwood Park Hotel. The woman you snogged! The blonde woman with the ridiculous veneers.'

Nothing. He pauses too long.

'How could you throw our marriage away like that, Andrew? How could you think so little of me?'

'No…I mean I didn't do anything.'

'And lying makes it worse. Were you or were you not with such a woman?'

'Well, yes, okay,' he says, *'I was with a woman.'* He's looking desperate and adds hurriedly, *'I don't know what you've been told, but it's a lie. It was purely a business meeting. Not that I got the contract, so it was a huge waste of time.'*

'You liar, there was no business meeting. It was a dirty rotten weekend away with your lover.'

'No, no, I'm not lying. Someone's been lying to you. Who was it? I want to speak to them. Call them out. This has something to do with Jo, hasn't it?'

'It was me who saw you, Andrew. I followed you – watched you. Saw you with my own eyes. (Well they wouldn't be anyone else's.) *And I have a witness. You can't get out of this. We are over.'*

His eyeballs jitter as he tries think up a way out, but eventually gives up, falling to his haunches, hands covering his face. *'Oh God, darling, I'm sorry. I never intended it to happen and it meant nothing. Please forgive me and give me another chance. It will never happen again, I promise. Don't leave me. I love you. You and only you. It's a midlife crisis or something. I've been so stupid.'*

'No, it won't happen again. I won't let it.'

It ends with me packing a bag and storming out, leaving him devastated.

The satisfaction I get from that little scene is mainly

because he admits to his sins and I get to make him suffer.

The second scene that plays out in my head is my worst nightmare of the soul-destroying type.

He comes in the door acting all exhausted after his terrible weekend of business.

'Why didn't you answer your phone yesterday? I missed you and wanted to chat.' ('Chat' should be 'whinge' maybe here.)

'Don't, Andrew, just don't. I know about you and that woman. You lied to me.'

'What woman? What the hell are you on about?'

'Don't act the innocent with me. The woman at the Northwood Park Hotel. The blonde woman dressed as a leprechaun. The woman you're having an affair with.'

'You know? How?'

'Doesn't matter for now, I know. How long has it been going on?'

He spins on his heel, pausing for a moment, his back to me, and runs both hands through his hair before suddenly spinning back. 'Six months. Oh Miranda, I'm so, so sorry but I'm in love with her. We met and fell in love. Neither of us could prevent it. It's not you, it's me, and I'm just a bastard. Not your fault. I wanted to tell you many times but couldn't.'

'What! You're in love! Andrew…darling. Our marriage. I love you. This is horrible. How did this happen to us?'

'The way it happens to most people – accidentally. I met Kate through another – erm – through someone else, Leticia her name is. She's Kate's best friend. Leticia is also a close

friend of mine and we talk to each other all the time about our problems. Work and such. And then one day I bumped into her and there was Kate, and we got friendly too. I'm sorry, I do love you, I'm just not in love with you anymore.'

And my marriage ends on a cliché, just like that.

My mobile rings. My stomach lurches but it's 'Rebel Rebel', Mum's ringtone

'Mum!'

'Hello, dear. Landed safely in Spain. Italy was fabulous.' Her voice is a tonic.

'Oh, great to hear that you survived the, er, ninety-minute journey. I bet you're sorry to leave Tuscany though.'

'Yes, but it'll be nice to see your aunt and introduce her to Steve. We're in the car-hire office right now and then we're driving to Auntie Barbara's villa. I'll phone you from there. But I'll visit when we get back, next month. We have some lovely news to tell you, but we want to tell you in person.'

Auntie Barbara is Mum's twin. So, she's staying at the villa with Steve and introducing him, and that's after a two-week holiday already in Italy. What can that mean? She never did that with previous boyfriends. And what's the news? Mum took early retirement last year from her bank job, so it's not that. No, it can't be. She can't be getting married; she didn't even marry my dad! She's only been seeing Steve for eighteen months. He's a nice enough guy and they do get on, still is that any excuse to get married at their ages? Always in the past Mum's relationships never progressed past a few months.

'You still there? It's gone a bit quiet.' My sigh must be audible as she asks, 'What's going on? Had a row with Andrew?'

Yes, but only in my head. Are all mums psychic or is it just mine? This means she didn't believe me when we spoke last week. 'No, and nothing's going on, Mum. A bit tired that's all. Andrew's not here. He's away on business again this weekend. Jo called down though and we had a day out. She bought me a lovely necklace, antique, and cost a bomb. Can't wait for you to visit and hear your news.' It all comes tumbling out too quickly and my pace has quickened as I'm agitated and walking the length of the kitchen and back.

'Hmm, Andrew's away a lot these days, isn't he?'

'Well, he has lots of new responsibilities, and he oversees bringing in new business.' I slow down my speech, doing my best to sound cheerful.

'And you sound weary as if speaking is an effort. You never stop working, slaving away at your desk with all your spare time doing stuff on the cottage, while Andrew swans off all over the place. I'll be having words with him.'

'No need, Mum, honestly. You know how it is with Jo, lots of wine, dragging me here and there and—'

'Are you pacing?'

'No.' I stop.

'Well, I'll be there soon enough to see for myself. You can take a weekend off to spend with your dear old mum – and dear old Steve.' She laughs.

'Cool, looking forward to it.'

Mum might see me sooner than she thinks if I flee to Spain. Auntie Barbara has enough room in that huge villa. Ah, the sunshine, palm trees and bougainvillea. Lying on the beach, swimming, day trips, and mooching around markets. To get away from it all – 'it all' being Andrew.

After lots of bye-byeing and blowing of kisses, we ring off.

As I have no idea what time Andrew will arrive 'Monday morning' covering several hours, I make a pot of tea to stop me pacing. Just as I'm pouring water into the teapot, the kitchen door slams open against the wall and Andrew strolls through it. I hadn't heard his car pull up and he catches me unawares and unprepared.

'Oh, hi,' I say, my heart pounding. The scowl on his face is disconcerting and I spill water onto the worktop, so put the kettle down not trusting myself. He drops his keys on the table and walks over to peck me on my lips, but I can sense his hostility. This throws me a bit, as out of the two of us, I should be the hostile one. With my hands trembling and feet shuffling in trepidation and awkwardness, I croak, 'How was your weekend?'

'Awful,' he says in a clipped tone, and leans against the fridge, staring at me without expression. He's wearing a white shirt open at the neck and black jeans but is still managing to appear commanding. 'And where were you yesterday that was so interesting you couldn't answer your phone?'

'With Jo. Her boyfriend dumped her. She arrived in

a panic and was upset, weeping, so I took her out into town.' I do the actions to match, waving my arms about.

'So, where is she now then?'

'Oh, she left this morning about eight thirty. Had an appointment. Arrived Saturday and stayed two nights.' His expression remains serious, his lips set tight. 'We didn't drink much. Sightseeing in Netherbury, that's all, and lunch.' Why am I being defensive? Get a grip. Turning, I grab a cloth and wipe up the spilled water before taking a breath and spinning back to stare him straight in the eye, saying in a coquettish way, 'And was it worth it, this whole weekend away from me? What was the woman like you were meeting?' An unintended emphasis on 'woman' causes him to blink, and I quickly add, 'Was she nice?' My smile is sickly sweet and I'm relying on the fact he won't remember what he told me or at least believe that he slipped up somewhere along the way.

He's frowning, his mind working overtime as he tries to recall what he said, wondering perhaps if I've heard something from someone else, his boss, Freddie, or his wife, or even if someone spotted him in the hotel. Whatever, I've rumpled his composure.

'Er, yes, that's right, Jane Maxwell. Has a cosmetic company, though I wouldn't say she was nice.' He laughs derisively. 'Turned out to be a right witch. Only drank champagne.'

'So what did Freddie think of her?'

He again frowns, trying to work out if I know something. 'He couldn't make it Friday, unfortunately, but he was there the rest of the weekend. Cost an arm and a leg that dinner, and I had to suck up to her to get her to sign the contract.' He adopts an indignant stance and crosses his arms. 'That's why I was trying to phone yesterday, to find out if you could transfer some funds to my account as I was running short and I couldn't stand my round of drinks. But you damned well didn't pick up. Something, you never do. That Joanne leads you astray. Can't bloody stand her.'

Always, without fail, he blames everything on Jo. My hackles rise. 'At least I enjoyed myself, seeing that you weren't here and instead spent the weekend with another woman, all the while eating expensive dinners, drinking champagne, and spending all your money on her with the intention of spending all mine too if I'd been able to answer my phone.' I gulp air in.

He unfolds his arms. 'What? Don't be stupid. It wasn't the entire weekend, it was Friday, and I didn't spend my money on her. Well, money was spent, but I'll get it back eventually. It was only one meal and the damned champagne, but there was a whole weekend to go after that with the team. What's this, a touch of the green-eyed monster?' A note of unease tinges his voice for all the anger.

And there was the kiss. If I'm jealous I have good reason to be. 'A couple of brief phone calls and texts were really all you could manage in three days? You were unwilling to answer simple questions such as where were you staying, coupled with putting me off going with you. It was supposed to be Friday evening and Saturday, then it was another night and another. Until recently, you would often suggest I go with you if you were staying at a plush hotel or staying in a lovely town like Bath. And if I didn't, you'd phone me to tell me how the meetings were progressing.'

He bristles. 'For God's sake, working for MI5 now? Do I have to report all I'm doing at work?'

'Do I ever ask you to do that? I never needed to!' This is not coming out the way I hoped. 'It would be nice if you told me where you were going to stay, in case of emergencies.'

'I didn't know until the last minute. Paula in the office booked the hotel. A three star dump. Do you want to see the receipt?'

'No, of course not.' Distress has crept into my voice. Mostly because of my frustration at myself for not being brave enough to admit I followed him. 'There was nothing unreasonable in what I asked,' I remark softly. 'You were being evasive and nothing made sense.'

He sighs heavily. 'It didn't make sense as nothing went as planned.'

'So what happened?'

'Freddie landed me with the client without warning and she's important as her company is about to go global.' His expression is pained, and he runs one hand over his face before continuing. 'He phoned and explained the plans had changed and he wasn't coming down until Saturday as his little girl was sick. He was supposed to meet Maxwell at the Northwood Park for dinner to butter her up and get the contract signed – told me to drive straight there.' He pauses momentarily. 'She asked for me personally. With thinking the meetings with the team weren't until Saturday morning and then Freddie would take the lead, I was totally unprepared. I wasn't even wearing my suit. When I saw the Northwood Park I knew it'd be exorbitant. Freddie really is the limit.'

Andrew did stop en route to answer a call. Perhaps he's telling the truth and that was Freddie telling him about the change of plans. 'Why didn't you just say.'

Andrew stares for second, and then blinks. 'You've no idea of the stress I'm under with these meetings, Miranda. I shouldn't need to explain myself. Are you pouring the tea or what? It'll go cold.' His face is flushed with indignation.

I grab an extra mug and can't help feeling a bit of a mug too as this conversation is not heading the way I expected. And he cleverly used his ploy of cutting me off.

When I turn to hand him his tea his expression is serious and he looks haggard as he hasn't shaven for a day or two. It adds a ruggedness to his usually smooth appearance. For a moment I'm reminded of Jack, though he carries the style in a natural way. With Andrew, he just looks ill.

He yawns. 'Good to be home. Hope you have some money left after your day out with Jo because I'll need some funds until my commission comes in. You know what Freddie's like. Keeps forgetting to organise my credit card – convenient.'

'Yes, it is.' I nod in sympathy. 'So, she was a pain this Jane Maxwell you said? What was she like?'

'A diva.'

'Look like?'

He rolls his eyes. 'Oh, middle-aged, bottle blonde, teetering about in impossibly high heels. And a bit scary to be honest for the size of her.' He takes a sip of tea.

'Why would she scare you?' I prompt.

'You've no idea,' he grumbles, and opening a drawer to the side of him, he roots out a teaspoon and stirs his tea.

'Try me,' I say, keeping my voice light-hearted.

He continues stirring his tea. 'Because she was a demanding bitch. Once she suggested champagne I could hardly say no.'

'So, did you have to conduct the meeting in your jeans?' I ask, remembering he took his suitcase into the hotel with him.

'No, there was a bit of time, so I had a quick change in the toilets, then slipped out and put my suitcase back in the car. Once I found a quiet corner in a lounge, there was only a few minutes to familiarise myself properly with the contract details.'

Hmm, I was outside for an hour and didn't spot him. Perhaps I was flicking through my social media. 'A bit of a trial then?'

'Bit?' He laughs. 'But at least she signed the contract and I'll get recognition for that. Talking of which, I have to go to the office.' He gulps his tea down and drops the mug into the sink before walking to the door.

I desperately rack my brain trying to delay him. 'How much sucking up did you have to do?'

He pauses in the doorway like a rabbit caught in headlights.

'She fancied you, didn't she?' I add, taking a chance.

He twists around and rests his hand on the doorframe and I can see in his eyes that he knows I know something. He recovers quickly and sneers in distaste. 'Yes, she did, and I had to pretend to reciprocate to secure the contract. Freddie wasn't stupid when he dropped me in it. He must have known.'

'That she fancied you?'

He frowns and my hurt expression is hard to hide. His eyes soften and he seems to come to a decision. He walks towards me, his mouth working. 'It was awful. And believe me, I did not fancy her back. She was all over me and even – even tried to kiss me. Well, did actually. Caught me unawares, but it was only a peck.' He pauses and shakes his head. 'As soon as dinner was over, I made my excuses and bolted. I pretended you'd phoned me with an emergency as a matter of fact.' He places his hand on my upper arm and my head drops, tears forming.

Oh God, there it is, almost an admission. If I'd only stayed a little longer I would have seen it. Surely, he would never admit such a thing if he was really guilty. But why was his car still there after they finished dinner? The answer comes almost immediately. Because he shot out of there and caught a taxi while I was drinking with Jack, which was exactly what I did myself later – left the car there because I'd been drinking. Yes, he lied about the kiss being only a peck but probably so as not to upset me. All Andrew was doing was trying to land the contract to help move up a notch within the company.

The tension drains from my shoulders, leaving me aching. 'Sucking up is off the agenda in future, I take it?' I ask. 'You'll have to tell Freddie, explain what happened.'

Andrew's expression is contrite, the relief also evident. 'Yes, of course. Sorry. I didn't mean to tell you all this and upset you. Thought it best you didn't know as I already intended that I'll never let anyone put me in that position again.'

He's acting so open and sincere that I readily believe him. Every blundering action flashes before me – checking his phone, following him, going off in hysterics like an idiot instead of waiting to discover what else unfolded, meeting Jack. Oh God, yes Jack. And later, switching off my phone for no good reason. I'm a jealous, paranoid, neurotic, stalking, jezebel!

I wheel away and add more hot water to my tea to hide my shame. 'I'm glad you told me actually,' I say over my shoulder. 'We should be honest with one another.' Jack's face looms up along with much guilt at being a hypocrite. I fiddle around with putting the kettle back and wiping up a few drips until I'm able to face Andrew again, eventually adding, 'Though, you could have done without me going on like this after such a nightmare weekend.'

'Well, not all the weekend, only Friday the rest was taken up with team meetings. God, I hated having to toady to the stupid woman.' His face brightens. 'On the good side, it's brought lots of money into the business. Wait until I tell Matthew, it'll make his latest contracts seem like chicken feed. And this points to a promotion and possibly an eventual partnership.'

Matthew's his older brother and there's a lot of rivalry between them. 'That's great, and congrats.'

He smiles. 'Glad you weren't on your own and enjoyed your weekend. Sorry, being away that long didn't put me in a very good mood.' He gathers me into his arms and his fingers come up to my face to tip up my chin. 'How sexy you are and how I neglect you.' His lips are soft and sensual, and I part my own, waiting for his kiss. When it comes, it's gentle, his tongue probing my mouth teasingly. My traitorous flesh responds, and I relax and melt into him as his kisses get more and more urgent, his hands stroking my back, turning me into mush, his body hard against mine. He abruptly frees me and grabs my hand. 'Bugger Freddie. I could do with shaving anyway.' He pulls me towards the stairs.

Afterwards as I lie in bed and Andrew is in the shower, I decide I'll make the first move to put our marriage back on track. I'll be in Netherbury anyway on Wednesday so can check out the lingerie shop. At the weekend I can surprise him. Spice things up a bit.

Newly shaved, Andrew comes out from the shower and grabs me as I'm putting on my bathrobe, pulling me close. 'Stay naked. I want to enjoy another few seconds of you.' His lips brush my forehead. 'Sorry I have to dash off so soon, darling, wish I could stay here and wallow in everything that's you. I'll make it up when I get back tonight, promise. Could be late though.' He plants a kiss on my lips and lets me go.

As he towel-dries his hair, the taut muscles work in his shoulders. My hungry gaze wanders down his athletic body to his tapered waist, firm bum, and strong thighs. When he notices me ogling in the mirror, he whips around and grabs me, making me giggle. His mouth comes down on mine and I lose myself in his kiss, this time long and lingering. I have one of those moments when I can't believe I'm married to such a handsome man. Putting in the same measure of attention he's given me lately is not the answer. Look where it has led – me blowing things up out of proportion. Mortification causes the heat to rise. Then there's Jack. God, what do I say to him if he asks me what happened Wednesday? He'll think I'm psychotic. A picture of his serious, intelligent, and disapproving face, appears in my mind.

Andrew's lips suddenly leave mine and I realise I've stopped joining in. Luckily, he doesn't notice and kisses the tip of my nose. 'Need to get dressed. I can still get you all hot and bothered, can't I,' he says, and he lets me go.

I frown for a second before it dawns on me, he's referring to my heightened colour. 'Er, yes, you certainly can.' Keeping my head down, I grab my bathrobe and head for the shower.

It's only later I remember the texts from Leticia. The reason I followed him in the first place. That piece of the puzzle wasn't resolved. In my imaginings I had seen her as a friend of Maxwell, but stupid me had forgotten that wasn't true. I was so relieved with Andrew's 'sort of' admission that it went out of my head. If he had wanted to meet up with Leticia though, surely this weekend would have been the perfect opportunity. No! I have to stop this. Most likely I was reading more into the texts than was meant. Andrew can be flirty, and friends are at times gushy with one another. Look at me kissing Jack like old friends and Andrew not knowing anything about him. Yet, there's nothing in that.

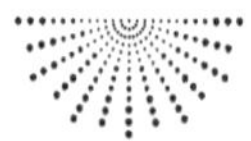

CHAPTER EIGHT

Wednesday has come around quickly and I've dressed in the most formal attire I can find, which in this case is a severe grey suit, several years old. No rock chick or slinky blouse for me today. Early for my appointment with Jack, I walk to the Netherbury Mall to buy new lingerie.

The promised 'I'll make it up when I get back tonight' didn't materialise as Andrew stayed working late Monday and Tuesday. Although he is no longer dealing with Miss High-Voltage Maxwell, it appears his input is still required. But the weekend will be one big date night.

In the lingerie shop I find there's so much choice I'm overwhelmed with indecision. I pick up a sheer white bra, similar to the one I was wearing when I imagined I was making love to Jack, there's a pair of tiny Brazilians to match.

Jack! Why am I bringing Jack into this? I'm buying for Andrew.

Black then, but when I pick up the bra, I recall Andrew with Miss Four-Hundred-Watt Smile on the four-poster at the hotel, so I hang it back. Must stop flashing back to situations that were never real in the first place, I could be here all day.

A raunchy red bra-and-knickers set catches my eye next. I'm a black or white girl, so this will a nice surprise for Andrew and there are no accompanying visions.

In the changing room I find the lacy bra is a snug fit and gives my small breasts a good boost. By the time I've paid it's two o'clock and I dash off up the road to Langford Gallery and rush in the door so fast I almost forget I'm anxious.

Hector greets me from the back. 'Jack's upstairs in the flat. Come through and you can go right up, he's expecting you.'

His flat! Doesn't he have an office then? With trepidation at being in Jack's home, his personal space, I negotiate my way past the display tables.

'I've had some great conversations with your friend Joanne over the past two days,' says Hector as he reaches to shake hands with me. He tries to be matter-of-fact but I can detect the excitement in his voice. 'She's such a live wire and is an absolute whizz at marketing.' He smiles warmly.

Yes, both.' Hector is obviously unaware that Joanne is fresh out of a relationship. He's not her usual type. And even if he was, she has to like a guy for years before deciding she will date him.

'She's coming back soon and we're going to discuss

the whole business, perhaps next weekend. Antique jewellery's an area she's interested in, she tells me.' His aqua eyes look to me for confirmation.

'Oh, um, yes, she likes jewellery. Loves…jewellery,' is all I can think of to say, but at least I'm telling the truth. I give him a quick smile and carry on to the room at the back, promising myself to have a word with Jo about flirting with and leading on the innocent.

The storeroom at the back is packed with stock, including enormous pictures probably too big to fit in the gallery. To the right, narrow stairs wind upwards. I climb them and knock on the door at the top even though it's open.

Jack shouts to come in and I hesitantly step into his personal domain to find he's not there. The room isn't quite how I imagined it would be. Yes, the windows don't let in much light but the room is long and spacious. Rather classy, I must say, with wood panelling, polished wood floor, and lots of old beams crisscrossing the walls. The ceiling is a bit low. How does Jack manage to avoid bumping his head? He doesn't fit with this place. It's also furnished with antiques, and only a modern comfy leather chair next to a small occasional table where a book lies, looks out of place. The desk is at the far end, an open laptop sitting on it along with a monitor, while a number of files stand at the back. The only other office furniture is a filing cabinet along with a chest of drawers. No, the flat doesn't suit him, the size or decor.

Jack appears through a door a tea towel in his hand. 'Tea?'

I turn into a nodding dog, bobbing my head up and down and then shaking it the other way. 'That would be nice, thank you. No sugar.'

'Not bad is it?' he says as I pretend to scan the room again, so I don't have to look directly at him. 'It was meant to be temporary but I stayed rather longer than I expected. The furniture is Hector's. I prefer something more modern. I'm looking for a property in the Winterfords.'

'The Winterfords are charming. Very picturesque.' I wouldn't mind living there myself, I think. There's a pause. We stand gazing at each other awkwardly, both smiling, though my own is stuck, and I must resemble the Cheshire Cat.

Jack starts. 'Right, I'll make the tea. Everything's over there.' He points to the desk. 'Bank statements are in the files. Do your worst.'

'Thanks. Should be a couple of hours.' Relieved to have something to focus on, I go to the desk. The office chair looks comfortable and I plonk myself on it and shove my handbag and shopping on the floor. I must drum this into my head – I'm here to work. I'm a married woman and need to remind myself I'm Mrs Jack Stone. Andrew! Mrs – Andrew – Stone! I make a mental note to de-fancy Jack Langford as swiftly as possible.

I get to work and am relieved when Jack brings my tea and, leaving me to it, disappears downstairs. Jack has a good bookkeeping system and I check invoices and bank statements against figures entered, finding it all straightforward enough. A couple of hours later I'm surprised to find the books of Langford Gallery are in excellent order and far from needing a spring-clean. I close the last file with a snap.

Jack's feet pound up the wooden staircase and he strolls into the room. I busy myself putting the file back. 'All good,' I say over my shoulder, 'from what I've seen so far.' In fact everything is so up to date I'm not sure why he needs me.

He's back to reading my mind when he says, 'It'll be a relief to have someone sensible and methodical looking after my books. Frees up time for my TV work. Assistants will insist on getting married.'

Sensible and methodical after our last two encounters? Well, I suppose that's an improvement on being the lush and psycho I imagined he must see. Still I'm a little peeved he couldn't have said something more flattering. 'The way you keep your accounts works well enough,' I say, sounding like a schoolteacher. 'Your assistant knew what she was doing.'

I move my foot and the bag with my underwear slips with a swish and rustle. Glancing down, I spot my scarlet bra trailing across the floor. Sweeping forwards, I scoop it up and shove it back in the bag, placing it upright against the desk leg. On the way back up I'm aware of Jack's thighs perilously close to my face. I raise my eyes to see if he spotted my ultra-sexy bra and they fall straight onto his ample crotch area. I blink. Shoot. Gulping, I bring my gaze up to his face and straighten up.

He gives me a wry smile, but puzzlement tinges his eyes. 'Everything better at home then?'

'Er, yes. I was mistaken about Andrew. A business colleague that's all she was.'

Jack raises his eyebrows as if to say, *really?*

Clearly, he doesn't believe me and his expression tells me he must have seen at least some of Andrew's wooing of that walking advert for whitening toothpaste. Suddenly it's important that he does believe me or I'll look an idiot. 'He – he had to act as if he was attracted to her to get the business. To persuade her to sign the contract. Harmless flirting. Business men have to do these things sometimes.'

'Do they?' His mouth is set in a grim line.

I'm indignant he's doubtful though the excuse sounds pathetic even to me. Jack wasn't there to listen to Andrew's explanation of events, which was perfectly logical at the time, even if it does sound as if I'm a gullible fool now. There's no point in elaborating further. 'My abridgement was quite obviously lost in translation,' I snap. 'Everything is back to normal at home. I was mistaken, but thanks again for coming to my rescue. Oh, and for the tea today.'

'Pleasure.'

A look of disappointment flashes over Jack's face and an unexpected feeling of tenderness towards him grips my chest, wiping away my pique. Could it be that rescuers are reluctant to give up those rescued because they feel eternally responsible for them? Or could it be the other way around and my imagination is running away with me?

'I have to get back,' I say, knowing either way he still

considers me gullible. 'The rush hour traffic, you know, want to avoid it. I'll phone you to arrange days to do your accounts, but as I'm squeezing you in, they might not be regular to start with.' Not waiting for an answer, I reach for my bags and flee.

Traffic is horrendous on the way home and I wished I hadn't stopped at the supermarket. It doesn't help that I have a car in front of me doing twenty in a forty-mile-an-hour zone. I'm not in the best of moods as I approach the cottage as I'm also still reeling from my hurt pride. Jack doesn't know Andrew, or how he conducts himself with people, or how it's just the way he is. In the hotel, striving to get the contract signed caused his unthinking behaviour – simply wanting to get promoted, to have something successful to throw at his talented brother. He wouldn't have thought about me when so focused.

As I turn off the main road and negotiate the blind bends in the small lanes, pictures of Andrew in the hotel reaching for the woman's hand, leaning in to kiss her, flash into my mind. But shouldn't he have thought of me? Every busy person can get single-minded at times. However, forgetting he's married? And there were other holes in his plot. Andrew said Freddie contacted him unexpectedly as he couldn't make it. Yet, I saw Andrew take the contract from his pocket to be signed. How did he get it?

For God's sake, there are those doubts again. Jack put

these suspicions into my head. Being married doesn't make you immune to attractive people; look at me with Jack for instance. But then I'm making an effort to keep it professional. Andrew should do the same. Perhaps I should remind him. And Jack no doubt believed Andrew should had more control too, and thinks I'm stupid to trust him. I shouldn't blame him for that.

The explanation Andrew gave me does mainly fit. He didn't go to meet Leticia Fuentes as I thought. My mind drifts back to the texts. Love you and miss you darling or something like that. Why was she so familiar with him? Andrew mentioned after the Claire episode that I also used to write, 'Love Miranda', often with kisses, to old Mr O'Brien the builder, and I'm sure I've done it with others. But, even so, I worried about that incident with Claire for years. And why did Leticia want to speak to him after work if she's connected with it? Office gossip? I shake the notion away. She might have been on a photo shoot; after all, she is a photographer.

Here I am, doing it again, tossing the thoughts back and forth like a ball in a tennis match. Must stop. The plan I have to move forward and work on my marriage is a good one. When that's on track, I can talk to Andrew on the subject of boundaries.

Andrew's car is in the driveway when I finally reach home and I park up behind him. He's home early and I glance at my bag of new lingerie on the seat beside me and can't help giving a furtive smile – a new start. Operation Save Marriage is about to get underway.

I jump out of the car. If he's lit the fire in the snug, I'll drag him straight in there. Perhaps it's time we took advantage of the new rug that lies in front of the hearth with no dog yet occupying it. Though I hope to rectify that soon. Once the cottage was finished, the plan was always to move on a stage in our relationship, and that's exactly what will happen, starting now with us focussing on each other more.

There's no sign of Andrew as I let myself in the front door, but I can hear the kettle boiling so he must be in the kitchen. I hide the bag of lingerie behind a cushion in the snug and carry on through.

I'm about to open the kitchen door when the kettle comes to the boil and switches off, leaving Andrew's voice echoing in the high-ceilinged room. It takes a few seconds to comprehend he isn't talking to me but is on the phone and hasn't heard me come in. Hearing the word 'darling', my instincts kick in. My hand freezes on the door handle, and finger by finger I loosen my grasp. My ear is sucked to the door like a magnet.

'Miss you too. Hated leaving you. Sorry it wasn't the whole weekend as planned. Bloody work got in the way Friday. Look, best not to call me at this time of day because sometimes I come home early. Time off for good behaviour.' He laughs softly. 'So, always text me first, hey.' There's a pause. 'Okay, I'll try to get over to you this weekend. It's a bit tricky two weekends on the trot, so don't know if I can swing it, but I'll damn well try.'

My stomach tumbles. In the early days of our

marriage he used that honeyed tone when speaking to me on the phone.

Andrew chuckles at something whoever he is speaking to says and replies, 'Can't wait, Tisha, you brazen hussy. Though you wearing nothing at all, would suit me better.'

My hand flies to my throat in distress. I'm such a fool and feel wretched realising that. How could he do this to me without a thought to how much it would hurt or injure me, destroy my life, our marriage… What an arsehole; monogamy obviously isn't part of his vocabulary. He's such a bastard liar.

He speaks again. 'Of course. Of course, I'll tell her. But Miranda can't handle it right now. It could send her over the edge. Soon though, I promise. Depends on what her counsellor says next time. Sorry, darling, have to go. She'll be back shortly.'

Counsellor! I've heard enough. I beat a hasty retreat to the front door and slip out. The anguish is crushing my heart. A few deep breaths help quell the rising panic as I struggle to compose myself. From the start I was right and my instincts are in perfect working order. There is someone else.

Tisha. Leticia. Leticia Fuentes! And what about Jane (The Teeth) Maxwell? There's no point in asking him as he will lie and lie again, he's so bloody practiced at it. But not practiced enough for me. Gosh, he's not even original. Counsellor! How can the stupid woman fall for that blatant lie? They were obviously discussing him telling me about the affair and he's making excuses not to. But then I can't blame her for believing him as that's what I did – readily accepted his lies as truths. The explanation he gave me about the hotel didn't sound ludicrous until I related it to Jack, and being impartial, he clearly didn't believe it. And there was I, stubbornly blocking the reality out. I can't believe how gullible I've been. Lowlife!

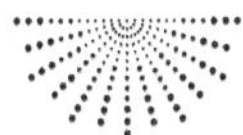

CHAPTER NINE

Anger has taken the place of pain by the time I've hauled a shopping bag from the boot of my car. I drag it into the cottage, slamming the front door after me, and shout from the hallway that I'm back. Bustling straight into the kitchen, I dump the shopping on the floor and throw off my jacket in the way a stressed person would when flustered with their day and is glad to be home. This I hope will hide my initial anguish, humiliation, and heartache. I deserve an Oscar.

'Hi, darling,' says Andrew, slipping his phone into his pocket. 'Decided to surprise you. Freddie flew to Berlin, so I came home early. He can't complain, especially not after that awful weekend.'

'Yeah, must have been so tough.'

He frowns. 'Tired? Shall I cook?'

I keep up the pretence. 'Not having to cook is fine by me. Traffic was hell coming back from Netherbury.'

'Netherbury? You didn't say you were going shopping today.'

I raise my eyebrows. 'Actually, I had an appointment at Langford Gallery.'

'Gallery? Been buying more stuff for the house? Glad, we still have money.' Sarcasm colours his voice.

In reply, he receives one of my slow blinks accompanied by pursed lips. 'To do the accounts. My new client.'

'Oh, sorry, talking at cross purposes. Well, great, more work. Every little helps. I could do with a few quid.'

'It *will* only be a little, so perhaps you should get onto Freddie about your expenses and commission, running short myself and we still need to eat for the rest of the month.' A feeble attempt to keep my tone neutral isn't working, but there's no way I'm handing over money so he can spend it on other women.

'Tetchy. It's not as if I'm spending it on me. Glass of wine help?'

'I'll do it.' The wine rack is almost empty, but I pull out a bottle of Malbec and make a big thing of searching for the corkscrew to avoid looking at his lying face. After a few deep breaths, I thrust the bottle at him along with the corkscrew before sticking my face in the fridge, concealing myself behind the door, my knees like jelly.

My face stays behind the fridge door as I mumble, 'It's been a long day with a difficult account.' This is becoming my standard excuse but will suffice here. I force a smile and appear with a bag of rocket. 'Still, I don't mind cooking if cajun chicken breast and salad is okay?'

'Yes, anything's good if you don't mind doing it.' He pours a good amount of wine into two balloon glasses. At this rate I'll become an alcoholic. I wish he would disappear into the sitting room and watch TV and leave me to consider my options, but instead he sits himself at the worktop on a barstool. 'I know how you feel regards work. Mine's so stressful, right now. It's good to be home, chill, laze around. Let's make the most of this evening. There'll be a lot of late nights coming up for me, and with your new account I bet you'll be dipping into the evenings too.'

How can he lay the groundwork for seeing his lover so coldly? I'm unable to scrutinise his expression but it's certainly devoid of guilt. If it wasn't for the fact I'd walked in at the very moment he happened to be on the phone to her, I'd think everything was normal and would probably be dragging him into the snug.

Not wanting him to see the pain in my eyes I spin back round to the cooker, but the devil in me wishes him to have a taste of how I feel. 'My new client's the TV personality Dr Jack Langford as it happens. He wants me to take care of his bookkeeping as he's working on a new series, so will be at the studios a lot. He's quite the heart-throb from what I understand.'

'Really? Jack Langford you say. Never heard of him.'

'No, you wouldn't, he's an art expert.' While speaking, I remain facing away from him, busily mixing some spices. 'He appears on those culture programmes you hate.'

'Old fart then?'

'Forties more like. I did say he was considered to be a heart-throb.' How did that go right over his head?

'Is he a tall bloke, by any chance?'

'Yes. So, you have seen him then.'

'How did you meet him? Did he find you online? You'd think he'd want to use an accountant if he's that important.'

Brilliant, it's little wonder his family trivialise my job when he does it constantly. 'Oh, I wandered into the gallery on Sunday with Jo,' I reply nonchalantly, 'while you were…in Bath. He was there, Jo recognised him immediately and then we got chatting and went to lunch to discuss business. Jo's doing some marketing for his colleague. You know how it is with clients. You have to get straight in there with them.' I pause for effect. 'During the conversation I mentioned I was a book-keeper and he said he needed one for his day-to-day stuff and asked me to come back Wednesday.' A blast of shame hits me for having left out half the information. Suddenly I find myself in Andrew's position, trying to act normal.

'Doesn't need an ad agency, does he?'

'Not that sort of business.' When I face him to access the knife drawer, he doesn't look in the least jealous. A TV personality couldn't possibly be a threat to him. Andrew doesn't consider me alluring enough to tempt anyone obviously.

'He'll be the next guy Jo sets her cap at,' he says, laughing. Obviously presuming Jo fancies him and I wouldn't, being married to him.

'Well, he is a hunk.' Somehow, I doubt Jack would be thrilled at being used in this way, so I search around my head for another subject to talk about. Perhaps, bringing up the weekend to ascertain if Andrew's planned anything might be too soon and could cause him to suspect I overheard.

As I murder a pepper and stab through cucumber with a santoku knife, I decide four things.

1. Try to get him to confess to cheating of his own accord.
2. Number one having failed, catch him in the act so he can't wriggle out of it, and in the process prevent him from making it somehow my fault (although I'm sure he'll still try).
3. Refuse to put myself in a position where I fall for his charm, his rationalising, and most of all, his body, sending my self-respect flying out the window.
4. Approach this in a calm manner. There must be steam coming out of my ears.

Andrew solves the problem of a new subject by yakking on about work, remaining in the kitchen until I've finished cooking.

While we're eating, he brings up the subject of the

weekend with a simple, 'Did you have any plans for this weekend?'

With the moment suspended and the atmosphere palpable, my heart skips a beat. Is he hoping to get away for a couple of days, even when again he's pleading poverty?

'Weren't you planning to make it up to me after being away the whole of last weekend,' I say with affected cheeriness. 'With no business meetings I thought I'd cook something special for dinner Saturday evening. Paella. There's a fabulous authentic recipe in one of my cookery books and you do so love eating Spanish.'

Silence.

My neutral expression greets him when he stares at me, unblinking. (I've learned how to do this having had a great teacher – him.) Calmly, I pick up my wine and take a huge gulp.

'Er, yes. Love paella, but—'

'And I'll make a jug of Sangria and root out some Spanish music. With no money we can't do much, but I can stretch to a simple dinner. We can have a cosy date-weekend in. Take time out for us. Husband and wife enjoying each other.' I concentrate on my food. 'We can keep up the Spanish theme. Pretend we're abroad especially as the weather looks promising.' I have no idea what the weather is going to be like.

With my next gulp of wine, I venture to peer over my wine-glass rim. Sure enough, this time fear is writ large in his eyes at the mention of all things Spanish, along with disconcertion as he's caught in a quandary –

Spanish out, Spanish in. Which will he choose? He actually planned to spend the weekend with her. How could he imagine he could get away with it twice?

He strokes down the side of his face, his gaze sweeping the room, buying himself time to mull over my suggestion. 'More wine.' His chair scrapes back as he gets up to fetch the bottle.

I'm right. A wave of emotion gushes up as I picture him with Leticia, my cheeks stinging as the blood rises. Sod it. I can't do this. Letting out a long trembling breath I say, 'Andrew, I know about—'

'Sounds great, a weekend in,' he says jauntily, coming back to the side of my chair. He pours the wine then pulls my head towards his side in a brief and suffocating hug before sitting back down. 'Sorry, what were you going to say?'

Sounds great? This throws me and my eyes widen. I'm confused and hesitate too long. Jo would be squawking like a chicken if she were here. 'Oh, just that you…you…that I know getting the contract at the weekend means a lot to you, and that we should celebrate…with Spanish food.'

'You've no idea how much.' He frowns, shakes his head, and stares at me fondly. 'God, that's such a standard saying, and so untrue. You do know how much. No one understands me like you do. It might be a cliché but you're my rock.' He chinks his glass against mine. 'Well, cheers, let's hope this contract I got leads to something bigger. Sunday we could go out for dinner if Freddie comes up with my payment before then. I'll tell you what, I'll push him on it, insist. The accountant's useless and a blasted nuisance. I've been with this company months now.'

'Well, I did offer to help with the accounts.'

'Don't be daft, darling. The company's too big for a mere bookkeeper. We have to have a qualified accountant. And best not to work with family and so on. You understand.'

I understand only too well and it's more to do with cramping of style. And now he's had second thoughts about Leticia I'm supposed to slot into the space again. At this point I'm sorely tempted to do a *Doctor Foster* on him. But Confucius said, 'Before embarking on a journey of revenge, dig two graves,' so perhaps not. To lower myself to his ground-hugging position will only cause me more grief.

Andrew clears the dishes and stacks them in the dishwasher before saying he's forgotten something and must email Freddie, and promptly shoots off to the snug. No doubt really to contact Leticia to say he can't make it as the mad woman needs support.

As I wipe the dining table, I wish I hadn't mentioned I'd make Spanish food. It's backfired and the last thing I want is to be in an intimate situation with Andrew, especially with paella on the menu. If anything, I want to move into the spare room. Better still, banish him to sleep there for ever more.

My phone rings, it's 'Miss Gulch's Theme' from *The Wizard of Oz*. I want to ignore it but know it's my mother-in-law, Felicity, who will keep on phoning until I answer.

'Hi, Fliss,' I say, trying to sound pleasant. Andrew, having recognised the ringtone, hurries into the kitchen shaking his head at me and mouths, 'I'm not here.'

After exchanging the usual pleasantries, Felicity says, 'Just a quick call as I'm on my way out. Did Andrew's tell you yet? Matthew just went into partnership with a huge IT company and he and Kate are having a little celebration at the weekend. Just nibbles and cocktails.'

'Congratulations to Matthew,' I say.

'Look, I know Andrew will be away on business this weekend but—'

'Away on business?' Andrew grimaces and nods his head vigorously. 'Er, yes, he did mention something.'

There's a loud tut at the other end. 'Yes, but perhaps you can persuade him not to go. You might be able to take time off whenever you want, working from home, but we don't see Andrew enough these days, and the trip to Chester's only four hours. And you can visit your mother while you're up here, can't you, and I can have Andrew to myself for a day.'

I bite my tongue knowing that Andrew would not want to be stuck there with Kate bragging throughout the evening about Matthew's achievements, and the resultant gloating from Matthew. Coupled with the fact he was originally hoping to meet Leticia, no doubt. However, I don't want to go either.

'Work has to take precedence, I'm afraid. Matthew should understand that.'

Andrew smiles and gives me a thumbs up.

'Even so, please do have a word.'

'I'll try, but he has work to do on the new big contract he's landed, and the extra money's handy.'

I can almost hear the steam escape from Felicity's lips as she says, 'Have you ever considered getting a proper job? It'd take the pressure off my son. He's probably worried about paying for all those renovations.'

Proper job! The hackles rise on the back of my neck. I earn almost the same as Andrew. I'm surprised Felicity can't hear me grinding my teeth as I state, 'I do have a proper job, my own business. And I doubt Andrew can get out of the meeting as he has an important position within his company and can't take time off on a whim.'

'Can't be that important, can it? I mean it's not his own business, not like Matthew,' she says sharply. 'He's entitled to time off, surely.'

'It is important,' I snap back. 'His next big promotion depends on it and there's a possible partnership in the offing. You wouldn't want him to miss out on that.'

This shuts her up and she says a curt goodbye. Andrew grimaces and refreshes his wine glass for the third time.

I've hardly had time to put down my phone away when I get a text message from his sister-in-law Kate. *Heard our news. What do you think of this?* Attached is a link to a pic of a sizeable house in Alderley Edge with a price tag of close to a million quid. A second message follows: *We've booked to view it Friday. So exciting. There's even a playroom for Oliver and Abigail. And three reception rooms. Hope you can make it to our little do.*

I suppose being an only child I'm not used to sibling rivalry. It wasn't easy for Andrew, as while he inherited good looks from his mother, Matthew inherited the brains and academic abilities from his father, achieving a first-class degree from Manchester University followed by an MBA while Andrew 'scraped through' with an upper second from a 'not-a-proper-university' meaning it was once a polytechnic. Andrew struggles to get any approval from his father with Howard favouring staid, sensible Matthew. On the good side, Howard likes me and often shows interest in what's going on with my business. Felicity, in turn, showers Andrew with attention to make up for it, always bragging about how he should have been famous with his looks. She constantly implies he only married me because I was pregnant. A little thing such as the truth doesn't stop her from spilling her bile as we lost the baby before we married. And when she introduces me to people, she tells them I'm an accountant.

So, I'm with Andrew on this one. We're not going. Matthew and Kate have made no effort to come to visit us during the past three years, apart from once. They turned up one day shortly after we bought the cottage and practically called it a dump. If I remember rightly, Kate said, 'It has charm, this little place, I suppose. You can sell it and buy something bigger in a few years. Consider it an adventure, like camping out.'

'Phew,' Andrew says, bringing the bottle of wine to me and topping up my glass. 'Thanks for that, darling.

Imagine a whole weekend of gloating and bragging, Mum fussing and Dad pointing out my failures. When I told him about winning the contract, I might well have said I just won a fiver on the Lotto for all the notice he took.'

I don't tell him his mother dismissed it too. No matter what Andrew does, in reality, he'll never be the self-made man his dad wants him to be. Why doesn't he tell them straight he's happy with his life?

Andrew stares thoughtfully into his wine. Is he happy with his life? With his job? Maybe not entirely. And happy with me? I thought I knew the answer. Shouldn't I know? Or have known because he can't be. I'm not enough. His job isn't enough. Nothing is enough.

It's Saturday and most of today we were both bombarded with pics from Felicity and Kate of the party and the house, and may as well have gone for all the peace we got.

Last night went okay, considering I far from wanted to celebrate and Andrew wished himself elsewhere. I'd told Andrew I fancied Italian instead of Spanish, so it was a creamy salmon linguine and a good chardonnay followed by a lemon mousse and Limoncello shot. Andrew was quiet and eventually complained he was tired and went to bed early with his phone. Later, I crept up and listened at the door. So much for being tired. He was clicking away, having not bothered to alter his keyboard settings. When I went in the room there was no sign of his phone so he must have shoved it under the duvet.

As Andrew found his expenses had been paid into his account, on Sunday morning I suggested the cinema for the evening, so I didn't have to go through another night of watching him regret his decision not to see Leticia. He said there were no films on of interest to him and suggested going out to dinner instead as planned.

I'd like to say Andrew's enthusiasm for together time only gradually waned throughout dinner, but there wasn't any enthusiasm to wane to begin with. He wasn't present at all, and either daydreamed or talked about himself and work or whinged about his family. Interestingly, he hadn't touched his phone all day that I saw, apart from once, and that wasn't for long.

It isn't until we get home that I decide enough is enough. Waiting for him to confess isn't working. He must be missing his lover and perhaps when he's vulnerable is the best time to confront him.

I wait until I've made cocoa and we're sitting having it in the snug, then say firmly, 'I need to talk to you.'

Andrew, suddenly alert, clangs his mug onto the coffee table and turns to me, placing his hand over mine. 'Sorry caught up in my own stuff again. Not asking how things are with you. Problems with clients? Jo having a crisis?'

'No, it's not about me directly. Are you happy? I mean, with me. This weekend—'

'Of course, why wouldn't I be?'

'You're distracted. I wondered if—'

Andrew drops my hand and gets up to pour himself a whisky. 'Oh, here we go. What? Wondered if what? No, there's nothing going on before you ask. I'm under stress. See how you've spoilt a lovely weekend?'

What lovely weekend? His reaction is extreme and not what I expected. But it shows something is the matter, so I stubbornly stick with it. 'Darling?' I stand up. 'I just meant, do I listen enough to any personal troubles you might have. You can talk to me about anything. Even if it…surprises me. I'm here to listen. We can work things out together.'

Andrew stiffens. 'Personal troubles? What the hell does that mean. Nothing wrong with me. What prompted you to say that? And the bit about whether I'm happy with you or not, why ask?'

He isn't ready to confess and the yellow streak down my back grows brighter as my mind whirls, searching for an answer. 'Do we talk enough? And are you happy with me working from home?'

'Don't be daft. We're always talking. And why wouldn't I be happy with you working from home? We agreed it was the best thing.'

'Oh, it was your mum. Told me to get a proper job again.' Brilliant escape even if I say so myself.

'Haven't you learnt to ignore her yet? She needs to understand I'm not a little boy anymore and can support us both.'

I finally snap. 'Don't I contribute then? Help support us both?'

'Maybe you should go to bed, the alcohol's making you argumentative.' He slams his glass down. 'That's exactly what I'm going to do. Some of us don't have the luxury of working from home and have to be up early.'

I didn't even have any alcohol. I give up. What's the point?

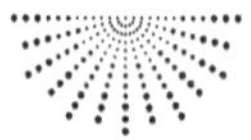

For the past two weeks until a couple of days ago, Andrew was irritable as work was stressful, so he said. Our sex life, admittedly, was non-existent with me avoiding him and him not noticing. I had begun to believe he had ended his affair as he didn't seem happy. But then the day before yesterday he became furtive and excited, occupying any room in the house as long as I wasn't in it, super possessive about his phone again.

In some ways I was glad of the respite when he wasn't attached to his phone and was home on time, until it was replaced by his low mood and ill temper. Now we're back to square one and that's hard to live with. Is he in contact with Leticia again? How can I confront him without solid proof?

Then there's Jack. Since our last encounter, I've avoided him too, and the invoices must be piling up if he's now leaving them for me to sort out. On the other hand, he hasn't contacted me either. Yes, I should have apologised to him and admitted he was right about Andrew, but now I've left it too long. Perhaps it's for the best. No matter what Andrew has done I can't counteract it by seeking the attentions of another man. Jack is attractive and was there when I needed help and support, and that puts me in dangerous territory.

My computer stares accusingly at me. A quick glance out the window shows a dull rainy day, not exactly motivating me into going for a walk. Now if I had a dog, I'd make more effort. Perhaps Jo is about, even for a short time. This last week or so she has practically lived in Wiltshire now that she has taken on Hector as a project, and her relationship with Phil is well and truly over.

After texts back and forth, I discover she's in Chester, so I phone her for some mutual support and sympathy.

'Why are we such fools?' she says when I tell her about Andrew's secretive and unhappy behaviour, followed by euphoria. 'Someone spotted Phil out in a pub with his ex too, last weekend.'

'Didn't she dump him?'

'Yes, but it looks as if it's back on. I was right. I was the rebound waiting like a lamb to the slaughter. When he comes running back, as I doubt their problems have been miraculously fixed, he'll find I haven't waited around. I'm no doormat to be trampled on.'

'Good for you, Jo. Well, I'm a walking, living doormat. My marriage is no longer much of a marriage, and I'm in limbo without proof. I have to wait for a slip up, no choice.'

'Wait? For God's sake, Randa! You're only prolonging

the agony by not acting. How can you stand it? Just confront him.'

With a deep breath in, and an even longer one out, I say, 'I've tried and he denied anything was going on. This is the only way, honestly. I now carry my phone around with me, and if I hear him talking to other women, I'm going to record it. He won't get away with that again. And if I spot emails or texts I'm going to photograph them.'

'Proper little Miss Marple aren't you?'

'I wish. There's no saying I'll catch him making calls again, to be honest. But something else might happen.'

'Wait a minute, you're not delaying the inevitable, are you? Holding out hope that he'll come running to you, apologising and begging forgiveness?'

'No way!' Strange Jo should think that, as not so long ago, I assumed that was what she wanted to do with Phil.

'Holly Cottage, is that it? After all the hard work, you don't want to give it up, but know you won't be able to keep it on by yourself?'

The consequences of divorce have occupied some of my time recently, but not in any detail. It's too scary to contemplate long. 'Haven't worked it out.'

'Maybe you should.'

'Hang on.' I swing around in my office chair and do a quick calculation on a notepad – the substantial deposit we paid, the equity from my first house added on, and approximately how much the cottage is worth now with the renovations. I take away the mortgage and divide the equity by two. Nightmare, no way I could take out a bigger mortgage to buy Andrew out, we'd have to sell. And I'm self-employed so it's harder to borrow. My life is unravelling faster than a ball of wool tugged by a kitten and tangling back up just as fast.

'And?' says Jo when she hears my sigh.

'Okay, we'd have to sell and start from scratch, but I'm not trying to delay the inevitable as you put it. But yes, a life without Andrew, all the plans gone, being single again, well, it's daunting. Would be for anyone.'

'You can do it. I have.'

'To be frank, your relationship was short lived, mine's a marriage of seven years. It's not easy to walk out and start again. Not that I'm trivialising your own hurt, it's just…less complicated.'

'No, you're right,' says Jo. 'You can always move in with me though. Come back up to Chester if that'd help.'

A picture flashes into my head of Jo's flat. Smart, on the outskirts of the town, lovely location overlooking the River Dee, but the mess – clothes everywhere, housework not a priority. 'I need my own place. My work's here and my business. Anyway, you've been down this end of the country a lot lately.'

'Yep, that's true. Perhaps I should be the one to move.'

Suspicion stomps in wearing hobnail boots. 'Jo, is there something going on with Hector? He seemed rather taken with you last time I saw him. Did you stay at his place when you came down? Well, you weren't here.'

'Not hiding anything from you, Sherlock, and don't intend to either. Okay, it's not that he *seemed* to be taken with me, he *is* taken with me. And he's sooo very… Anyway, yes, I like him too.' Her voice sounds defensive.

'And staying at his place?'

'Are these questions a practice run for Andrew?' I don't answer. 'He did offer to put me up, yes, but I stayed in the local hotel. Well, I could hardly have stayed with you at your house with Andrew shooting daggers from his eyes. And with everything going on there…'

'Sorry.'

'Nothing to be sorry about, it's not your fault. The hotel was rather plush and Hector paid my expenses. He's a perfect gent, and such fun. And those eyes.' She's gushing now. 'We've been Face Timing each other. I'm considering going into business with him. Jewellery's only one of the businesses he deals in, he buys and sells antiques online too. And –' she coughs – 'he's already asked me if I'd like to.'

'You know zilch about antique jewellery. It'll be one of your five-minute fads.'

'Oh, ye of little faith. Not this time. And I'm a quick learner and have some creative marketing ideas. We're discussing it again over dinner Saturday.'

God help Hector, but at least she's moved on from Phil, lucky her. But with Jo staying locally, it's the perfect escape from me having to spend another awkward weekend alone with Andrew. I picture her sitting between us. That should provoke a response from him. Failing that, shopping would be good therapy. 'Sounds fab. When do you arrive? Can we meet up for a couple of hours?'

'Erm, I'll call you from Hector's.'

'Hector's!'

'Yes, what I didn't say was he's invited me to stay at his house for the weekend, and this time I've agreed.'

'Weekend?'

'It's all above board, and I'll have my own room. He said it's silly for me to stay in a hotel when he has so much space. I'm leaving here first thing Saturday and should arrive mid-morning.'

'Mid-morning, right.'

'Are you going to keep repeating everything I say? I – am – staying – at – Hector's – and – will – have – my – own – room.'

'Sorry, Jo, I just don't fancy spending the whole weekend with Andrew, picturing what he's up to. Time away from him would be great. Even an hour.'

'I'll see what I can do.'

'Thanks. You're a darling.'

'I know.'

It's Saturday morning and I'm lying in bed next to Andrew waiting for him to declare he's planning to write reports, and hiding away somewhere to do it.

Thursday, he phoned to tell me that he would be late in again. His tone was dismissive. Most likely he was meeting Barcelona Sex Kitten or Jane *You-Need-*

Sunglasses-to-Look-at-Me Maxwell. I was wondering which one it was when Freddie's voice sounded in the background along with another man's murmurings and I had to shelve my suspicions and tell myself to get a grip.

Yesterday, Andrew phoned me with good news. Freddie finally got around to giving him a business credit card so there wouldn't be any problems going forward with expenses. Somehow I didn't find that as much of a relief as he did. There was also talk of his future in the company and hints he was about to be given more important accounts. He sounded happy about that. When he got home, he disappeared into the snug with his laptop 'to get creative' he said.

Avoiding Andrew then wasn't a problem but now I have the whole weekend to get through. I'm just thinking of getting up when the landline rings from the top of the chest of drawers, and Andrew springs out of bed, giving me a perfect view of his alluringly toned backside. His back muscles work as he picks up the phone and turns towards me, providing a second perfect view, this time of his impressive morning erection. For a minute I regret I'm trying to avoid him, and then shocked at betraying myself, dive under the duvet.

'Yes, Freddie. Okay, I'll put her on.'

Andrew tugs the duvet back and I get a second, closer look. He passes the phone to me.

I clear my throat, but croak, 'Er, hello, Freddie.'

'Hi, Miranda, so sorry, need to borrow Andrew this morning. Something's come up. I know there's been a few late nights already, but it won't be for much longer, I promise.'

'That's – that's fine. My friend's in town visiting on business, so I'll track her down and spend some time with her.'

'Much appreciated. Oh, and I expect Andrew's already told you, but you're invited to the celebratory dinner next month, date to be confirmed. We don't want partners to miss out on all the fun. It's entirely owing to him we gained the extra business – talented husband you have there – so we're booking a rather nice restaurant. We'll combine it with the senior staff Christmas dinner. Bit early I know, but there's a lot on in December. Anyway, it's just a few people here in the office and their partners, and maybe a client or two. Nothing too scary for you.'

The patronising pig. What prompted that? 'No, he hasn't mentioned a dinner,' I say brightly, staring at Andrew, 'but great, I'm looking forward to it.' I pass the phone back. The thought of the celebratory evening might not scare me, but it is scaring Andrew. He's gone pale.

'Er, yes,' Andrew says to Freddie. 'Within the hour.' He replaces the phone in its holder, then shrugs at me. 'Well, it's more points towards that promotion.' With renewed energy he heads to the shower.

When he comes out, I'm pretending to read.

'So, there's a dinner,' I say, and continue to stare at the page.

'Sorry, I forgot about it. Same old stuff, you'll probably hate it. Skip it if you want.'

Nice try. 'No, wouldn't dream of it. I could do with a night out.' When I glance up, he's frowning and grinding his teeth. There's no chance I'll miss it now.

He shrugs again and begins to dry himself. 'Who's the friend coming down on business?' He stops and looks me directly in the eyes, questioningly.

'Just Jo. She's meeting someone to discuss marketing. He owns the building where the gallery is. The one where I do the accounts.'

He finishes drying himself, turns to his underwear drawer and while rooting for socks says over his shoulder, 'So you took Jo into that gallery last time she was here you said, and then went to lunch and made new friends with what's-his-name, the TV guy?'

'Jack Langford – and she went in herself. We passed the place going to the cathedral and she got talking to the owner. And no, not new friends, new clients. I've had no time to make new friends working all the hours God sends to do up this cottage.'

'Well, it's finished now.' He turns to the wardrobe. 'If you are getting out more, socialising, I'd like to be part of it.'

I don't get it. He's having an affair with one woman and smooched with another, and even that most likely progressed to sex, but he's wishing our social life would improve? The cynic in me is bursting to get out and achieving it. He just wants more opportunities to meet new women to add to his harem. Cupcakes or even muffins, anything but sticking with bloody wedding cake.

He finishes dressing without further questions, and five minutes later leaves the room and I finally drag myself out of bed.

Before I reach the bathroom, he's back standing in the doorway catching me unawares. 'Didn't kiss you goodbye. Tomorrow we'll spend some quality time together, I promise.' He strides over, grabs me by the back of the neck, and yanks me into his arms. 'I miss you with all this work. Sometimes I miss being in Chester. Miss the old life.'

With no choice, I accept his firm kiss on my lips.

'Best you have dinner with Jo,' he says when he lets go. 'Could be a late one. Enjoy the day and say hello to her from me.' And with that he's gone.

He never says to say hello to Jo. And why is he saying he won't be back until tonight when Freddie said he only needed to borrow him 'this morning'? Confusing signals. Is the sudden affection guilt? My stomach churns at the thought he might be using this an excuse to meet Leticia.

He missed 'the old life' he said. A time when we had more fun and less stress, he must mean. Family and friends close by. Jobs starting at the same time each morning and finishing at the same time each night without worrying about our positions within the companies we worked for, the goal to earn money to live. A means to an end. A time when he still loved me. When we shared troubles and did everything together.

The implication our lives have become mundane is

obvious. He's found fun elsewhere. And would he give his women up if we had more fun? Wouldn't matter, deep in my heart I know it's too late.

Jo phones late morning and I update her. 'Can he possibly miss the way we used to be? Did we take on too much too soon? Or was that guilt because this afternoon he's with someone else?'

'The last one. He's putting you off the track, believe me. Oust him from your head for the day. Don't start blaming yourself, do you hear me?'

'Yes, I'll try.' It doesn't work as a vision of him with Leticia charges into my head. My heart rate goes into sprint mode and the sinking feeling returns to the pit of my stomach. This is stupid, he's probably in the office. Doubts creep in. 'You don't think I imagined all this?'

'Don't be gullible. Wait there, back in a sec.'

I wait and hear mumblings.

'Right, Hector suggests you come down here for lunch. There's plenty for three and probably a lot more people besides.'

'Oh no, Jo, it's your day. I couldn't intrude like that.' We both know I'm lying.

'You won't be. In fact –' she lowers her voice – 'you'd be doing me a favour. It'll help me get over that initial awkwardness of being alone with Hector for the first time in his home. You know what I mean – when you're talking chitchat and the weather and you begin running out of things to say, especially as we both know there's something more going on here. Anyway this place needs to be seen to be believed!'

'Okay, you win, give me the address.'

Turns out he lives not only in Upper Winterford, which is impressive, but at a place called Winterford House no less. A quick check on Google to find the best route reveals the house is a country estate. So, it's with relish that I take care getting ready as lunch at a country estate calls for something special to wear. The weather is cool, so I've chosen a vintage, bottle-green jersey shirt dress with a large buckled belt. Beige flats match well and with my wavy hair loose over my shoulders, I look smart and feminine.

An hour later I'm sitting in the car staring at the incredible Palladian-style mansion before me. It's enormous with three floors and multiple windows. The beautiful formal garden has a handsome hedge, crisply trimmed and shaped with geometric precision.

Movement at one of the upstairs windows galvanises me into action and, grabbing my bag and shawl, in seconds I'm out of the car and mounting several steps to a portico, wondering if it's the right entrance. I knock and Hector opens the door. I'm surprised as I expected a butler. It's probably his day off. Greeting Hector in this impressive setting unnerves me and I feel a little out of my depth.

'Come in, come in,' Hector says cheerfully, allaying my fears. 'You're most welcome. Come and join Joanne in the saloon. We thought you'd like to see it. I'll be there in a jiffy. Wine? Oh, of course, you're driving. I have some alcohol free.'

'Perfect,' I say, and follow him across a drawing room and into a magnificent hall with a sweeping cantilevered staircase and through into what he calls the saloon. It's a spacious room with powder-blue walls, white wood panelling and a gorgeous pink and blue Axminster rug, covering most of the floor. Jo is standing staring through French windows and down onto the garden.

'O-M-G, Randa!' she says when Hector, having let her know I've arrived, excuses himself and disappears through the door. 'What do you think? I've died and gone to house heaven. I assumed I'd be staying in the attic of some large city-centre Victorian semi. There are twelve bedrooms. You want to see my room! Overlooks the back garden – I mean grounds at the back. There's even a pool house with a hot tub and sauna. And he has staff! A gardener, under gardeners, a housekeeper, though she's off today, and cleaners. Just think of that, no cleaning! There's also an estate manager.'

We sit down on one of the couches. I catch her excitement, and I'm glad I made an effort with dressing. 'Hector has a new hairstyle. Is that for you, Jo?' I'd noticed it the moment he'd opened the door. Much more stylish and tamed.

'Haven't a clue, but I can't tell you how charming he is. Kind, sweet, intelligent, and he teases me in such a cute way when I'm being thick. Things happen for a reason. This is the cosmos at work. Phil was meant to leave me and—'

'Andrew was meant to play around so we could commiserate together?'

'No, of course not. Just the Phil bit. The rest was coincidental. This is a dream, a fairy tale. I really like Hector honestly. He's so, so—'

'I believe you.' I smile at her happiness.

'He inherited this gorgeous house five years ago from a grandparent.'

'It is a beautiful place.'

At the sound of footsteps and men's voices mumbling, we both stand. The mumbling becomes louder. 'Good timing – come through to the saloon,' we hear Hector say. 'I have visitors you happen to know.'

We both stare at the doorway. The hairs stand up on the back of my neck as my extra sensory perception kicks in and I'm not surprised when Jack strolls into the room.

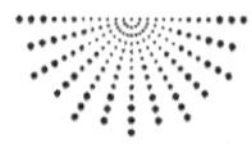

CHAPTER ELEVEN

'Sorry to interrupt,' Jack says. He freezes, abashed when his gaze alights on Jo and me. 'Hi, Joanne – Miranda.' Standing just in the doorway, he nods his head at me as if acknowledging someone he knows well but doesn't like, and I colour. His shoulders are huge in the chunky moss-green sweater he's wearing, and even in the large room he's a considerable presence.

Jo nudges me. We both say hello. Mine is feeble.

'I forgot you were entertaining today, Hector,' Jack says, turning back to him. 'Just called to ask if you fancied coming along to view a house with me in Lower Winterford. Second opinion and all that. But no matter, I'll shoot along there on my own.' He pats the side of Hector's arm as he attempts to pass.

'Not so fast,' Hector says. 'When's the appointment?'

'Two thirty.'

'Then there's time to join us for lunch. Splendid. And then perhaps…?' Hector stares at Jo and me expectantly.

'I'm up for it,' says Jo. 'Third opinion is always helpful –' she thumbs towards me – 'and a fourth.'

I could kill her. She knows I wouldn't want to go and I'm sure Jack doesn't want to be in my company either after our last confrontation. Along with my complete lack of contact it would be awkward, and that's putting it mildly. Frown lines appearing between Jack's eyes confirm my thoughts. The tense atmosphere between us increases, but I try to smile to save us both from embarrassment.

Hector clears his throat and nudges Jack. 'Come and help me with the drinks. Let's leave the girls to chat.' He throws me a glance of sympathy at Jack's hostility.

When they've left the room, I say to Jo, 'What made you suggest that? And Hector – you've told him, haven't you?'

'Maybe a teensy-weensy bit of what occurred.' She indicates with her finger and thumb how much that is. 'But it was all in a good cause, to win you lunch.'

I'm about to give her a piece of my mind when Jack comes back with my imitation alcohol. To my frustration, Jo saunters to the French windows and steps out onto the terrace.

With Jo blocking my escape route, knowing I can't join her as someone needs to stay to be polite to Jack, I grit my teeth and accept the glass from him. I open my mouth, hoping something sensible will come tumbling out, and manage a rather mumbled, 'Thank you.'

Jack returning smile doesn't reach his eyes and he fixes his attention on the windows and gestures to where

Jo is standing on the terrace. 'The grounds are exquisite. You should grab the opportunity to explore them before lunch. You have a few minutes until it's ready. Take the path to the left across the lawn and it'll bring you down to the river, or the one to the right and you'll discover a walled garden.' He points into the hallway. 'Meanwhile, Hector needs help in the kitchen.' He turns and strides out like the lord of the manor. So bloody stiff and formal.

Jack isn't just annoyed, he's avoiding me. He needed an excuse to leave the room, wanting to keep a distance from me that's both mental and physical. If he was sending me a message, such as get lost, it's worked. I rush out on the terrace to tell Jo he hates me.

'Hates you? You twit. He likes you a lot. But as you say yourself, you're a married woman and have made that clear. Make some decisions, you ditherer.' She raises her eyebrows and purses her lips. Another message, this time reiterating the need for me to sort out my life and fast.

'The only decision to make is about Andrew, not Jack,' I say, miffed. 'I'm going for a walk around the grounds.' Although it's a growing chilly, I don't return for my shawl, which hangs over the arm of a chair in the saloon, and instead stomp down the steps.

After circuiting the lawn, I soon come to a fork and take the narrow winding path to the right through rhododendron trees coming out close to a long, red-brick wall. I suspect it's the walled garden, Victorian at a guess. Halfway along the wall I locate the door and turn the rusty, iron ring to open it. Stepping through I find the garden is laid out with winding pathways and long flowerbeds, housing cheerful orange, red, white, and yellow roses with more climbing up the old walls. It's so sheltered they have ample protection and are probably at the end of their second flush. The scent is delicious and calming in the enclosed space.

Four wrought iron and wooden benches sit around the sides of the garden and I choose one and sit on it, content to hide away.

I ponder my recent unfortunate behaviour, and wonder if I'm alienating Jo now as well as Jack. Dithering, or whatever Jo called it, is exactly what I am doing, and fear is the cause. Then stubbornness is also a fault of mine. Once I decide something I stick it out to the end.

Was it only a couple of months ago everything was normal? Holly Cottage was completed – most of the renovations, anyway. I was looking forward to choosing a pet and hoping I would be pregnant by Christmas. Life would progress. Then there were those texts to Andrew from Leticia, and I met Jack, and ever since it's as if someone has taken all the little parts of my life and thrown them up in the air like a handful of rice and it's anyone's guess where each piece will land.

Where is Andrew right now? Pictures loom up in my mind and then the pain takes hold and I'm filled with confusion. I can't recall the last time we shared hopes and dreams, made plans together. Cosy cottage, a dog, and children had been among my own, but Andrew's? Were they different?

Admittedly we haven't talked about children much

since I miscarried, even though that was seven years ago, but it was always there, unspoken, or so I thought. Anyway, we didn't have to speak of it with Fliss never letting it drop and hinting I must be infertile. Andrew would always laugh and reply, 'All in good time, Mother.' Coupled with the fact he was fine with my last pregnancy, there was little reason to think otherwise. And now? My chance has gone and the time and investment wasted.

What would have happened if I hadn't have miscarried? It didn't encourage my own father to settle. He ran like the wind when Mum told him she was pregnant. Andrew's behaviour was admittedly better, but would the novelty have worn off eventually, even with children?

A leopard never changes its spots, people say, and Andrew hasn't exactly trodden softly on my dreams. When he proposed, I imagined we would grow old together – the perfect couple. Instead, he is a stranger to me. And underneath all the immediate pain, I'm mourning for what might have been. How will we ever unravel this tangled mess?

I sit for a few minutes mulling it all over until a breeze begins to blow, and darker clouds appear. I should return to the house, but facing Jack is daunting. My day isn't going as I expected with him here. But he's right to play it cool, I can't blame him for that. I must control my attraction to him. My vulnerability is drawing me to him, a sort of clutching at the straws of having someone to lean on. And straws won't bear my weight long.

Shivering now the sun has disappeared and because

I'm no further in deciding what to do except for perhaps sticking to my plan to catch Andrew out with proof of his cheating and take it from there, I pull myself up, knowing I can't delay going back any longer. I'm rubbing feeling back into my cold arms when I spot Jack standing at the door in the wall, watching me across the garden, my shawl in his hands.

'Thought you'd be chilly, and it looks as if I'm right,' he calls. 'Lunch is ready.' Strolling over, he places the shawl around my shoulders.

We walk in silence as we return to the house. His reserved demeanour makes me feel insignificant, miserable and alone. Rejected by men in general. All too soon we're back at the terrace and I steal a glance at him, wondering how to phrase my apology for snapping at him, as we must surely clear the air for the sake of the others. Jack senses it and his returning expression is far from what I expected, his eyes exuding sympathy. The familiar lump forms in my throat. Jo or Hector must have said something to him.

He sighs, and taking my hand, tucks it firmly around his arm before escorting me up the steps and back into the saloon. He appears to have brushed off our tiff without me having to explain.

Lunch is in the morning room, a smorgasbord of delightful dishes. Jack is sociable and smiles at something I say. It heartens me that we're still friends and I'm soon joining in the enthusiasm of Hector and Jo as they unveil a few of their plans. Their passion is catching. It's extraordinary the way they bounce ideas around, each in harmony with the other. Although I worry there might be an element of rebound involved on Jo's part, they do hit it off remarkably well. How lovely to feel the way they look – safe, relaxed, happy and with a sense of peace. When she sees me scrutinising them, Jo winks at me. She's happy.

While we're getting on well, I take the opportunity to arrange a day the following week to catch up with Jack's accounts. 'Hope it won't be too daunting a task,' he says. 'The gallery's been busy and I've just bought some new stock, so the mess on the desk could do with your expert touch. I've had no time to file anything.'

It crosses my mind that he has let invoices pile up deliberately in order to see me more. Then common sense tells me I shouldn't flatter myself.

At two fifteen we realise the time and begin to stack plates. 'Leave it,' says Hector. 'No time. We'll have to drive down, and we'll do the washing up when we get back.' Hector indicates Jo and her eyes twinkle in amusement. What will happen is Hector will wash dishes and Jo will sit sipping wine.

Outside, Jack offers to drive. I'm relieved he has a smart BMW estate as well as a van. Jo hops in the back while I walk to other side, but before reaching the door Jo has scooted over and Hector jumps in beside her.

Having no choice, I get in the front. It's strange being in a car next to Jack with friends in the back. I haven't done this for a long time. First eating a delicious lunch, then shooting off together with another couple somewhere. A taste of what Andrew wanted back, except it's not Andrew but Jack, and I'm glad, and that causes a sudden rush of guilt. Control is not my forte when it comes to Jack.

Lower Winterford is not far and we soon reach a property with a for-sale sign in the garden. The house is a good-sized detached family home with lots of character. The exterior is white, and the ample windows indicate light and space. Even after we've parked behind a little red Peugeot, there's room on the drive for several more cars.

A smartly dressed middle-aged woman with immaculate makeup is standing waiting for us on the doorstep with a file in her hand. The estate agent I presume.

Do I wait for Jack to open the door for me? Say he doesn't come around and leaves me sitting here. Quickly deciding, I jump out and start walking.

As I approach the door, Jack's feet sound on the path behind me. The woman standing on the step catches a glimpse of my wedding ring, beams me a big smile and holds out her hand. 'Good afternoon, Mrs Langford, so delighted to meet you. Catherine Walker.' By now she has my hand in hers, having grabbed it, and is shaking it vigorously. The shock of being called Mrs Langford prevents me from speaking clearly and all I can manage is a croaky, 'Hello, but I'm—'

'And pleased to meet you again, Mr Langford,' Catherine blusters, abandoning me and shaking Jack's hand. 'I think we've cracked it with this house. Fabulous isn't it. Fits your specifications most splendidly.'

'Call me Jack, please. Yes, it looks perfect from the outside, Catherine, I'm impressed.'

'Come inside, Jack – Mrs Langford – and you'll find it's just as perfect.'

Panicking, I glance around for support from Jo. But she's wandered off with Hector to view the garden though she turns and grins at me, and I know she's heard and has deliberately left me to it.

Jack nudges me forward and I have no choice but to enter. His spear of disapproval pierces my clothing and sends a shiver along my spine. As soon as I can get a word in edgeways, I'll correct her and make sure he hears.

Meanwhile, Catherine floats along the hallway prattling a non-stop descriptive commentary. 'And such a spacious hallway. This cupboard is handy for visitors coats, and there's a boot room off the kitchen for wellies and rainwear.'

We follow her and I don't get another chance to speak as she keeps gabbing, showing us the kitchen-diner with its Aga, granite worktops, lots of cupboard space and plenty of room for a large table. 'The patio doors open right out and bring the garden in, don't you think,' she enthuses, and unlocks them to demonstrate, letting cool air rush in.

The chattering carries on into the long sitting room which has an inglenook fireplace and wood burner with an opening leading into the sunroom, a newer extension, and French windows leading out onto another part of the 'extensive' garden. There's a study downstairs, and I imagine that will be Jack's office or perhaps Sophie's study room.

Catherine leads us up the wide staircase and into the master bedroom, still not giving me a chance to tell her I'm not Jack's wife. But it's too late anyway as it would sound odd. As Jo and Hector come upstairs and into the room, I turn and grimace at them, opening my hands and shrugging, indicating there's nothing I can do. They both laugh. Catherine is in the walk-in wardrobe, showing Jack its magic. The room is spacious and light with a bathroom en suite and views over the garden, the river beyond, and spectacular countryside. I love it.

Jo and I follow Catherine into a second spacious bedroom while Jack and Hector continue to inspect the master.

Catherine beams at me. 'This room will be perfect for your daughter, Mrs Langford. Plenty of space and she'd have her own bathroom too.' She winks. 'Teenagers, eh?'

Behind me, Jo stifles a giggle.

Daughter! Do I look old enough to be the mother of an eighteen-year-old? Jo clears her throat. Catherine is awaiting my answer. I should tell her now that I'm not Mrs Langford but instead find myself cheekily saying, 'Oh yes, it's the perfect size. Sophie will love it.' I roll my eyes skywards. 'Yes, and teenage daughters, always taking hours in the bathroom. Ours is no different.'

There's a small movement behind me and I spin around to see Jack standing in the doorway. Blood rushes to my face and I want to fall into a volcano and let it burn me up. He comes forward and puts his arm around my shoulders, turning me back towards Catherine.

'Yes, a perfect room for our daughter, isn't it, darling?' He plants a kiss on the top of my head. He's mocking me and I could die with shame and embarrassment. What must he think of me? Not only didn't I correct Catherine in the first place that I'm not Jack's wife, but I'm caught in the act of pretending I'm Sophie's mother. Perhaps he's seeing the funny side and is joining in the joke. I hang onto that thought in vain hope.

'And there's one more double bedroom and an ever so slightly smaller single, just in case we hear the patter of tiny feet again.' Catherine hunches her shoulders and screws up her eyes, her mouth forming into a broad smile. 'You never know, you two lovebirds.'

'You never know,' Jack says, squeezing my shoulders and pulling me closer. He pats my stomach. 'There's room perhaps for two more in there.'

Catherine gives us an indulgent smile.

I know I deserve it, and by Jack's tone of voice he doesn't see the joke, but he doesn't have to be so cruel. He must know children are off my agenda now through no fault of my own. When Catherine leaves the room, I pull away from him.

Jack walks ahead to view the other rooms while talking details with Catherine, and I run downstairs and straight through the kitchen and into the garden. Jo comes up behind me.

'Don't take umbrage, Randa,' she says, panting. 'I'm sure he was just teasing you.'

'Nope, he's had a sense-of-humour-ectomy. For God's sake, it was a joke.'

My colour heightens and I pretend to examine the rear of the house. Jack must think I'm exacting revenge on Andrew by saying what I did and should have understood that I was just responding in jest to Gung-ho Catherine's remarks. I'm dying with shame at his reaction.

What on earth made me say I was Sophie's mother? I could have told her the truth or kept my big mouth shut. Jack surely would have been okay with either. Where's the Tardis when you need it?

In my imagination I rewind to what I would do if I could I travel back in time to half an hour ago.

I walk to the door and Catherine calls me Mrs Langford and introduces herself. I shout over her chatting, 'Actually I'm just a friend.' No, hang on that sounds dodgy.

I rewind again. *This time I wait to see if Jack opens the car door. He doesn't so I get out slowly and make sure I'm behind Jo and Hector as we approach the house. Jack introduces us as friends.*

Now that's better. Just one little thing – no Tardis!

For the rest of the viewing I'm everywhere that Jack isn't.

Once he's examined the garden and declared it the perfect house, he promises to get back to Catherine later in the day with an offer.

The atmosphere is so tense it's sliceable on the five-minute return journey. My leg is tight up against the door as I gaze out of the window to avoid seeing Jack's cross expression, or heaven forbid, I accidentally touch him.

As soon as we step from his car outside Winterford House, Jack thanks Hector for letting him gatecrash lunch and says he has to rush home to work out some figures. No one gets a kiss goodbye and I know it's because he's avoiding kissing me.

Thanking Hector, I make my own excuses. Jo promises to call me, and I kiss and hug them both knowing Jack is already driving away. I'm relieved when my satnav takes me in the opposite direction.

On the journey back, I cringe as the day's events play out in my head. How could the pleasant afternoon I expected, both start and end in such a disaster? If only the middle bit had prevailed.

When I arrive home, I keep reliving my excruciating *faux pas* moment. Then pictures of Andrew having dinner with Leticia or Maxwell flood in. They force me to break open the Baileys as I can't find any wine in the house. One small glass and I find I'm not in the mood as December is Baileys month – a month of Christmassy feelings, joy, parties, family and love. Dance music then while I indulge in some cleaning therapy.

Singing every song I know, being mindful, concentrating on remembering the words, and zoning out, I clean surfaces, floors, windows, everything that doesn't move.

The snug is the last room to tackle. There's spider in her newly spun web in the corner of the window. I'm about to fetch my spider catcher when a gentleman caller appears. He attaches a string to her web and starts plucking to gain her attention. Lady spider bides her time. Taking this as a good sign, he carries on plucking. Fascinated, I watch the mating ritual only to jump as she suddenly makes her move, shooting onto his thread. He tries to make a quick getaway, but she attaches a thread to him and whips him back, and he meets a grim end. That's the price of sex in spider land, I guess. He gambled and lost. You have to admire her in some ways. I name her Jane Gnasher Maxwell and leave her where she is.

While fluffing up cushions, I find the bag with my new red lingerie behind one of them, having slipped down the back of the sofa, the edge of the handle just showing. A waste of money as now it's just a reminder of Andrew's infidelity. I drag the bag out and bin it. With the cleaning complete I retreat to my office and throw myself into tackling an account.

I'm so exhausted, mentally and physically, that by the time Andrew arrives home at ten I'm showered and in bed. When he sticks his head into the room, I breathe steadily and feign sleep. He gently closes the door again, but not before my sixth sense kicks in. I can almost smell another woman on him.

CHAPTER TWELVE

During the next week, I mull over my erratic actions when around Jack, eventually deciding he's the most impossible person: sanctimonious, austere, and judgemental. He would make anyone behave impetuously. Still, I'm appalled at myself and depressed. Especially as I chickened out and texted him saying I couldn't make the appointment and I would come the following week instead. He replied, *That's fine.*

Andrew is unhappy too, repeatedly putting his head in his hands, suddenly rising then sitting again, agitated, often short-tempered, and continually wanting to be alone. A woman problem? And by that I don't mean me.

Sunday evening arrives and we're forced to spend time together, having no other choice, as Andrew is not working and we have to eat. So, sitting across from him in the kitchen, I fish for reasons, asking if work or something else is troubling him though I'm wondering if it's me.

'Work? What makes you say that,' he snaps. 'No, work's fine. Great even.'

'Oh, sorry. No need to be prickly. You just seemed low this last week.'

'Do I have to be constantly cheerful? You don't. Face like a long, wet weekend for several days. A right misery guts.' His curled lip would give Elvis a run for his money. And I thought he hadn't noticed.

Refusing to become riled, I give a short laugh and say, 'Like you, I'm fine. Work's boring, same old, same old.'

'Don't you have exciting new clients to hang out with?' The rising acerbity in his tone leaves me wishing I hadn't spoken. 'Going out to lunch with them etcetera etcetera.'

'Exciting? One lunch with one client? Hardly living the high life.' What a cheek after what he did and probably still is doing. Cool lost, the cynic in me makes a bid for freedom. 'What about your clients or colleagues? Isn't it you who becomes *good* friends with them? Have regular lunches out and dinners too, etcetera?'

'Maybe you should find yourself another job then,' Andrew says, pretending he hasn't heard the questions. Snatching his whiskey glass from the table, he takes it through to the sitting room. Two minutes later the TV is blaring out. Another vain attempt to get him to talk sadly fails. Looks as if I'm washing up even though I cooked, not that I intend to argue about it.

Thursday afternoon and I'm waiting for Mum and Steve to arrive with their news. The visit will be awkward with Andrew's behaviour, but I can't put it off. Anyway, I want to see Mum.

I postpone my appointment with Jack again, sending him a short text saying I can't make it as I'm expecting visitors, but receive no reply. How can I face him? A year or two and I might build up enough courage to visit the gallery.

This week was a trial. Tuesday I guiltily took the day off and spent several hours in the garden pulling up the last few weeds and sweeping up fallen leaves, finding gardening, like cleaning, is good for the soul. For all the hard work, I'm sorry the landscaping is complete. A garden to work on now would keep my mind and hands occupied.

Jo suggested taking up meditation to reduce my stress, so Wednesday morning I pulled out a pair of crumpled Thai pants from the back of the wardrobe and searched on YouTube for suitable meditation music. A stick of incense and I was ready to go. Within five minutes the incense was choking me and the music grinding on my nerves, my mind too active to concentrate. Eventually, I gave up and scrubbed the kitchen floor, deciding men were the bane of my life.

During my splurges of housework, I kept an eye on my resident spider Jane Gnasher Maxwell. She was doing fine, though still standoffish, and yesterday another male was making threads on her web, plucking away like there was no tomorrow (which there probably wasn't). Swinging across she made a beeline for him but missed and he retreated into the peace lily. 'If you don't stop thinking with your penis,' I shouted into the plant. 'Gnasher will have you.' I fetched the vacuum and cleaned up the remains of her other dead prospective mates. She'd been busy.

With the week not going well so far, it's not surprising that today I'm impatient for Mum to arrive. To keep occupied I make a coffee, but my thoughts soon drift to Jack. My daydreaming has taken on an element of escapism mostly revolving around my effortlessly sophisticated self, fitting perfectly into the world of Art, television appearances, and mansions. Except for one that ends with me impressing Jack so much he pulls me into a passionate clinch as we walk together in the walled garden in Winterford. Well, everyone needs a distraction sometimes.

Could I be developing a seven-year itch? More a seven-year glitch, I would think, as my romantic liaisons with Jack are purely imaginary. And therein lies the crux of the matter. Andrew does have a seven-year itch and is scratching away. If he doesn't love me anymore, he should have the decency to tell me and then, despite the prospect of another woman coming between us, I'll respect him more. It's not as if I haven't given him time or encouragement. Meanwhile, completely keeping my hands off Jack other than in my head is the least I can do to live by my own rules and avoid being a hypocrite.

· · ·

Another half-hour goes past. Where are Mum and Steve? The moment I glance out of the sitting-room window a car pulls onto the driveway and I hurry out, relieved the waiting is over. There's a flurry of hugs and kisses and I usher them in.

Mum looks fabulous: healthy, attractive, and younger than her sixty-three years. Steve walks in behind her, smiling and glancing around enthusiastically, having never visited before. For the first time I examine him through Mum's eyes – he's good-looking, average height with a slim build. He's few years older than Mum and a retired lecturer of English, one with an abundance of energy. He has two grown up children, one married with a child, but I've never met them.

'Sorry, we're late,' Mum gushes. 'You know what Auntie Barbara's like, goodbyes go on forever.'

'Just glad you're here, Mum.'

I glimpse myself in the hall mirror as we pass, and a washed-out face reflects. I've been frowning so much there's a line etched between my brows. Knowing Mum will notice with her third eye, or maybe just her normal eyes, I fix a smile to my face and direct them through into the kitchen.

'Scrubbed to within an inch of its life, this floor,' Mum says, seating herself on a stool. 'Anyone would think you were stressed.'

Didn't take her long. 'I'll make tea while you tell me your news,' I say brightly, both distracting her and stealing myself for the worst. My imagination runs wild as I picture myself in a grotesque, peach bridesmaid dress walking behind Mum wearing a huge white creation as she trips smiling down the aisle. The reality would be Mum in a simple frock in the registry office, but my head just won't compute that happy scene. For years it's just been Mum and me. Mum kept her previous relationships separate from our own lives, but now Steve is here in my house.

Mum smiles nervously. 'Best to come straight out with it. Steve and I are moving in together. No reason why not, we're never apart.' She states this as if expecting me to protest.

With no mention of a wedding I splutter, 'That's… lovely news.' They both get huge hugs and a kiss. Nothing can be worse than Mum getting married, but I can cope with them living together, and Steve can always move out again. Just to confirm, I ask, 'So, who's moving in with whom?'

'Steve's moving in with me and he'll rent out his place.'

Again, that's welcome news. With Steve not selling his flat this doesn't disrupt Mum. We moved into her smart, good-sized three-bedroomed semi on the outskirts of Chester while I was still at primary school, and a piece of my heart will always remain there.

'And this way we can both pool resources,' Mum continues with heightened exuberance at my encouraging response. 'And there'll be an income from Steve's flat which means more travel, leisure pursuits, and money to pay for an eventual wedding, if that's what we decide. I'll get the cups.' She opens a cupboard and takes out three mugs.

For crying out loud, Mum slipped in the marriage bit, hoping I didn't notice. But she said, 'eventual wedding', obviously that's years away and might not happen. Still, I'm ruffled as they have obviously discussed it, but I keep my thoughts to myself, not wanting to ruin Mum's joy. 'All lovely. And great to travel more.'

While I finish making the tea, I puzzle over why I wouldn't want Mum to be happy and secure in a stable relationship. Why should she be alone? The answer comes into my head immediately. It's because I'm insecure in my marriage. Home was always somewhere I could retreat to if needed, just Mum and me like before, which would be difficult with Steve living there. I'd have to move in with Jo. Nightmare. I sigh wearily. That's stupid. If my marriage breaks up, I can't expect other people to rescue me. In three years I'll be forty and should fend for myself, fully embracing independence – single and self-sufficient the way I was before meeting Andrew. Time to stop being selfish. Mum's news is highlighting my misery, that's all. And I am miserable. When was I happy last? Really happy? It escapes me it's been so long.

'Okay, what's going on with you?' Mum jerks me out of my reverie. 'I know when something's wrong. You can't hide it from me.'

'Just popping out to have a wander around your

spectacular garden,' Steve says tactfully, disappearing out the back door.

'Well.'

'Nothing, honestly, Mum,' I reply, a this-is-a-real smile fixed to my face. 'It's just work. The new account means added stress until it's worked into my routine.'

'Don't deflect. You know what I mean. Is everything okay between you and Andrew?'

'Mum, everything's fine – good.' My mobile rings. Saved by the bell. As I answer, the name coming up on the screen doesn't register immediately.

'Miranda, it's Jack.' The phone slips from my hand and drops onto the worktop and I fumble to pick it up. He's caught me off-guard. A flush travels up my neck, flooding my cheeks, and my stomach wobbles. The phone is on bloody loudspeaker again and I stab at it, trying to turn it off while smiling at Mum, hoping she takes a hint and leaves me to speak privately. Her lips curve into a smile but shrewdness glows in her eyes and she doesn't budge.

'Hi, Jack, 'tis I,' I say lightly, trying to sound casual, but sounding stupid. Oh God.

'Shame you couldn't come this week,' he says. 'You were looking for a sculpture, I remember? Only one's just come in. Contemporary, but as you described, tall, bronze, elegant with a skilfully done grey and green patina. A work of art. Someone else was interested, a couple actually, but if you want to come and see it...' His voice sounds normal, even pleasant. What a relief.

'A sculpture? Right. And contemporary?' This is for Mum's benefit who's on full psychic alert. 'Yes, sounds just the thing. But I have visitors today, so can't come, and you must be closing soon.'

Mum moves in closer.

'I can keep the gallery open if you have time to drive over. Bring your visitors for a private viewing. The other customers said they'll return over the weekend.'

Bad timing, I so desperately want to go and not just to see the sculpture. With the current turmoil, what's the point in buying such an investment for the home? No, it's more that I want to ensure Jack and I are still friends and go forward as such with him seeing me acting sensible around him again. I'm disappointed. 'Kind of you, but my visitors only arrived a few minutes ago, and I don't want to put you out or lose you a sale.'

Mum butts in. 'Where is it?' She's curious.

'Netherbury.'

'Well, then, let's go along, seeing that Mr…?' She shouts this out as if Jack must be deaf.

'It's Dr Langford. Jack Langford,' I say. 'He's my new client.'

'Seeing that Jack is so good as to keep the gallery open just for you.'

'But Andrew will be home soon.'

'No, he won't. He'll do the usual and make an excuse to avoid me.' Her shoulders come up as she chuckles. Jack coughs.

I put my hand over the phone, not that it'll prevent

Jack from hearing me. 'It's fine, Mum, and you must be tired after your journey.'

'Oh, don't be silly. It was barely an hour. We only drove from Surrey. It'd be a shame to let the sculpture go. If you like it, I'll put something towards it. I'll fetch Steve.' She moves towards the door.

'No, Mum, it's fine. Anyway, I mightn't like it.'

'Well, let's go and find out.' And off she goes while I tell Jack we'll be there in half an hour.

How many years do you get for matricide? Before I forget, I rip the screen cover from my phone.

When we arrive in Netherbury, Mum walks ahead she's so eager to get to the gallery. It's a wonder antennae aren't popping out the top of her skull. Meanwhile, I drag my feet, dreading Mum meeting Jack and using her mind-reading abilities. Steve, sensing my uneasiness, pats me reassuringly on the arm, indicating he'll keep Mum in check. That's funny, though I appreciate the thought.

When we reach the gallery there's a closed-sign hanging on the door. Jack is at the back and hears me tapping on the glass. He strides over and turns a key in the lock. He shows no sign of his earlier animosity when I enter, and smiles broadly, but is astute enough not to greet me with a kiss. My psychic abilities must be selective as I've no inkling what's going through his mind.

Inside the gallery I step aside so Mum and Steve can come through. 'Jack, this is my mother, Annette, and

Steve, her…' What? Stepdad? No way. Boyfriend? He's hardly a boy. 'Partner,' I finish, satisfied with that, and feeling proud Mum is so attractive.

Everyone shakes hands.

'You're from the TV,' Mum accuses Jack.

Great, everyone recognises him except me.

'Most likely,' Jack replies with a deep chortle. 'Come through, you won't be disappointed.' He leads us to the counter where the sculpture stands in all its glory, lustrous and beautiful. 'Here she is. A personification of the south wind.'

'The South Wind.' Wistfully, I stroke the tactile bronze of the naked figure gracefully balancing on her tiptoes on the slim granite base, her head and arms thrown back, hair blowing behind her, material winding gracefully around her legs. It's so perfect and the blue-grey patina with a blush of green is fabulous. There's no way it can be within the amount of money I allocated, but I love it.

'Stunning,' I gasp, 'but clearly over my budget.'

'Don't let that put you off,' Jack replies, coming to stand beside me. 'We can work something out. No rush.'

'How generous, dear.' Mum smiles indulgently. 'It's perfect for the snug. What do you think, Steve?'

'Totally agree.' Steve has zero control over Mum.

'There you go,' says Jack. 'Everyone agrees. Not that I've seen the snug.'

What does he mean by that? Mum will spot the implication a mile off – that he's covering up an affair! As for the snug, the sculpture is far too tall and grand and needs a bigger room.

'Miranda?' Mum prompts after an awkward pause.

I can't be in debt to Jack and would feel beholden. And the money would be better remaining in my account with all that's going on. 'It's very generous of you, but I can't, just can't.'

Jack's expression changes from one of being pleased with himself to one of disappointment, and I deduct from that he didn't just come across the sculpture. He's trying to make amends.

'Ah, darling, why not,' says Mum. 'Look, I'll give you something towards it. How can you turn down such a beautiful work of art? What an opportunity.'

'Me too,' says Steve. I turn and stare at him. How kind. He continues to examine the sculpture to save us both embarrassment, no doubt.

Mum strokes the figure. 'With your own contribution you'll be well on the way. It's truly a work of art.'

Jack has a message in his eyes saying he wants to do this. 'Sophie, my daughter, loves it. She said she was eager to know your reaction to it.'

I don't understand his complete change of attitude as it was my own previous behaviour that was inexcusable or, at the least, inconsiderate.

I turn to Mum and Steve. 'Thanks…both of you. And you, Jack. Generous, but I can't honestly.'

Jack studies me, and I try to communicate with puppy eyes it's too much and inappropriate, my senses telling me the 'we can work something out' will never materialise. He holds his hands up. 'Okay, I give in, but I'll keep it a while in case you change your mind.'

'What about your prospective buyers?' I protest.

'Hard luck.' He grins and turns to Mum and Steve. 'Feel free to wander around while I sort out with Miranda a regular day to do my bookkeeping. We haven't arranged one yet.'

Oh my God! He's getting rid of them. Mum smiles and, taking the hint, walks down the gallery with Steve in tow to study the paintings, out of earshot but keeping one eye on me.

'Sorry, Jack, I couldn't allow… You're too kind,' I say hurriedly, shaking my head. 'It's lovely of you to consider me, especially after—'

Jack presses a finger briefly to my lips and I shiver at his touch. 'No need. My reaction was shameful. I normally pride myself on my sense of humour.' He grimaces. 'Both Hector and Jo berated me. In a nice way. Quite fiery your friend.'

I redden and play with a piece of string on the counter, intermittently glancing at him. 'You could have done without my antics when you were seriously viewing your future home. I invaded your privacy. Sorry.' I screw up my nose. 'The estate agent presumed I was. And well—'

'My fault. It was unintentional I assure you, but sorry also for making you nervous with my general atrocious and arrogant behaviour.' He grimaces. 'Jo told me that too.' He scans the room to check where Mum and Steve are to ensure they can't overhear. With his voice low and tugging at the other end of the string I'm playing with he adds, 'There was a reason I reacted the way I did that made your joke rather painful. But it's not appropriate to reveal it at the present time.' He touches my arm, so I pay full attention. 'Do you understand what I'm saying?' Frown lines crease his forehead.

Oh, gosh. Is he saying he has feelings for me and that's what caused his reaction when I pretended to be his wife? The fact I'm married to someone else? I look intently at Jack and read in his eyes that I'm right. Whatever I say about my own feelings now could push our friendship into the danger zone. Better to stay silent and accept being happy we resolved the issue. Now I can turn up to do his accounts with no accompanying anxiety and with everything else that's happening that's no small thing.

'Yes, I understand,' I simply say.

Jack relaxes and lays a hand on my shoulder. 'We're good then?' His touch has an intimacy that makes my stomach somersault. As I return his earnest gaze, we have what I can only describe as a 'moment'. A fluttering in the pit of my stomach intensifies and Jack drops his hand and runs his fingers through his hair.

'Yes, we're good.' When I look over, Mum is watching us. Quickly changing my expression, I say loudly, 'Wednesdays and fortnightly then. Great. Suits me.'

Jack and I join Mum and Steve and we say our goodbyes.

'Again, thank you,' Mum directs at Jack as we walk

out the door. 'Lovely gallery you have here. Thank you for your thoughtfulness regarding my daughter.'

'My pleasure. See you next time, Miranda,' he says. The door shuts.

Mum waits until we're out of hearing distance before saying, 'That was a good offer, darling.'

How can I explain myself? 'You don't understand, Mum. I can't be under such obligation, especially with that sculpture costing a small fortune.'

'I understand more than you give me credit for, love.'

We're barely home when I receive a text from Andrew. *'Stuck at work. Apologies to your mum. Sorry to miss dinner. I'll grab something xxx.'*

I tell Mum and she gives me an I-told-you-so look. Steve goes off to the kitchen to find a bottle of wine at her request.

As soon as he's out of the room, I feel the need to excuse Andrew. 'He has a lot on right now. Busy, you know, with work. Promotion…'

'What's going on, dear? Really?'

'Nothing. His work means he has to go away a lot. Not his fault – that's the job.'

'Not nothing, Miranda, there's something's wrong.' I know what's coming as there's no endearment. 'Is Andrew having an affair?'

'Mum, I don't want to discuss him. You don't like him, never did.'

'I've never said I don't like him!'

'Okay, tell me something, anything, you do like?'

'Works hard – he's never here.'

'Mum!'

She sighs. 'He's handsome – very. Polite and charming. See, there are many things I like.' I glare at her. 'Okay, I never believed he was right for you, but most parents think that, surely. I thought you'd marry someone like – like Jack for instance. He's a genuinely good person. The family type. Thoughtful, intelligent, and handsome. And on TV.'

'Mum! I'm trying to hang onto my marriage, not trade Andrew in for a TV personality.'

'Hang on? Is that what you're doing? Shouldn't you be enjoying your marriage and living it, not just hanging on?'

There's no point in continuing as Mum has me sussed. Despair must show in my face as she takes me in her arms for a tight hug, stroking my hair, and I bite my lip, having not intended to be so transparent. 'Sorry, darling. Your marriage and its problems are for you to figure out. No one can do it for you. Just be careful. I'm here if you need me.' She releases me.

Mum thinks I'm besotted with Andrew and blind to his faults. Why did I defend him and say I was hanging on? Is that what I'm doing? I imagine a future with us still together after his eventual confession and my subsequent forgiveness. The two of us – me the model wife and Andrew the attentive husband (making amends) – a baby, a family pet, and entertaining friends in the garden. That's the problem, it would be make-believe, surface happiness, the damage persistently lurking, and I'd be forever wondering when he would cheat again.

Whatever the results, the only thing I'm hoping for now is the truth from him.

For the moment I intend to enjoy the two days with Mum. As for Andrew, he's welcome to stay away.

CHAPTER THIRTEEN

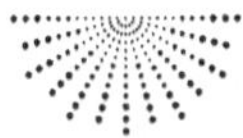

Friday, for the short time they spent together, both Andrew and Mum made an effort to be civil to one another. Andrew's mood lifted and I became visible to him again. Having found me irritating for the past two weeks, he couldn't have been more the opposite and was pleasant and considerate.

Saturday afternoon with Mum and Steve gone, Andrew apologises saying he has an important report to do that he should have done yesterday. His phone has been buzzing like mad, so I'm immediately suspicious. To take my mind off it, I set off to Southampton for early Christmas shopping.

On the drive there, I pass the dog rescue centre. It's open and there are few cars parked. I drive on but can't get it out of my head. Surely it won't hurt to enquire. With Christmas coming up there will be an influx of dogs, so perhaps making space for at least one will be helpful to them. Turning my car around, I go back.

A smiling man greets me in the reception area and asks if he can help.

'To be honest, I was passing and saw you were open,' I admit. 'I've wanted a dog for ages and thought I might take a quick peek.'

'Yes, of course, prospective adopters are always welcome. Would you mind filling in a form first? We like to be certain visitors are both serious and suitable.'

Sounds like a firm commitment. Instead of saying I'd best return when I'm ready to choose, I take the form from him and fill it in. Yes, I have had a dog before, but years ago, and yes, I do have an enclosed garden but no other pets or children. I'm tempted to write 'and not likely to', but refrain.

When I've finished, the receptionist peruses my form and, satisfied, calls a young man to take me through to the back.

Both the noise and smell of the dogs assault me as I walk up and down the rows of kennels. The number of dogs is overwhelming with mostly large ones and a fair amount of medium sized. Making a choice will be difficult. They all need homes. An older couple are also meandering up and down and a man with an excited little boy are preparing to leave with an overactive spaniel.

'Do you have any smaller dogs?' I say to the kennel boy after walking up and down lanes, but at a loss over what to do with so many bigger dogs needing homes. 'Most rooms in my cottage are quite small.'

'Sorry, 'fraid the littlies go faster,' the boy replies.

'Keep checking online. Things can change from day to day. Why don't you take another look?'

Perhaps I should consider a medium-sized dog. But as I haven't even mentioned it to Andrew yet, I say, 'Better speak to my husband first and we'll come back together another day. Yes, I'll check your website meanwhile too.'

Leaving is hard. All the way to the city, dog whimpers echo in my ears. One of those dogs will find a home with me whatever happens.

Sunday morning with Andrew asleep, I slip into the bathroom to shower. When I emerge again his phone buzzes at me from the bedside table. He's softly snoring and facing away from it. It buzzes again. Stealthily moving to his side of the bed, I'm reaching out to turn it over to see if a message is showing on the home screen when he snorts. His breathing becomes shallower, so I shoot away. God, it's as if he's protective of it, even in his sleep. I retreat upstairs to my office and waste time reading the news and catching up on social media.

Half an hour later, he's up and in the shower. When he comes out of the bedroom, I wait for him to work out I'm in the attic, but instead his footsteps sound on the stairs followed by the kitchen door opening and closing.

I wait a few minutes before following, the aroma of coffee greeting me as I walk through the kitchen door. Andrew is squeezing oranges, dapper in jeans and a casual navy-blue shirt, his sleeves rolled back. Clothes hang off him like a male model. He'd look good in a bin bag. On the worktop his phone flashes and buzzes. I'm close by, and it glares at me in amusement, knowing I won't get possession of it a second time. Andrew ignores the buzz. He won't check if that was a message while I'm around.

Andrew used to greet me with a kiss first thing in the morning, but he remains put, so I do the same. 'Been working?' he asks. 'Thought you'd stopped at weekends?'

'You can talk.'

'Good point. And knowing that, I've made breakfast for you,' he says, smiling. 'Smoked salmon, scrambled egg, and spinach. Let's go for a late Sunday lunch at the Fox and Hounds too. We haven't done it for a while. Then when we get back…' With a smouldering look on his face, he moves towards me. That look would have had me weak at the knees once.

I dart to the kitchen window. 'No cooking today. Great with me.' My head's doing the nodding dog thing. 'There are a few spring bulbs to plant still – mainly narcissus. You can never have enough spring flowers.' I turn and roll my eyes exaggeratedly.

'You mean daffs?'

'Yeah, that's them. I'll do it straight after breakfast. Can't leave it any later than this week.' The bulbs are tulips, but he won't know that, and my narcissus remark goes right over his head. The danger has passed though as the water is coming to the boil for the spinach, and Andrew has to root around for a whisk to beat the eggs. Meanwhile, I busy myself setting the table.

Once breakfast is finished, I find the few dried up tulip bulbs from last year hiding in a plant pot in the shed and spend as long as possible searching for the best place to put them, eventually shoving them into the herbaceous border, not caring if they are the right way up. In time, they will find a way to the light.

At two o'clock after having had another shower and doing my nails, it's time to leave. Andrew might be acting normal, but normal probably means he's cheating again. I think I've figured out his behaviour patterns. At the time Leticia texted him and he received her phone call, he may have been secretive but he was pleasant to me, except when challenged. So, my guess is the affair is back on and his sweet behaviour is prompted by guilt. When his affair is at a standstill he must blame me in some way and hence his irritation towards me. Or he's taking his foul mood out on me. He'd better not approach me again later as I wouldn't touch him with a ten-foot barge pole.

The Fox and Hounds is busy when we arrive, and we push ourselves through a sea of flat caps and wax jackets to get to the bar. While Andrew is trying to catch the eye of the bar person, I scan the room to check if there's anyone I'm acquainted with to say hello to.

A woman with a whippet stands by the door, having just come in. First scanning the room she waves before making her away over. Slowly turning, I peer behind me to see who's she targeting, maybe even Andrew, but there's no one paying her any attention. She's middle-aged, casually dressed in trousers and sweater, and devoid of make-up. I recognise her but can't place where from and rack my brain trying to recall before she reaches me. Then her face lights up with a broad smile and I remember her with horror – the estate agent. I try to warn her, my eyes widening, frantically shaking my head, but she just keeps on coming.

'Mrs Langford!' she shouts over the buzz of voices when she's a metre away. 'How lovely to bump into you. Out for Sunday lunch? Is Jack with you? Just want to congratulate you both on gaining the house. Cash buyers, no chain, it will be through in no time.'

My heart stops for a moment and a look of alarm must be visible on my face as I frantically shake my head. Catherine at last catches on, her expression perplexed. My head flashes around to see if Andrew has heard, not knowing how I'm to explain this to him. I can't believe my luck that he's moved forward and is ordering the drinks while chattering away to the woman behind the bar. I spin back, grab Catherine's arm, and pull her to one side. The whippet looks at me so I give it a reassuring pat on the head.

'Actually, I'm – I'm not Mrs Langford,' I stammer at her in somewhat of a whisper while gesturing with my eyes and head towards the bar. 'I should have told you but was too embarrassed. You see—'

'Oh?' She stares at Andrew. 'OH! He's your…?'

'Husband, yes. You see—'

'Ahh. Don't worry, my lips are sealed.' She does a dainty zip up thing across her mouth with the tip of her forefinger and thumb. 'Strange, Jack doesn't seem the type.'

I do then? 'But—'

She leans in. 'A word of advice, my dear. Best to come clean. Webs have a habit of rapidly untangling themselves, catching one unawares.' She pats and squeezes my hand before striding off.

I'm astounded. She doesn't realise how true that is, except she's the bloody spider in this case, putting two and two together and getting five! It doesn't help that as soon as we sit down, she is right in my line of vision and keeps winking at me.

'Strange woman over there,' Andrew whispers out the side of his mouth, and laughs. 'She fancies you.'

'Can't say I've noticed,' I answer in panic, and start prattling on about bulbs and gardening until Andrew zones out.

Although I'm dying for the loo, I daren't walk past Catherine. It's an hour until she leaves and I manage to make my way there. When I return, Andrew is tapping rapidly on his phone. I creep up behind him and peer over his shoulder, but he senses I'm there and presses the off button, forcing me to carry on to my seat, making a big thing of putting my handbag beside me while chatting about the queue in the loos. There must be another way to find out what he's up to now and confront him with it.

Andrew has a big week at work. Every evening he has papers and posters spread out on the kitchen table and types away on his laptop, his mood still buoyant. Sex isn't an issue as he hasn't noticed I'm avoiding him.

I spend some time each day in the fresh air, sweeping up the never-ending leaves in the garden, preparing it for winter. A few petunias in their hanging basket cling onto life, and two chrysanthemums bloom in a sheltered corner. A cold spell finished off many of the others.

Andrew and I are like two house sharers, each doing our own thing, not a couple who find time for each other to talk stresses away.

I'm increasingly lonely and even Andrew would be better than no one to talk to, but still I fight it. How can I act normal around him? Doing so would be dishonest and there's enough of that already.

Wednesday comes around and I finally go to the gallery to tackle Jack's books. When I arrive, he's not there.

'Oh, you just missed him,' says Hector. 'I'm sure he'd have hung around had he known you were coming today. Thought he mentioned it was next week.'

Blast, he must have counted fortnightly from last week. What a disappointment. 'That's okay, I can come back.'

Hector smiles kindly at me. 'I could let you into the flat. Jack won't mind.'

'Thanks, but I'll need to speak to him. He prepared everything for me last time. How are things with you?' We both know I'm asking how things are with Jo.

'Life's bright. Come and view our latest jewellery display. There's so much rubbish out there, but we're gathering together a lovely collection of wearable pieces.' *We* must be Jo and him.

He unlocks the cabinet and I instantly spot Jo's influence. The collection is smart. Gone are the cumbersome Victorian items that were there before. I foresee Hector's corner being the go-to place for elegant antique jewellery.

'We're planning to keep a few items here and the rest we'll buy and sell relatively quickly,' says Hector. 'What was a hobby could now grow into a thriving business thanks to Joanne. We're building up a bespoke cliental. Jo's a whizz on social media and has a group of art deco fans in the middle-market range.'

'How is it working out with Jo living up in Chester?' Jo is freelance but with this new business I wonder how she will manage logistics and fitting it in with her other work.

'Oh, I travel up to her too, but yes, we're discussing a better solution. Jo's considering relocating to help more with my side of the work. Visiting clients and so forth.'

Jo hasn't mentioned any of this. 'How lovely.'

Hector grins with pride. 'We're quite a couple now, you know, and not just in business.'

So they got together. Hector's in love. Jo didn't tell me when I spoke to her last. I do so hope she isn't using this relationship to distract her from her break up with Phil. She might not recognise she's doing it. I'd hate Hector to get hurt, he's such a lovely person. But then I should give Jo credit. I've never known her to hurt any man.

With that in mind, I try to answer in the same spirit. 'Lovely for you both. And it'll be fantastic having Jo living close by.' My smile is real enough as Hector's sheer joy is catching. So, another couple are getting together with only Andrew and me drifting apart. I can't help feeling envious.

'I'm not normally here so much, but stepped in to help out when the assistant left. We'll have to employ someone soon. Jack's filming a new TV series, you know. Quite popular with the female viewers he's been told. Much in demand.'

'No, I didn't know, but that's great.' If Jack is increasing his TV work I expect I won't see much of him anymore. My heart jerks and I'm surprised it hasn't landed on the floor for everyone to walk on. Even my imaginary beau is deserting me for female viewers.

As soon I get back home, I phone Jo to congratulate her, telling her how great it will be to have her living close by. Of course, I'm nosing and she knows it.

'That was quick,' she says. 'We only decided at the weekend. You must have seen Hector.'

'He was in the gallery this morning and he let it slip,' I add by way of explanation.

'Yeah, taking it slow wasn't working. Let's just say we fit each other very well. He asked me to move in with him, even if it's just to use it as a second base.' Her voice rises with the excitement. 'There's a vacant self-contained flat within Winterford House if I want it. The house-keeper used to live there, but she's moved into a cottage in the grounds. He admitted he'd prefer it if I just came to live with him in the house though.'

'It's rather quick. You hardly know him.'

'Doesn't feel like that. He's lovely and I've fallen for him. I'm considering saying yes to moving into the main house. I can't be bothered going back and forth, and anyway, you're down here. I'll keep the flat on. Rent it out.'

'And Phil? Over him?'

'Who's that? Honestly, ever since I met Hector, he hasn't come into my thoughts. You talk about him more than I do. I was in love with someone who didn't exist. A phantom. He used me. And anyone who can do that, well, is basically a shit. Hector is real.'

'How do you know Hector is real? He's not your usual type of man.'

'That's the whole point. My usual type of man lets me down. Now it turns out they weren't my type at all. Hector is the most straight up, honest man I've ever met.'

Hard though it is, I must admit I do like Hector myself and he comes across as a kind man. 'Still, it's early to be moving in together. But knowing you, you'll make your own decisions, right or wrong.'

'You know me well. Anything new on the Andrew front?'

'Nothing. He's busy with work. One minute it's almost as if he knows we're drifting and attempts to do something about it, then the next he's off in his own world again and acting guilty.'

'Get on with your own life, Randa, and out of the doldrums. Make changes. You're becalmed on an endless ocean of speculation and self-doubt. And instead of rowing to land, you're drifting and going with the flow wherever it may take you.'

'Sailing off the edge of the world,' I reply. 'What shall I do?'

'Start with your job. Happy? If not get a different one and meet new people.'

She's beginning to sound like Andrew. 'I enjoy working for me.'

'Then take on a new project.'

'And Andrew?'

'That's up to you. Don't just float around aimlessly waiting for something to happen to force you into a decision. Live life. Make new plans, or get on with the ones you already made before all this. I mean personally. Get it?'

'Got it.'

I wish I were more like Jo. Even when she was fixated on some unobtainable man or another, she managed to live her life to the full.

To change the subject, I ask about Jack.

'Oh, the new TV series. Didn't he tell you? It's his own show. One series to start.'

'No, he didn't mention it.' Why should he tell me? Although he's admitted having feelings for me, I haven't admitted anything back. Jo is more to him than I am. She's now the girlfriend of his best friend. I'm just the bookkeeper, and, as I made the decision that's what I'll only ever be to him, I can't complain. From now on he can't exist in a romantic way even in my day dreams. There can be no more 'moments'.

CHAPTER FOURTEEN

The rest of the week I follow Jo's advice and instead of moping while waiting for a storm that might be a long time coming, I turn to my garden to see if there's something new I can add that will occupy my full attention. Jo had in mind something more drastic, a change in career, or husband, but I'm not that impulsive. This gardening project will probably be a waste of time and money. But as Jo said, there's a life to be lived, and it can't just stay on hold forever.

After scouring my gardening books, I choose two things which will add interest to the garden without overwhelming the already well-stocked space. First is to buy a tree and I can't quite make up my mind between an elder, which will provide flowers for cordial or berries for wine, whichever I have time to make, and a crab apple for autumn jam (overly confident I know, but some miracle might happen where I get to keep the cottage or, failing that, I can dig them back up). Both can be pruned and won't overpower the other shrubs and trees. The second thing is to buy more solar lighting for the darker nights to light up the areas where I have evergreen or winter-flowering plants.

Jo was right. Time spent at the garden centre carefully choosing lighting and buying both the elder and crab apple, which I'm sure I can squeeze in somewhere, is welcomingly distracting. On Saturday, I finish tidying the garden ready for planting while Andrew disappears into town to buy a new shirt for the work dinner tomorrow. A darker mood has descended on him once more, so I take great pains to avoid him.

By dusk the garden work is complete and I stand back and admit Jo was right. It wasn't a big enough project. Christmas will occupy me making decorations and preparing treats, but again it won't last forever and I'll be adrift again and there's all the time before then to fill. The spark of enthusiasm lasted all of five minutes. What's the point?

Not wanting to make any relationship decisions right now, I make a deal with myself that in the New Year if nothing has progressed, I'll have to make changes. Sweeping ones. By leaving it until then, I've given myself permission not to stress over it for a few weeks and, in between, life has a chance to sort itself out, the cosmos taking a hand and doing it for me hopefully.

My thoughts drift back to trying to live life and the plans I had before all the upset. I so want a dog. With everything that's happening, would it be fair? Then plenty of marriages break up where there are pets. They go with you. Andrew wouldn't be bothered, so there would be no custody arguments. And if I lived alone, I would definitely want a pet for companionship anyway. In fact, I'm alone now.

Sunday evening has come around too quickly and I dress carefully for the dinner with Andrew's colleagues. A 'just in case' as Andrew hasn't tried to deter me from going. So if someone were to be there who was a threat, namely Jane Maxwell, she probably isn't going to attend now. By the time the night is over, I'm sure I'll wish I hadn't bothered.

My black, flared dress comes just above the knee and the back has a V-shaped opening. It dips up at the front hem making the most of my long legs and I've matched it simply with a clutch bag and high-heeled shoes. I decided to have my abundant hair in a messy up-do. The pearl and moonstone necklace that Jo bought me and river pearl and gold drop earrings finish off my ensemble.

The overall effect is better than I'd hoped. I'll do. Well, more than do. I look hot. I wait downstairs as Andrew is still in the shower. Once there, I grab a glass of wine, needing Dutch courage.

When Andrew appears looking handsome and sexy in the grey suit he wore on the night at the Northwood Park Hotel, my heart skips a beat. He's not aware I'm watching him as he fastens a cufflink, a worried look fleetingly crossing his features.

'Well, do I pass muster?' I venture.

His dutifully checks me over. 'Yeah, same as always.'

That's it? Well, it's a step up from 'fine' or 'okay'. Still, I'm glad I've made the extra effort. Whoever is there tonight, I'm ready for battle. Andrew isn't looking worried for nothing.

'That necklace you're wearing,' he remarks offhandedly, 'new is it? Antique at a guess?'

I'm amazed he's noticed something new I'm wearing, and that it's antique. Funny, I could have sworn I told him about my gift. He must have forgotten. 'It was a birthday gift from Jo. I told you, remember?'

'No, I don't. Expensive gift. Gold, isn't it?'

'Yes, but—'

'First time I've seen you in it.'

'First time I've worn it. It's special so—'

'Special. Who are you trying to impress – Freddie?' He snorts.

What's got into him? My outfit is stylish and elegant and I'm not overdressed, the necklace not at all flashy. 'No one,' I snap. 'I have to wear the necklace sometime and we never go anywhere.' Then it dawns on me. Jane Maxwell is going, or worse, Leticia Fuentes. 'And you? New suit? I haven't seen it before.' Yes, it's a blatant lie.

'Had it for ages. It's just a work suit.'

How can I argue with that? The evening he was with Jane Maxwell did include work. 'Why so grumpy? This dinner – clients going? Expecting it to be stressful?'

'No, why should I?' Despite the offhanded way he says this, he remains tight-lipped as he fastens his second cufflink. The fearful expression that follows, briefly flickering in his eyes, confirms my suspicions. My sixth sense is working full out. If Jane Maxwell is going to be there, it's strange he hasn't mentioned it after his admissions. And he criticised me for dressing up. Could it be he doesn't want to upset her? Rock the work boat? Perhaps it is Leticia Fuentes who's going then, not Maxwell. I take another gulp of wine while we wait for the taxi.

We arrive at the restaurant to find Freddie and his wife Sarah, and Hannah the creative accounts manager and her husband Jason are already there. Ben, who is young, eager, and up-and-coming in the artistic team and Andrew's main rival, arrives behind us. Paula the office manager, a single woman in her early fifties, is the last one in, a woman of few words. With her I recognise Jane Maxwell who is accompanied by her assistant, introduced as Leon. My stomach churns.

While Freddie is greeting me with an appreciative glance, and Sarah giving me a warm hug, Maxwell throws herself at Andrew and kisses him on both cheeks with a 'mwah' sound. Andrew pulls away from her and swiftly introduces me as his wife. Realisation dawns on Maxwell's face and she can't hide her surprise. She didn't expect to see me here.

Even though she has towering heels, she stands short next to me. Her plain, white, figure-hugging dress highlights her lack of waist. More confident, I shake her hand but don't smile. This woman flirted with my husband

and he, in turn, kissed her, and the situation is unreal. Where's the antibacterial gel when you need it?

Ben is suddenly there beside me taking my coat. 'Looking stunning tonight if you don't mind my saying so.' He adds loudly, 'You're a lucky guy, Andrew.'

Andrew frowns. He's clearly uncomfortable and so he should be. 'Er, yes, I am.' Maxwell's glance flits from him to me.

A waiter shows us to a long table at the back of the restaurant. Freddie takes the centre chair on the other side and pulls a chair out for Sarah on his left and Jane Maxwell on his right. Freddie indicates that Andrew sit on Maxwell's other side. Paula takes the remaining seat. When Ben pulls out a chair for me opposite Maxwell, I have no choice but to sit with him on my left and Leon to my right with Hannah and Jason taking end seats next to each other. The waiter goes around the table pouring wine.

Ben has a fiancée who's not with him. I ask how she is, so I don't sit awkwardly silent as Leon is chatting away to Sarah across the table.

'Got the flu,' he replies. 'I'm not complaining though if I get to sit next you.' I ignore him. This isn't the first time he's tried to flirt with me. At the company barbecue in the summer, he buzzed around me like an annoying wasp and I had to swat him away more than once. He's far too touchy-feely for my liking, doesn't respect boundaries.

Maxwell is busy chatting to Freddie and Andrew, switching from one to the other, managing to sound business-like and intelligent combined with vivacious-ness. She certainly livens up dreary conversation, and enjoys being the centre of attention.

How old did Andrew say she was? Early forties? Her Tinder age might be, but her real age is closer to fifty. Her teeth are remarkable though. A work of art. My gaze keeps drifting to them.

'You should grace us with your presence at these dinners more often,' Ben suddenly says. 'How many have you come to? One, Two? So that's at least three more you could have attended.' He smiles slyly. 'Why should we be deprived of your beauty?'

Three? Apart from the barbecue, there haven't been any. I'm seething with outrage. If it wasn't for Freddie inviting me, I wouldn't know about this one. Why doesn't Andrew take me? Cramping his style maybe? To save face, I mumble an answer along the lines of being very busy with my business. Still, I'm not that stupid that I don't know Ben is mischief making. He knows something.

Amusement bubbles in Maxwell's eyes. She must have been watching us. Saw me disconcerted.

She makes a remark to Andrew and laughs heartily. Not receiving much response, she continues to chat away to him. A picture flashes up in my mind of them canoodling in the hotel in Bath: the way Andrew behaved; the way he worked his charm on her leading up to that kiss; the way she stares at him now so adoringly and familiar. This is horrible. I bet she's secretly reliving it, believing I don't know. She must have known he was married. Her demeanour screams smug. And Andrew has no clue to the humiliation I'm feeling. I gulp some wine.

The conversation among everyone else is no longer focussed on business and has become general. Holidays.

'We're going away for our wedding anniversary, aren't we, darling?' It's out of my mouth before I can stop it. Desperation. Wanting to stop Maxwell's flirting.

Andrew frowns. 'Are we?'

'Yes, to Rome or Paris. We haven't yet made up our minds. But somewhere romantic.' I give a light laugh and then stare at Andrew with what must be panic in my eyes, begging him not to deny it.

He's flustered, his mind working. 'Yes, Rome or…er Paris, that's right.' He must see this as a way to get Maxwell off his back though as he adds, 'Venice was mentioned too, I believe.' For the first time in a long time we communicate, make a connection.

'Yes, Venice…and Santorini too.'

Maxwell throws an indulgent smile Andrew's way. Urgh! I've gone too far and sound so false. No one is buying this. Especially not her. 'Sounds fab,' she says. She turns towards Freddie. 'We should hold the next meeting in Italy. Rome or Florence perhaps.' She gestures towards me, her hand palm up. 'You should come…'

'Miranda,' Freddie and Andrew say simultaneously. She damn well knows my name.

'Yes, you should come, Miranda. It would be better than hotels in rainy Bath, wouldn't it, Andrew?'

She's deliberately trying to make Andrew feel uncomfortable. Panic registers in his face and he glances at me, but I pretend not to have heard for his undeserved bene-fit, intensely studying the menu.

When he speaks, his voice teems with false joviality. 'Well, that'll be up to Freddie. He handles your account now. You're an important client, you know. I'm just a minion.'

'Oh, I'm sure that's not true, is it, Freddie?'

'No, indeed. Andrew has a lot to offer your company.'

Beads of sweat break out on Andrew's forehead and he takes a sip of wine, squirming.

Freddie changes the subject back to business matters, for which I'm thankful, and I decide to regroup.

I grab my bag and trip off to the loo. The room is empty so I drop my handbag on a table top and root out my phone to send a message to Jo.

The Maxwell woman is here, I tap. *She's well into middle age and those teeth.*

Jo answers straight back. *Oooh, saucer of milk for table two*, followed by a cat emoji.

At least have some sympathy, meany.

Get a photo of her, she types back.

I'll try to sneak one.

When I come out, everyone appears to be listening intently to Leon, a flamboyant, creative type of guy with oodles of ideas. Phone in hand I direct it at the table, quickly clicking as soon as I have Maxwell focussed in my frame. Suddenly, she glances my way, clearly astounded. Everyone sees her face and looks my way. Coolly turning, so I get a general view of the restaurant, I click, click, click, and take pictures of everything.

I stroll back, confident and composed, sit down and say, 'For an important client. They asked me to report on this restaurant as a possible venue for their annual dinner, after I mentioned I was coming. That's life when you run your own business – you never stop. I'm considering moving into event organising, so offered to help.'

Freddie frowns and Andrew doesn't know where to look.

'Lovely,' says Sarah, coming to my rescue. She's so nice.

'What's the nature of the business?' asks Maxwell.

'Bookkeeping.'

'I mean the photos. Who are they for?'

'A…a plumbing business.' Oh God. An annual dinner for a plumber! 'I mean builder of course. Which includes plumbing.'

Panicking, I turn and take a photo of the bar, then the ceiling (can't think why), and a general overview of the restaurant. Then running out of things to photograph I start on the table, beginning with the cutlery, picking a fork up and turning it this way and that. Click, click, click. All the while everyone stares at me in disbelief except Freddie and Ben who weigh me up, unsure if I'm a genius or crazy. I'm going to murder Jo.

After a quick check of my photos, I nod with pretend satisfaction and return my phone to my bag. My glass of wine stares at me accusingly. That's it for the rest of the night or this can only get worse.

Andrew is flushed with embarrassment and Maxwell is smirking.

If only I could start the evening again where I'm super sophisticated and only saying and doing intelligent things. Why is this always the position I find myself in – wishing I had a time machine? Hopefully, the rest of the table will forget my antics if I just blend into the background.

As the first course arrives, Freddie asks me about my business, saying how dedicated I am to my clients, business matters never leaving me, even at social events.

Encouraged I spout, 'Bookkeeping might appear on the surface boring but there are elements one can add to the business to make it more dynamic. To build it into something more. An essential service. My latest client is a TV personality.' Where in heavens is this coming from? It sounds good even to me.

'Really? Admirable work ethic,' Freddie says. 'You'd be an asset to the company should you ever wish to join us.'

Ben agrees and chinks his glass with me, staring at me even more admiringly than before. Meanwhile, Freddie redirects the conversation to the annual company dinner in the spring with everyone attending.

Reprieve.

'So, we can expect to see you there?' Ben says to me alone.

'Certainly,' I reply, knowing it's unlikely. Then an idea strikes me. 'Do you have to work and socialise a lot within your position at the company at weekends? With clients, I mean. Conferences, meetings and so forth? Just researching for future reference, in case I ever consider Freddie's kind offer. I hate working weekends.'

'Rarely. In fact, I can't remember the last time we had to do a weekend meeting. Yes, weekdays, same as Andrew. We generally work on the same accounts. Will you take Freddie up on his offer?'

Ben may as well have picked me up and shaken me, as my heart has come loose and is jangling around inside me like a bead in a rattle. After what I've discovered lately, I can't believe I'm hurt by this revelation. I knew the answer before I asked.

'Probably not,' I reply. 'It's never a good idea to work with your significant other.'

'It'll be our loss.'

The rest of the dinner goes well, considering my mind and body is in shock. While we're waiting for coffee, I trot off to the loo for respite, wishing we could go home. My reflection in the mirror reveals a wan face, the strain showing. I've just pulled my makeup bag out when Maxwell bursts through the door like a thespian making a grand entrance onto a stage.

She sashays over on her impossible heels and stands beside me. The little smile she gives me after catching my eye in the mirror, tells me she's followed me on purpose, and I mentally prepare myself for whatever demoralising comment she will throw my way. With what Ben told me earlier, it can't be any worse. I'm not in the mood for her nonsense.

She opens her handbag and plucks out a lipstick,

applying it to her pouted lips while critically appraising me, then slips it back into its sleeve. 'We haven't had time to chat, have we?'

'No.'

'You're not what I expected. As Andrew's wife, I mean. I imagined someone sophisticated and in control. But your behaviour was rather odd earlier. Wives are generally an asset to their husbands, not a hindrance.' She daintily wipes the edge of her bottom lip with a red, acrylic, talon-like nail. 'Taking photographs at dinner. Bit of a faux pas.' She has a laugh in her voice.

The knives are out and I've had enough. 'It's a work dinner and I know everyone here well. And as for being an asset, that's rather an out-dated view with you being a businesswoman yourself. Men don't expect that these days. Maybe they did in your time.'

Her eyes glow with venom. 'Some do. Andrew's that sort. Good appearances matter to him. Having a supportive wife would surely be part of that, to help him succeed in his career, instead of being selfish and self-seeking.'

'How would you know what Andrew's sort is? He's not a Neanderthal.'

She sneers derisively and pats her hair, fixing an imaginary stray lock behind her ear. 'You'd be surprised. For a start, he admires a successful woman who can demonstrate self-control while recognising his needs. That I do know.'

What a bitch. Keeping my anger in check, I say calmly, 'Yes, that's true. Andrew does admire successful women, plural, me being one of them. We don't live in each other's pockets.' Realising that I've accidentally implied we have an open marriage I add, 'Do you know Leticia Fuentes? She's a very close friend of his. Twenties, stunning – a natural beauty, and runs a successful business. As you say yourself, he admires that very, very much. She must satisfy some needs as he never stops talking about her. Funny, he's never mentioned you though.'

Maxwell's face reddens.

'Are you all right? Hot flush? Menopause can be a bitch, so I've heard. Better leave you to cool off in private.'

Not waiting for her reaction, I grab my bag and flee.

As I hurry back to the table, Andrew watches me. For all my bitchiness, I'm shaking, and my face must be deathly white. He doesn't miss it and knows there's something wrong, especially when Maxwell joins us, her face still showing signs of a flush and her lips set tight as they can be, stretched over her big teeth.

Andrew twists uncomfortably in his seat. And when his eyes catch mine, a flash of concern registers briefly. Did I just use one of his mistresses against the other? This is getting stupid.

Sarah asks me to tell her more about my work ideas. She's astute. I take one deep calming breath and enthuse about extending my business, now that I have more time as our beautiful cottage is perfect. What I won't do is give Maxwell the satisfaction of knowing she upset me. That she and Andrew have both upset me.

With Maxwell silent, Freddie, hearing some of the conversation between Sarah and me, gives me his full attention. He's genuinely interested in my job. My confidence builds as I tell him my imaginary new plans, explaining nothing is on paper yet as they are just ideas. Not that I admit I only thought of them this evening. They sound convincing though, so why don't I do it – expand? Not exactly a new business, but an extension of it?

'Sounds exciting,' Sarah remarks when I finish. 'If I hear of anyone that needs such a service, I'll put you in touch with them.'

'Me too,' Ben agrees, and pats my leg under the table. At least I think it was a pat. Could have been a grope. I move my knee away just in case and calm down. The distraction worked already, both for taking the emphasis off the spat, and helping me to compose myself.

Maxwell is quiet, so Andrew attempts to placate her, probably worried about how it will affect business, but she's having none of it. She probably eats men like him for breakfast. And he let her do it. In the end, I'm the one here who's suffering. There's no real satisfaction in getting the better of her. A bitchy remark or two can't overshadow a full on snog and probably worse. There was plenty of implication in her words.

Inwardly sighing, I refuse to let her occupy any more of my time or thoughts. There's no way of knowing if Andrew had sex with her, though I expect he did and is regretting it now.

Across the table Andrew's expression is one of resignation. Maxwell is no longer of interest to him sexually, that's for sure. Leticia though – my intuition tells me – is another matter. When I mentioned her to Maxwell, I wasn't indicating her as a possible threat to her. She is a threat, but to me only, most likely heralding the end of my marriage.

CHAPTER FIFTEEN

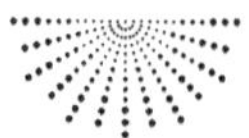

The next morning, I wake to find Andrew has left for work. He didn't mention any of the night's incidents on the way home last evening, if anything he was pleasant. As soon as we arrived back, I ran straight upstairs to divest myself of my finery and have a shower. When I emerged Andrew was in bed and already asleep. Men seem to sleep regardless of any stresses.

A headache prompts me now to stagger to the kitchen to make coffee. The clock reads nine o'clock, so I haven't overslept too long, even after lying awake for a couple of hours, wondering if I should be proud or ashamed of my behaviour before deciding it was understandable.

Once the coffee has brewed, I pour myself a cup and plonk myself at the kitchen table. While I'm gulping the reviving fluid, I examine my oh-so perfect kitchen. Not a thing is out of place. It's sterile – looks almost unlived in.

Curious, I wander into the sitting room, then the

snug, but each room is immaculate. Am I that fastidious about cleaning? Suddenly I want to mess it up, so throw a few cushions around. It's a start. In the corner of the window, the spider web is empty and Jane Gnasher Maxwell lies dead on the window ledge. Well, that's what happens when winter is coming in spider land, you run out of mates. I fetch the vacuum and clean up both her and her web. And not being able to help myself, I also straighten the cushions.

Why am I so bothered about how the house looks? I recall my old friends with their growing families. They never bothered excusing the mess. Even Kate when we visited her and Matthew last year, moved a few things for me so I could sit on the sofa. 'Kids,' she said. 'But you wouldn't know how impossible it is to keep a tidy house.' It was a dig of course. A dig at the lack of offspring.

Andrew comes in before six and there's a thumping up the stairs. At a guess he's going up to talk to me. 'I'm in the kitchen,' I call, and pour him a glass of wine, hoping to soften him up. Not wanting a confrontation as my head is still foggy.

As he enters the room, he notices the two glasses and the bottle. He raises his eyebrows. 'Celebrating?'

'Er, no. More hair of the dog. Just a small one though.'

'Oh, is that all. Good. Freddie said he might contact you to try to persuade you to join the company. Wants to make a new position for a part-time freelance event organiser and travel coordinator. If he offers you the position, I trust you'll turn it down.' He waits but I don't react. 'Best not to work together. And why give up your own business? You do okay.' Andrew isn't even trying to hide the fact he doesn't want me working with him.

At least, there is no mention of my general behaviour last night. Good job too as he would get short shrift. Rolling my eyes, I say, 'I've no intentions of working for Freddie. Nice of him to think I'm worth it though.' I put emphasis on 'him'.

'Great.' Satisfied I'm not going to discover his extracurricular activities he leans against the island and picks up his glass.

Am I so thick in his eyes? Something explodes inside me. 'We have to talk.'

'Oh?' He takes a gulp of wine.

'Tell me the truth. Are you having an affair?' I say this assertively rather than aggressively.

He chokes and splutters, 'For God's sake, not again. No.' He clears his throat and takes another drink. 'No, I am not.' His voice softens. 'Of course not.'

Did I really think he was going to admit it? Really? 'Well—'

'It's that bloody woman, Maxwell, isn't it? What did she say last night? She's a liar if she's implied anything.' Thrusting down his glass, he steps towards me, his face flushed with anger, and even though it's not aimed at me, I back away. He can get angry in his own space.

'No, it's not all her. But yes, she did imply something. She was doing it all evening.' This is not strictly true, but it was in her manner.

'Bitch, isn't she? Why would I want burger when I have steak at home? She's not even burger, she's a…chipolata.'

Did he really just use that? 'Andrew, honestly.'

'Sorry, Ben said something like that today. He'd noticed Maxwell's behaviour and mentioned it. He called you steak and truffles with champagne.'

Why would Ben say that? Why would anyone? Steak, burger, it's horrible. Is that what I'm reduced to, food?

My face must tell all as he adds, 'Sorry for subjecting you to her. Didn't know she was going. Today I told Freddie about her, er, earlier behaviour, with everyone at the office talking about her attitude towards you. I guessed she'd upset you and he's assured me he'll keep her away, saying he wouldn't have that.' He gestures with his hands outstretched, his shoulders coming up. 'So, nothing to worry about.'

'Well, that's good to know. But I actually meant is there someone other than her? Someone at work? You're away so often at weekends. It never used to be like this. You can talk to me.' Why did he start the steak and burger thing? Now I've lost momentum.

Still, it has impact as his face blanches. 'Did Maxwell imply that too? She's jealous of you. Of course there's no one else. That woman has you overwrought. Don't believe a word she says.' He turns to the island and pours himself more wine. 'You're the only woman for me as I'm the only man for you. Isn't that so?' He turns and holds my gaze, a question in his eyes.

'What? Don't be stupid, Andrew.' Typical of him to try to turn it back on me.

'Same for us both then. Here you are.' He hands me my glass. 'Now, let's enjoy our evening and not let any stupid client or anyone else come between us.'

It's too late, two women already have, but he's not ready to admit it. From his reaction I can surmise Jane Maxwell knows something. Could that be why she was so shocked when I mentioned Leticia's name? Did I inadvertently expunge a hold she had over him?

After a pause, I say, 'Okay, better start dinner.' I busy myself gathering ingredients to make a risotto. He moves to leave the room, so I ask, 'Now we've ascertained we're the only ones for each other and the time being right, I'm considering getting a dog again. What are your thoughts? And starting a family – we need to talk about that soon. The clock is ticking.'

'Of course, we can discuss them both, but not tonight please, darling. I've had a hard day. What's that you're making?'

I pick up my cookery book and show it to him, knowing he's trying to distract me.

'Great. Love risotto.' He quickly leaves the room.

To have children with him is off my wish list so I'm not bothered that he's avoiding long-term plans. I feel so detached from him – from everything now in our lives. Brick wall or resigned to an eventual break up? Both? I'm unsure.

Later while we're eating, Andrew says, 'By the way, here's something to cheer you up. I've bought a seventy-five-inch, ultra HD TV with my commission. You'll love it. There's plenty of space in the sitting room. We hardly use it, and you prefer the snug anyway. Can you stay in Thursday, it's getting delivered?' He gives a deep, satisfying sigh. 'Matthew can stuff his cinema room.'

Oh, so it's okay to make unilateral decisions around here. Horrendous.

'Let's have a gander at the photos then,' Jo says, the next day as we sit nursing coffees in the kitchen. She called unexpectedly, interrupting me in the middle of tackling a mobile hairdresser's muddled account. Working from home is as good as being on a permanent holiday to some people who presume you're constantly available, but Jo understands this and is only here to comfort me after I phoned and told her about Sunday night.

I show her the photos. The one I have of Maxwell is blurred. The other photos don't make sense: a crack in the restaurant ceiling, a waiter's bum, the end of the bar, a skewed general view of the tables, and the back of a fork. I hope Freddie never asks for them to see how much they helped my imaginary builder client choose a venue.

'Not a patch on you. What was he thinking?'

'He wasn't thinking with his head. And don't

mention burger or steak or even sausages.' I roll my eyes and explain.

She laughs and flicks through the photos again. 'Event organising is a cracking idea but you might need to improve your photography skills or find a photographer—' She pauses. 'Sorry, forgot about the photographer woman. Still it could work, expanding your business. Take your mind off stuff.'

'I am considering it. I even made real notes. It would get me out sometimes. I'd rather have had a baby and the ever-elusive dog, but it won't happen.'

'The baby or the dog?'

'Probably both.'

Jo puts her arm around my shoulders. 'Never say never. There are at least four years until you're forty.'

'Three.'

'Oh yeah, same here. When did we get a year older? Thirties are going in a flash.'

We both sip our coffees while pondering on this.

'What if it doesn't happen?' I put to Jo. 'Can you imagine a life without children?'

'We can always adopt or foster.'

'Or take advantage of sperm donation.'

'Can you imagine that – choosing a guy to be the father?' Jo laughs. 'Some tall Dane, a handsome doctor.'

'You never told me you were considering going it alone.'

'I'm not. I mean, I wasn't. Rather, I could have imagined that type of guy being the father of my baby. Now that's Hector.'

'Do be careful, Jo.'

Jo laughs. 'I will, but this is the real thing.'

'Okay, I do admit there's something magical between you and Hector.' I narrow my eyes. 'You went back that day using the necklace as an excuse, didn't you?'

Jo glances upwards innocently. 'It wasn't just the way he looked at me, like looking into my soul. It was those eyes. Aqua like the Mediterranean Sea on a cloudless summer's day.' She puts on a mock dreamy expression to cover up her flowery words. 'Anyway, you got a necklace out of it.'

'I did and I love it.'

'There might be more jewellery gifts now I'm in the business.' She grins. 'We're so in sync with one another.' Her eyes are alight with happiness. 'Sorry, I hate harping on about us with all that's going on with Andrew. You must be so fed up.'

'Don't be daft, it's good to hear.'

'There is life beyond a broken relationship,' she gushes. 'Look at me!'

For some reason an image of Jack comes into my head. I shake it away. 'So much to face. I can't just say goodbye and walk away. Even if I could, if there's to be a divorce I need good grounds. I wouldn't want to wait years for that. But most of all, hearing the truth would help me heal. The lies are the worst thing. They eat you up. Eat into your soul. Somehow it becomes more important to know the truth than anything else.'

'Yes, I see that. But don't let the situation go on too long. You need out so you can start healing.'

'Yes, and eight years together is hardly a shallow relationship to get over quickly.'

'No, of course not. And you truly worshipped Andrew.'

'And was blinded by it.'

'Top and bottom of it, yes. You cut too much out of your life to concentrate on him. Invested so much, it's making it harder to leave it all behind.'

'Cynical. What else was I supposed to do? I did marry him. We all take chances in relationships. If you don't have faith in your partner, why get married?'

'Yeah, I get your point. Like having a prenup which is like saying, "When this fails, I'm covered".'

'Exactly.'

Jo wags a finger at me. 'So, don't have regrets then, but don't dwell on the investment either or it'll hold you back. Move on – kick him into oblivion. We'll support you. Be there.'

'After I have the truth.'

Jo rolls her eyes. 'Stubborn. What about a private investigator to speed up the process?'

'I considered it, but the little money I've saved should stay in the bank. Come January, I promise I'll make decisions regardless.'

The sun makes its first appearance of the day, a shaft of sparkling light shining across the table. 'Come and see what I've done in the garden.'

Jo follows me outside and from her perspective, apart from the new trees, there's nothing different to see. I gesture. 'Those two trees are new and there's more solar lighting. Winter's laying everything bare,' I say. 'Cycle of life. Autumn's almost over so there's only tidying to do while waiting for the spring flowers to appear.' Then I remember. 'Did you know daffodils came up in January last year? Perhaps they will again and I can take it as a good omen for the New Year. *And then my heart with pleasure will fill,*' I paraphrase from Wordsworth, '*and will dance with the golden daffodils.*'

Jo's silent for a moment before saying, 'Soppy thing, but I'll dance with you.' She points to the silver birch leaning over from next door. 'You have that gorgeous gold now to tide you over. Shouldn't that be a good omen? Looks fabulous but I don't envy you all that mess when those leaves decide to let go of their moorings and float down.'

'You're joking. The atmosphere, wood smoke and musty smells, a misty frosty morning, sweeping up crunchy fallen leaves…'

'I'm not sure Hector's gardeners would agree.'

'Autumn can be fun, just not this year. To be honest, spring can't come quickly enough.'

'And talking about Hector, I'd better get back. I'll leaf you to it.'

'Funny.'

'I know.'

Once Jo has gone, and having changed clothes, I head for the garden again. At this rate I'll have to work over the weekend to catch up with accounts. But the fresh air beckons. I rake the lawn of leaves and put them in the compost bin, then sweep the pathways, and even get the hedge trimmer out and tackle a conifer.

Time slips by and suddenly Andrew is home. Early for him as it isn't yet dark. 'Hang on, I'll help,' he says when he comes outside and sees me struggling to put the clippings in a bag.

Five minutes later he's back and changed. Together we finish up. The last time he helped in the garden was a year ago.

'Been a while,' Andrew says, echoing my thoughts. 'Let's not cook. Fancy the pub tonight?'

'Don't you have work?'

'Freddie can wait for once.'

Definitely news to break – first the garden and now dinner. A confession? Could it be tonight? My heart races.

Later, at our usual table in the Fox and Hounds and having ordered food, I use event organising as an excuse to speed things up. I'd rather get it over with. 'So, Freddie hasn't found his event-organiser-come-travel-coordinator yet?'

'Nope, Paula could handle it easily.' He's still trying to put me off. 'Freddie needs other people more urgently in my opinion. Another admin assistant, for instance, to save us having to do it, and another person in Creative. Someone actually creative though, not like Ben.'

'If it's any help, I know a photographer if he needs one?' This is a prompt.

'Freddie has one he uses already.' Andrew's lips are set tight.

'Is he any good?'

'It's a she and she does the job well enough.' My stomach churns. He gets up and goes to the bar to order two glasses of elderflower presse, even though there's table service.

When he arrives back, he pulls his phone from his pocket. After flicking though several screens, shows me pictures of a butter-yellow villa on a Greek island. All deep blue skies, turquoise waters and sandy beaches. 'Let's make the fib we told at the work dinner become a reality. We could go in the spring.' He places a hand over mine and strokes it.

Any other time I would have loved the attention, but instead my head is full of pictures of him with Maxwell. It's superficial – a move. Means nothing. I want to pull my hand away.

When I don't answer, he adds, 'A romantic week away, discovering secret coves, eating freshly caught fish in the local restaurants, swimming, making love. His fingers intertwine with mine.'

'Yes, and time to discuss the future. The next big step in our relationship.'

He withdraws his hand, puts his phone back in his jacket pocket and shrugs. 'Or just revel in the moment. Not worry about anything except enjoying each other's company.'

I stare directly into his eyes and say, 'Making plans isn't worrying, it's exciting – isn't that what couples do?' I say enthusiastically. 'The house is finished and we're both established in work.'

Andrew chews on his bottom lip, thoughts racing, and then, his expression brightening, he reaches for my hand with both of his. 'Okay, if you want a dog, I can't see why not, the garden's big enough. Might be fun, though we'll have to find sitters if we're both away. And there's all that walking and the extra mess for you. Hard work dogs.'

The sacrifices he doesn't make to avoid having children. Shouldn't he be saying a dog would give us an excuse to walk together, help bring us closer? 'Perhaps this isn't the right time for a pet,' I say. 'And there are other considerations as you say.'

'Stop being contrary. It's a good idea when I think about it. A dog would be company for you when I'm travelling. And that'll be for longer periods being long haul. With a dog here I wouldn't worry so much about you being alone. Holly Cottage is a good distance from the village.'

Bloody hell! And there it is. The holiday idea was indeed a softener, as was me having a dog. 'Ah, so, you're going away more often?'

'Yes, 'fraid so. Freddie has trips planned to the US. Hannah's side of the business. She's my new direct superior. A move up. Not as high as I hoped, but this is a stepping stone, Freddie says, for hard work and dedication. Going above and beyond was how he put it.' So, no choice on the travel, sorry, but it's all good for the career. The New York trip is in January but this week it's just

London – Thursday to Saturday. Should be back in the evening.'

Ben said no one works weekends. And Andrew hasn't suggested I tag along on any long-haul trips either. 'You're right, a dog would be an excellent companion. People say dogs are better than humans. I might go to the rescue centre tomorrow.'

'The sooner the better. It's a great idea.'

During the rest of the evening Andrew doesn't mention the holiday again. My compensation sorted in his eyes. He chats about work animatedly, his eyes shining. My own eyes must be dull in comparison. They feel vacant of any happiness.

CHAPTER SIXTEEN

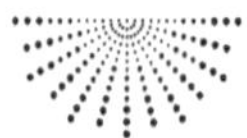

The next morning, after doing a few errands in town, I park at the back of Langford Gallery. This time Jack will be there as I texted him and he answered. For all our ups and downs, Jack no longer confuses me. The misunderstandings were caused by his feelings for me, and that makes me feel good. Jack is a light in my otherwise cheerless existence. We both know where we stand, and that's as friends. So why not enjoy that for what it is? Okay, I know I'm kidding myself. But I have to get used to it.

Having walked around to the front of the gallery, I'm approaching the door when a familiar face emerges. It takes me a second to recognise Jack's ex wife, Stephanie, who frowns and carries on walking past.

'You?' she calls, and I spin around. 'You…?' She shakes her head. 'I'm such a dolt. So sorry, I've forgotten your name. But you came to my pub with Jack one evening. A bit upset from what I remember. You'd only just met?'

'It's Miranda. Yes, we had just met, but I'm now Jack's bookkeeper.' Why do I feel the need to explain the reason I'm about to enter the gallery? 'And you're Stephanie.'

Sporting a wide smile, she walks the few steps back and we shake hands. 'I'm afraid I was a little rude when you called that evening. Jack's such a pain. He does that, you know, turns up with friends and no prior warning. Regardless of The Three Horseshoes being a pub, it's also my home, and being the ex, I'm scrutinised by his companions. The proverbial goldfish in a bowl.' Her expression is sincere, her brows knitted. 'The place was so busy that evening, what a fright I must have looked, and with no time to chat or explain.'

How wrong can you be about someone? I make a mental note not to have a bad opinion of the whole female population just because Andrew cheated. 'Don't worry. You can't have looked as much of a fright as I did.' I laugh as it's true.

Stephanie laughs back as she also knows it's true. 'That would take some beating.' My smile fades as suddenly as it appears, forming into a mock frown. We stare at each other momentarily and burst out laughing.

'Hey,' she says. 'Will you be long in the knight's court? How about meeting up again for a coffee later? Haven't had a good natter with another female for absolutely ages. We must have a few things in common.'

I'm not sure what she means by 'knight's court' or

'few things in common', but I find myself assenting. 'A couple of hours?'

'Shall we make it one o'clock? That should give you plenty of time. The Mall Coffee Shop?'

Once I agree, she hurries off. For some reason the encounter raises my spirits even more.

Hector is by the door as I walk into the gallery and greets me. 'Thank you,' he says. And when I show puzzlement, he smiles. 'For bringing Jo into my life. I can't tell you how much it's changed since I met her.'

'Ha, more that she brought herself in.'

'Like a whirlwind,' says Hector.

'Or at the least, a force-nine gale,' I reply, and we both laugh.

Jack's busy at the back, and, hearing my voice, looks over and frowns, probably wondering if I saw or spoke to Stephanie. Feeling playful, I decide to wind him up. Ruffle his standing as an exemplar of knightly virtues.

'Just saw Steph,' I say gaily, walking over and taking a chance on the shorter version of her name. 'We're going for coffee later.' Jack's body tenses. He's rattled. Smiling, I sail past him and into the back without stopping. 'Shall I go up?' Not waiting for an answer, I run up the stairs and have reached the top before his footsteps sound behind me.

On entering his sitting room, I almost trip over a box, several of which litter the floor.

'Whoops, careful, I'm packing. It's going through quickly on that house we viewed.'

We. Then I recall what Jack said to me in the

gallery last time. A flush creeps up my neck and I breathe deeply, hoping it will dissipate before showing. 'Oh, erm, congratulations. Lovely house. Hope you'll be happy there.' I pick my way towards the desk which, thankfully, hasn't been packed away. And there, in the middle of the room, sitting on a little occasional table hidden behind a tall box, is the South Wind sculpture. 'Oh!' My exclamation is out before I can stop it.

'Yes, the sculpture. I did say I'd keep it in case in case you might want it at some point in the future, or I could keep it if you don't. We have similar tastes. Big house to fill.'

'Oh, yes, of course,' I croak, my powers of resistance wavering as I know Jack was thinking only of me.

He clears his throat. 'So, you're meeting Stephanie?'

'Yes, she apologised for if she appeared rude that night. You know the night—'

'I know which night. How can I ever forget it?'

That could be bad or good, depending. 'That night –' I chuckle at the absurdity of it – 'I thought she was still interested in you as she seemed hostile towards me, but that's simply not the case.'

Jack ignores the fact I've just admitted I was jealous. 'Hostile towards me, more like. Yes, that boat has well sailed,' he replies in a reassuring manner. 'We both moved on. I'm the one who found it hard out of the two of us. The loss of the family unit, I suppose. Suddenly, I was a single parent as Sophie stayed with me, or did until university. But I missed the togetherness. Do you know what I mean? Building, planning and the day-to-day business of living together.'

Very much so, and I wish Andrew had such an attitude. To be a family man like Jack, focussed on his wife. A child. That boat has sailed too.

There's a sudden commotion downstairs. Voices drift up through the open door. That can't be! It sounds like Andrew. What on earth is he doing here?

'Hellooooo!'

For God's sake!

Footsteps sound on the stairs. We stare at the door and Hector appears. 'Miranda's hubby is here. Urgent apparently.' He glances sideways, a glimmer of mischief in his eyes as he steps aside to let Andrew through before disappearing down the stairs, but I'm sure he doesn't make it to the bottom.

'Sorry to interrupt,' Andrew directs at Jack while examining him. Jack stares hard at him in return. They're like two bulls sizing each other up. What is Andrew playing at arriving unannounced at a client's business premises – home even?

'Something wrong?' I ask. Perhaps I shouldn't, but I can't help feeling proud that such a handsome man is my husband. Reflects on me, I suppose. I know, it's bad.

Meanwhile, the handsome man is not amused or even pleased to see me, he's glaring, and I fall straight back down among the uglies. 'Darling, your phone's off again.'

A blush rises, stinging my cheeks. Again? Twice, actually, twice. How embarrassing. He's the cheat not me. 'I switch the phone off when I'm with a client, same as you,' I say sharply.

'Well, it's a good job you mentioned where you were going last night. Change of plans. Remember I mentioned a trip to Manchester? I have to travel today instead and need to pack.' His voice rises with stress and he slips into what I call his cave man stance – arms folded, in chest-beating mode. 'This diversion has slowed me down. Trust you not to be in today. I left my house keys on the kitchen table. Didn't you see them when you washed up?'

My face grows scarlet. How can Andrew do this to me? Make me look like both an imbecile and a skivvy. I bristle. 'No, I didn't. But yes, you failed to lock the door when you left and I was still in bed. Anyone could have walked in.' I can't believe we're arguing in front of a virtual stranger. But when I turn, Jack has thankfully disappeared into the kitchen.

Andrew's anger ebbs. On the seven-mile journey here he must have been simmering until boiling point. This is normal for him, short-lived tempers, which once vented, quickly evaporate. Still, he didn't have to do this in front of a client, and that client Jack. Even from the kitchen he could have overheard.

Andrew sighs and rolls his eyes. 'Yes, sorry, was in a hurry. Well, give me the key to the back door and I'll leave it on the table. It's Freddie again. Last minute as usual. Wants me to go along with Hannah. She's waiting in the car park. Sorry for snapping.'

After taking my keys from my pocket, I pull one off the ring and hand it to him.

'Thanks.' Andrew pecks me on the lips. 'Back Saturday. Friday I'll be working late, and it's a bit of a drive from Manchester.'

Didn't he say he was going to London, last night?

Jack reappears across the room.

'Again, sorry to interrupt,' Andrew shouts over the top of my head.

As Jack makes his way through the boxes, I say, 'Andrew, Jack Langford. Jack, this is Andrew, my husband.'

'I gathered that,' says Jack, his face deadpan, but he holds out a hand.

Andrews shakes it. 'Er, yes. Urgent and all that.' He turns back to me. 'You will remember to stay in tomorrow, won't you? The delivery?'

He excuses himself and I show him out. Hector scurries out of sight as I reach the top of the stairs and I'm sure Jo will get to hear all about this little incident. How mortifying. Jack and Hector must think Andrew walks over me in more ways than the one. He wouldn't usually do this – embarrass me in front of people. Things have certainly changed between us.

As we reach the door onto the road, Andrew says, 'Strange office Langford has. More like a home.'

'There's a desk in the corner. It'll be more of an office when he moves out. The flat was temporary while he… they, looked for a house.' Now that was sneaky, knowing he'll infer Jack's married. Of course, I'm referring to Sophie who technically will live there too.

'Well, enjoy your day. Any plans this week?'

'Just today. Once I finish here, I'm meeting my new friend Stephanie for a coffee, then it's off to the rescue centre.'

'The dog.' He smiles.

'Yes, the dog.'

'Pick a good'un.' He pecks me again and sets off up the road.

I dread going back upstairs, but when I do, Jack's in the kitchen. 'I'll be doing some work here at the kitchen table if you need anything,' he calls. Relieved I hurry directly to the desk and open the folder of invoices.

My reprieve is short-lived. An hour later Jack brings me a mug of tea and a cheese and salad sandwich. Not just for me, but for himself too. He's intends to have lunch with me. What happened to enjoying being friends? I'm struggling with it.

Casually, he leans against the desk and his thighs are there again. I desperately scour my brain for something intelligent to say.

'Both our spouses here embarrassing us, hey,' he says while I'm still thinking. 'Hector was here when Stephanie came in spouting off about Sophie threatening to drop out of her course. Blamed me for encouraging her to do what she wants, and demanding I should stop her.'

How considerate. He's trying to lessen my embarrassment.

'Of course, in my case, it's *ex*-spouse,' he continues, leaving that dangling in the air.

'Yes, better if it's an ex speaking in that way, I suppose, not your actual husband or wife.'

'Still, when you have a child together with someone, you never really split up, do you? Even though you're no longer a family.' He's being philosophical. 'Not until the child grows up and is independent.'

That peeves me for some odd reason. 'We're getting a dog,' I say as if that's the same as having a child with someone.

'Really? A dog, wow. In time, I hoped to get another golden retriever.'

At this point I'm reluctant to mention the bichon frise or similar I was hoping to get. 'Retrievers – love them. In fact, a big dog would be perfect.' He probably thinks I'm making it up as I go along, which I am. 'After I've had coffee with Stephanie, I'm driving to the rescue centre. No time like the present.'

'Really. Would you like company? Now I'm moving into a house there's nothing stopping me from having another dog, and Sophie would love it. And, of course, the extra exercise wouldn't go amiss.' He pats his flat stomach. 'I'll be settled soon enough.'

'Your last dog…?'

'Died, yes. Molly stayed with me at first. Then once the house sold and I moved into the flat, she went to live with Stephanie.' He shrugs. 'Passed away a year later. She was twelve. We had hoped to have her a little longer. Sophie was so cut up.' The sadness shows in his eyes.

'So sorry.' I want to hug him but stay glued to the seat. I daren't look at Jack for too long, but then again lowering my eyes doesn't work either. Those jeans stretched over his muscly thighs… Instead I take a bite of the sandwich.

'Well, perhaps it's time for another. So, that's a date this afternoon?'

I swallow. 'A date?'

'Rescue centre later?'

'Yes. I'll come back here.' This is so nuts and soooo weird.

'Brilliant. Shall we go in your car? I only have the van with me.'

I agree. Jack's van isn't the most comfortable one I've travelled in. But I'm galvanised into action now we've made arrangements, and continue with the invoices.

Jack goes down to the gallery.

An hour later, as I'm hurrying out of the door as I'm late for my meet up with Stephanie, I bump into a mousy-looking woman who is straining to see into the gallery through the window, but the sunlight is glaring on the glass. She almost drops her phone, and a startled expression crosses her face when her eyes meet mine. She turns her glance away as if uncomfortable. I apologise. The woman mumbles something which I lipread as 'no worries', lowers her head and scurries away.

A horrifying thought strikes me. Did I know her and failed to recognise her? Her hair was cut in a bob, and with her thick-rimmed glasses, she closely resembled Velma from *Scooby-Doo*. No, I don't think so. Perhaps she was a Jack groupie. I laugh to myself, but this is how it could be with his new TV series – fans ogling him through windows. Oh God, I'm jealous, how silly.

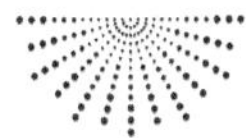

CHAPTER SEVENTEEN

The coffee shop is popular being in the middle of town, catering for a wide range of food allergies and preferences. Jo would love it. Stephanie is already standing at the counter, so I hurry over.

'So, you're Jack's bookkeeper as well as using his shoulder to cry on?' she asks when we've bought our coffee and find a sofa that's free. Her expression is devilish suggesting deliberate nosiness.

My mouth opens and closes, and I laugh. 'Something like that. Yes, fell into doing his accounts out of gratitude for being rescued.' With the slight emphasis on 'rescued' I'm hoping she'll explain her remark in the pub along with the 'knight's court' comment of this morning.

'I'm not surprised. Jack rescued me once, and I was so grateful I married him. I expect that's how he'll meet his next wife.'

Next wife! My curiosity intensifies. 'Does he make a

habit of it?' Saying this in a jokey way makes me a comrade-in-arms, hopefully.

She leans forward and says conspiratorially, 'He met the girlfriend before me on holiday when he rescued her from a particularly powerful wave. Holiday romance, so it didn't last long. '

'Ah, I see. So, want to swap stories?'

'Yes, sure. Mine's a classic. Jack came across my car on a lonely country road precariously parked on a grass verge with a flat tyre. Petrified, as it was growing dark, and not having a mobile phone with me, I was at a loss at what to do next. When he pulled up behind, I was even more terrified. But he was lovely. Called from his open window, asked if I was okay and could he contact someone. He looked…safe.'

I laugh. 'Yes, it sucks you in.'

'Such a big man. Anyway, he changed the tyre, and with me just out of a relationship, well, our own started. Rebound. Young. Then Sophie came along.'

'How long were you married for?' Cheeky I know, but applicable.

'Eleven years. We didn't marry immediately. Sophie was fourteen when we split. My fault we broke up. Met someone else.'

So, she cheated. That's why he reacted in such a hostile way about Andrew. I nod in sympathy, hoping to encourage more information.

Stephanie is happy to and continues, 'Once I met Chris I wanted more from a relationship. Jack and I had lost our closeness, just muddled along, and I met a man who was the perfect fit.' She sighs. 'You know how it is when you meet your soul mate. Deep inside you know this is the person for you. Your lifetime partner. I suddenly found excuses to eat at Chris's pub. Did a similar thing happen with you and going to the gallery?'

She's guessing I'm involved with Jack or have fallen for him. 'Not exactly,' I reply. 'Jack's just a friend.'

She raises her eyebrows. 'Well, with Chris I was in hook, line and sinker. As soon as the sex happened, I told Jack straight away there was someone else. I didn't know if it would work out with Chris or even if we'd get together eventually, but it was over for Jack and me. Chris and I did marry, so I made the right choice.'

'Do Chris and Jack get on?' I'm taking a chance as there was no sign of a man at the pub, giving me the impression Stephanie was alone.

'Oh no, well that is, they did eventually. Chris died last year. Heart attack. Fifty-one. My night off. The next morning… He hadn't come to bed. That feeling of dread you get. We were only married a few months.'

'Oh, my goodness, I'm so sorry. Must be so hard.' Guilt rises for bringing the subject up.

Stephanie's eyes fill with tears and she tries to laugh them away. 'I'm coming to terms with it, but yes, it's hard. The Three Horseshoes was Chris's dream. Built it up from nothing and made it into the popular place it is today. Lots of mentions in the broadsheets. Now I feel obliged to carry it on, but it's too much at times.' She shrugs as if it's her lot now. 'Perhaps I got my punishment. But enough about me. What about you? You were rather distraught when you came in that evening with Jack. And very much like a couple at first, to be frank, but then I noticed you wore a wedding ring. Thought it odd you'd just met and were eating together with you clearly weepy, so guessed you were a rescue job.'

I laugh. 'I was. I'd followed my husband to a hotel and then watched him cheat with someone else. Massive shock. Panicked, literally ran into Jack, and he filled me with brandy and took me home. Needed the loo, so we stopped off at your place.'

'Oh! Blast. Sorry if I sounded flippant about cheating.'

I don't know why but I find myself telling her the whole story. She listens and is suitably sympathetic.

'Life often gets in the way of happiness,' she says. 'So, and now you do Jack's books in return for being rescued. Could do with being rescued myself. For a start I need a new bookkeeping system, ours – mine is outdated. Advice would be helpful.'

'No problem, I can help with that. Not an easy life running a pub.'

For a moment Stephanie's silent and then says wistfully, 'No it isn't. Perhaps I should sell up?' Her frown tells me she's asking my advice.

'Life goes on,' I say. 'You have to do what's best for you now. Surely Chris would want that. Want you to be happy.'

'Sounds sensible on the surface,' she says. 'And it's what everyone keeps telling me, even Jack. Hard though when you're still grieving and can feel his presence about the place. Perhaps I should mull it over more. There's time enough to make decisions.'

As it's exactly what I'm doing myself there's little more to say. The conversation changes and I mention the flowers outside the pub in the summer, the lovely colourful window boxes and cart, and the subject shifts to gardening.

Soon, having checked the time, I tell her about going to the rescue centre before it closes. We swap phone numbers and promise to meet up again.

I'm rooting for my handbag ready to leave when a girl plonks herself down on the end of the sofa next to me. With a jolt I recognise her as Sophie, Jack's daughter. I remember her from the gallery.

'Hi,' she says to me before leaning forward to speak to her mother. 'Dad said you'd be here with the bookkeeper.'

The bookkeeper! So detached and formal.

'Miranda,' Stephanie says, and Sophie smiles.

'Nice name. So, Mum, what did Dad say? I bet he agreed with me.'

Stephanie rolls her eyes. 'That's not the point, Sophie. You've already put a lot of time and effort into getting onto that course and have hardly given it a chance.'

'Mum, it bores me silly. Stupidly, I thought I could be like Dad. You know, go on TV and stuff.'

'Well, I could say, "I told you so" and that the art business isn't as romantic as it appears. And now the money and time you've already invested will be wasted.

Sometimes, all we need is to give things a fair go, to make sure we're making the right decision. What do you think, Miranda?'

Stephanie is right as we're both doing that, but I'm not qualified to answer, not being a parent. Neither do I want to upset either Jack or Stephanie by saying the wrong thing. 'What do you intend to do instead, Sophie? Do you have a plan?'

'Sort of. Take a gap year, travel to Australia, a couple of friends are there and having a brilliant time. I can work while deciding what course to do. Something a lot more exciting though, like drama.'

'Drama!' Stephanie cries.

'Just joking, Mum. I don't know what I want to study. Haven't decided yet.'

'Well, in my opinion you're giving up too quickly. But doesn't look as if I have any choice. Just promise me to leave the decision until the end of this first year. Then perhaps you could take a gap year and afterwards go back to the same course…or not.'

Sophie screws up her nose. 'Okay then, I'll think about it. Thanks, Mum, I love you forever.'

During this natural break in the conversation, I mention I must leave. 'Need to see a man about a dog.'

Stephanie laughs. Sophie is puzzled as to why I'm announcing I need to wee.

'Dog rescue,' I explain. I don't mention that Jack's going with me as that will put me into a different category than just Jack's bookkeeper.

'Wow, brill, says Sophie.' And with those two words I've scored a point with her as she's grinning with delight.

We say our goodbyes with kisses, and Sophie adds, 'Glad Mum has new friends.' And with that she elevates me from lowly bookkeeper.

When I arrive back at the gallery, Jack is waiting to go, and stares at me curiously, wondering perhaps what Stephanie divulged about him. If the situation had been the other way around and Jack had been meeting Andrew for coffee, would I have worried? Hell, yes.

As we walk back around to the car, I explain how Stephanie and I both found we shared a mutual interest in gardening, and that she had roped me in to help with her bookkeeping too. Whether this puts him at ease or not, is hard to tell.

Jack offers to drive and I agree, as sitting in the car with him alone is nerve-racking enough, after what has transpired between us so far.

'Exciting, isn't it?' says Jack, reading the atmosphere in the car as we drive off, rather than my mind. 'Of course, we might not find a suitable dog first visit.'

We! Does this mean there will be further visits? The thought excites me more than it should. 'And what if we both want the same dog?' I ask though I know it's unlikely as a big dog is out of the question. But it occurs to me that it will be a difficult task surreptitiously searching for little dogs while ignoring the retrievers.

'Perhaps if we both like a bigger dog, you get first choice.'

'Oh, no, this was your idea. It's your dream I'm trespassing on.'

'No,' I say firmly, feeling a little more Godzilla-ish. 'You mentioned golden retrievers first, so if we find one that's suitable, it's yours. There'll be dogs of all shapes and sizes needing homes.'

'Okay, whatever.' He grins.

The trip to the rescue centre is half an hour. My car is small and sitting in close proximity to Jack is torture. Butterflies attack my stomach with gusto, and I'm puzzled to why his masculine presence affects me the way it does when Andrew is so very handsome. Wanting to keep occupied, and not become too intimate, I root out my phone and switch it on. All the messages Andrew sent this morning come pouring in, bleeping like mad.

I giggle. 'Methinks Andrew was panicking earlier.'

After switching off the sound, my attention turns to what's out the window, and I remark on the weather.

When you meet your prospective mother-in-law, or when in the local shop, or when you're waiting for a bus and there's one person standing there with you and it's late, the only thing to say is, 'Lovely (or awful) weather today, isn't it?' prompting an answer. Or when you fancy someone and you want to distract yourself, like before, and like now. However, it's failing to work.

There's a smile in Jack's voice as he asks, 'Is your mother still around?'

It takes me a minute to grasp that he means is she in

the vicinity rather than is she dead. 'Oh, no. They only stayed a couple of days. And they'd already visited Aunt Barbara, Mum's twin, in Spain, and they all returned together to Surrey where my aunt lives, so they travelled straight back to Chester.'

'Twins in the family.'

'Yes, but I'm an only child myself. My dad ran off before I was born and we've had little contact over the years.' The next thing I'm telling him all about Mum and Steve moving in together and perhaps in the future, getting married. And add how disconcerting it all is as it's always been just Mum and me.

'You're not happy for them?' he asks when I finish spouting my grief.

'It's not that. It's just that well you'd think what's the point at their age—'

'Your mum isn't old. In fact, she looks fabulous.'

'Really?' I'm proud.

'You *are* happy for them,' he continues. 'You're just not happy for you. Feel insecure.' He pauses. 'How many years ago did you marry?'

'Seven.'

'So, for seven years she's been alone?'

'Ten. I bought a little house before that. Lived close by. If I'd have had siblings, it might have been different. Perhaps I wouldn't be so possessive.' I sound like a nutcase and hope Jack doesn't glean from that I'm generally possessive and Andrew is innocent. 'Do you have any brothers or sisters?'

'One younger sister, Livvy, married and living in

Cardiff. Has three children. I don't see her as much as I'd like, but when I move, at least I'll be able to put them all up comfortably.'

I don't know Jack at all – nothing about his background or family. 'Parents?'

'Alive and well and retired to Dorset.'

A proper functional family, I should have known. Not that Mum is dysfunctional, just different, and she did teach me to be independent until that went to pot. How on earth, as Jo says, did I end up with my life revolving around Andrew's? At least Mum has bided her time looking for the right person. 'Were your parents in the art business too?'

'Antiques. They had a place in Netherbury and I shared it, using the first floor for my gallery. Then when they wanted to retire and sell up, Hector suggested I move lock, stock and barrel into his building as he wanted to pull back a bit. He'd inherited the Winterford estate at that point.'

'The estate must take a lot of management.'

'Yes, that was it. Hundreds of acres. Woodland too. A lot of work.' He smiles then concentrates for a moment on steering into another lane as we pass a junction. The road to Southampton is busy. After a short pause, he continues. 'Anyway, it worked out perfectly for us both, and when the house had to be sold, Sophie and I moved into the flat as it was handy for school. Didn't quite intend it to be for so long. Three years. So, it's high time for me to have a more permanent base.

'I suppose that's all Mum wants. To get on with her

life. Steve's all right. He has two children from his previous marriage. Haven't met them yet.' My sigh is audible. 'Never had to consider them as siblings, but I suppose now I might have to. As stepparents go, Steve could be worse. And he and Mum have plenty in common.'

'Companionship would be key. As well as love. Isn't that what most of us want? And talking about companionship, we're here.' He pulls off the main road and around into the rescue centre, parking up in front.

The man I saw on the previous visit greets us in the reception area. He smiles when we say we'd both like to adopt a dog. 'We have you on file already, I believe,' the man says to me. 'Never forget a pretty face.'

Having asked him a few verbal questions, the man hands Jack a form to complete. Once done, he peruses it, and says he'll find someone to take us around. He picks up a phone. A woman in overalls soon appears and leads us through to the back.

The stench of urine is powerful as we walk up and down the rows of kennels. The dogs of all breeds and sizes run up to the doors, wagging their tails and barking. With Jack for company, and knowing I am now seriously seeking a dog, I'm less apprehensive and more enthusiastic.

A few larger dogs bark loudly, making me jump as we pass. I imagine a *Beethoven*-type situation in my lovely home: the shaking of a head, the slobber hitting walls, rugs, and my cream sofas. But at least I'd have something to clean for a change.

The noise increases as other dogs join in with the barking and yelping. Poor things all wanting a forever home. I visualise myself playing with one on the local field, then coming back to cocoa in the snug with me curled up in a chair in front of the wood burner while he lies on the rug with a treat. But there are so many to choose from. 'How do we know which is the right one,' I say to Jack. 'I haven't had a dog since I was young teenager.'

'You'll know, believe me.'

'There aren't any retrievers so far. I suppose people don't give up their dogs just to suit your tastes.'

Jack stops at a kennel holding a rather large cream Labrador who reacts eagerly and is friendly if a little hesitant. Jack squats down and calls her over.

A card outside the kennel states her name is Duchess. I read it out. 'Three years old, is good with other dogs, cats and children.' She wags her tail and pokes her nose through the wire. I bend down and shuffle closer, and her paw comes up to try to touch me. She's a heart-stealer.

Jack jumps to his feet and asks for more information. The woman tells him she's new in, and that the owner, a middle-aged woman, took ill and could no longer care for her, but was eager to find her a good home. 'Why don't you take her for a walk in the back field and see how you get on,' she says encouragingly. 'She could be the perfect dog for you both.'

Both! Should I have corrected her? Especially after

the last time. Jack's expression is neutral. He hasn't corrected her either.

The woman goes to fetch a lead and a couple of minutes later arrives back and lets Duchess out. We follow her outside to a fenced-off field.

'I'll leave you to it then,' she says, handing the lead to Jack. 'Duchess is such a lovely dog, I'd have her myself if I didn't have three dogs already. When you're ready, come back to the reception desk.'

Jack pats Duchess's rump firmly and we walk around the field.

'She pulls on the lead a bit,' he says, 'but that shouldn't be a problem.'

'Probably just eager to get out of the kennel,' I reply. Jack must be seriously considering taking Duchess.

'Could be. Here, have a go…' Jack hands me the lead. Duchess loves being out and reacts happily to my combination of walking and trotting, her sad eyes looking up at me as she runs alongside, her tail wagging furiously. I stop to give her a big hug, knowing for sure that having a canine friend is what I want right now.

We carry on trotting and I break into a run, laughing with glee with Duchess at my heels. She suddenly runs around in front of me then behind, the lead tangling around my ankles. Abruptly coming to a halt, I lean down to unravel it, but in her keenness to get going again, Duchess leaps at me. I try to straighten up, but feel myself falling backwards. Then Jack is behind me, his hands under my arms, accidentally gripping my boobs as he tries to prevent me from falling onto the ground. The shock makes me wriggle my feet as I try to gain purchase, but I'm making things worse. Jack can't let go or I'll fall. Meanwhile, Duchess tries to lick my face as I squeal. I stop struggling and let Jack manoeuvre me back up while at the same time, trying to reposition his hands. It's seconds but feels longer.

'Ehem, sorry about that. Didn't mean to. It was—'

'Accidental I know. Thanks for saving me.' We're both embarrassed but laugh. Jack unravels the lead and we both chuckle as Duchess jumps all over us. Jack takes her again. He's just as smitten as I am.

Twenty minutes later, having both taken turns, Jack leads Duchess over to a bench. We sit for a while making a big fuss of her. Jack rubs her ears and receives a big lick. Then she jumps up to me, puts two muddy paws on my smart black trousers, and licks my own face, leaving slobber all over me. Duchess is so trusting and affectionate. I rub her ears and receive more slobbery kisses.

'She's perfect,' I say.

'Yes, she is. That's decided then. She's yours. And I'm a little jealous.'

Duchess is mine, not Jack's! Duchess senses it and puts her head on one side as if pleading. Then gives me another hug to confirm she's the right dog. Perhaps I want a large dog after all. 'What about you?'

'Definitely. I mean want one. Might be best to wait until I move though.' Jack must have known that already. 'At least I know there are plenty of dogs needing homes. Might hold out for a golden retriever for Sophie. Anytime you want a dog sitter though, call me. I'd be happy to help.' A devilish look forms in his eyes. 'And if you need someone to catch you, should she knock you over, well...'

My stomach leaps, my eyes widening in amused shock as I shove him in the arm. Jack felt my boobs. Briefly, for a few seconds, but oh God! The fact he referred to it just now confirms he's as aware of it as I am.

When we go back into reception, I arrange a home visit with the receptionist for tomorrow. Luckily there's been a cancellation and he offers me the appointment. I accept with gratitude. Jack tells him he'll be back in a couple of weeks.

The kennel woman in overalls appears. 'A perfect match then?'

'Yes,' I say, 'a perfect match.'

She writes something in a book and beams us a smile. 'Duchess's previous owner will be so relieved. If you let us know how she's doing and send some photos, we can send them on. After your home visit if all's well – and there's no reason why not from your form – you can come and collect her straightaway.'

Reluctantly, we watch the woman lead Duchess away. As we open the door to leave, she makes a break for it and lollops over. We give her one last hug each and she whimpers, dismaying us both. I feel like a traitor leaving her.

On the way back to Netherbury, the chat is about dogs,

and Jack relates stories of happier times with Molly when he was still with Stephanie.

When we pull up outside the back of the gallery, we remain in the car, reluctant to move, and Jack asks, 'So what will Andrew say, d'you think? Was he expecting a large dog?'

The question takes me by surprise. I hadn't considered Andrew. I hesitate before answering and then be as truthful as I can. 'He'll be fine.' What I mean is he won't care. 'Though yes, I expect he'll be surprised she's so big.'

'You didn't discuss it in depth?'

'You mean actually communicate? No.' I snigger at the ridiculousness of it. 'But Andrew agreed I should get a dog as he's going to be away more.' I pause. 'Duchess will be all mine as he has already stipulated he won't have time. Demanding job. Long-haul trips.' Realising I've knowingly hinted to Jack that Andrew is living his own life away from me, I blush furiously in case he thinks I'm coming on to him. I can't be much of a catch in anyone's eyes if my own husband would prefer to be anywhere else except with me. Sadly, I admit, 'The dog is to keep me occupied, I suspect.'

The two creases furrowing his brow tell me Jack is mulling over what I just said. 'I'm here if you need me, right?' he says after a pause. 'Both you and Duchess. Andrew's a bloody idiot. Blind to what he has. I wouldn't risk you so easily.'

Bloody hell. My heart hammers in my chest as I absorb what he said. All he has to do is open his arms and I'll be in them I'm so overcome with emotion at his kindness. To hell with it. 'Jack…' In one swift movement as I move towards him, he opens the door and steps out, and my hand lands on his empty seat. Gulping, I grab my bag from the footwell, pretending that's what I intended all along.

Jack comes around and opens my door.

Stepping out, I stammer, 'Thanks, I – I have to get home.' Thank goodness I had those few seconds to come to my senses.

We say goodbye with a kiss on each cheek. Kisses are strange and can mean many things. And our kisses, innocent on the surface, are laden with meaning. My lips linger on his skin, my hands on his chest. His lips are firm on my cheeks, his hands squeezing my shoulders, causing all manner of warming twinges deep within me, fleeting but intense.

The look Jack gives me as I slip into the driver's seat is questioning. The answering flutter in my belly in not the reaction I should be having. As much as I'm attracted to Jack, he can't come into any decisions I have to make. If I leave my marriage it must be because of what is going on within it, not because of any outside influences. Eight years in a relationship, seven years of marriage, a lost baby, and a beautiful hard-won home – none can be thrown away on a whim. Nothing could justify me having an affair with Jack. Not that he's expecting that, and hence why he left the car when he sensed he'd said too much and my willpower was wavering. After what Stephanie did to him, he wouldn't be a hypocrite, I'm sure. Andrew cheating doesn't make it all right for me to cheat either, and Jack isn't the only one not wanting to be hypocritical. I should be more careful.

'Thanks for going with me and helping me choose such a lovely dog,' I say. 'Not sure when I'll be back.'

'Thought you might say that. I understand.'

My heart jumps. What was I hoping for, that he'd protest? Whatever was between us just now, it was fleeting and is clearly over, so I can't have regrets. But when I drive away it's with a horrible sense of loss.

CHAPTER EIGHTEEN

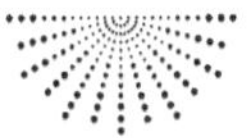

After a sleepless night tossing and turning, persuading myself I'm doing the right thing, I'm determined to improve my life regardless of errant husbands and lost potential lovers. So, I spend couple of hours working out a new routine. A bit of juggling here and there and I'm pleasantly surprised by my new schedule, and have managed to factor in a long walk with Duchess.

The TV arrives mid-morning and luckily there are two men to carry it into the sitting room and prop it up against the wall, though a crane might have been easier. It's enormous. What was Andrew thinking? From now on, I'll avoid the sitting room, dominated as it will be by that monstrosity in it.

Just before lunchtime a woman comes out from the rescue centre, checks the house and garden and approves me as an adopter. Easy peasy. I can collect Duchess tomorrow afternoon already as her vaccinations are up to date and she is neutered and chipped.

When I rang Andrew last night to tell him about Duchess, he was surprisingly non-phased by the breed, saying he was looking forward to meeting her.

As for Jack, I'm trying not to waver. The longer I leave seeing him, the better.

I shut them out of my head. No Andrew, no Jack, no confusing thoughts. Just me.

Feeling the need to get out for a while I decide to call on Stephanie to help her install a new system for her bookkeeping. It's almost lunchtime. If I leave now, I can have lunch at the pub and be back to spend a few hours on my car mechanic's account before dinner. And if she's not there I'm going out for lunch anyway, the cottage is beginning to feel like a prison.

When I draw up at The Three Horseshoes, the car park is full, and I wished I'd phoned ahead. Stephanie must be run off her feet. The place looks rather shabby and the window boxes and cart need a good tidy. A few flowers lie in among lots of dead foliage.

On entering, I can immediately see the reason for the full car park. Two parties are in progress, both business dinners at a guess. Stephanie is talking to a waitress and looking extremely harassed. There are a couple of empty tables but they are laden with dirty dishes.

Stephanie spots me, and I hurry over and greet her. 'One of my waiters fell ill and one bar person left,' she says. 'Typical when it's so close to party season. Businesses like to start early now.'

'Can I do anything?' I say, my clean-freak side kicking in. 'Let me clear those tables for you. Perhaps you can direct me to the kitchen.'

Instead of demurring, Stephanie in her desperation says, 'Oh, would you? Oh no, that's awful of me.' A customer signals to her and she sends the waitress over. 'Oh, all right. Come through here and I'll show you.' She takes me through to the back where there is a boy dedicated to washing dishes.

Stephanie returns to the restaurant and I ask the young man where I can find trays and cleaning materials and he points these out.

Clearing away, taking out dishes, coming back and wiping tables, I suddenly feel part of something. A team. I don't ask Stephanie anything else, but keep checking tables, clearing any dishes where the customers have finished. There's a dresser with cutlery, napkins, and condiments, so I refresh these as needed.

An hour later most people have left and I pop outside to the window boxes and give them a good tidy. Once I've pulled out all the debris, I venture into the back garden and find a shed with gardening tools. Armed with a trowel and fork I remove the last stubborn bits of root and weeds and clear the rubbish away. I'm not exactly dressed for it, but feeling as if I'm being useful outweighs getting dusty marks on my serviceable grey sweater and skirt.

I've just finished when Stephanie appears. 'Gosh!

Thanks so much. I keep meaning to come and do it. When I saw you out here, I decided not to stop you.' She laughs. 'Well, it was such a mess. I do feel awful though. You don't need a job, do you?' She laughs again.

'Perhaps I should have been a housekeeper or a gardener rather than a bookkeeper. I've thoroughly enjoyed myself.'

Stephanie smiles and nods towards the door. 'It's quieter now, come and have some lunch.'

While sitting eating a delicious lunch I decide to stop work for the day. Being out is preferable to being stuck in the attic. I can always go back to my accounts this evening to keep on schedule. Strange that before this problem with Andrew I kept to a routine and was methodical, almost obsessive. Now there's a lack of purpose. Working to live is different from working to build a home and future.

'It is getting too much,' says Stephanie as we tuck into our tuna salads. 'This place needs a manager. But Christmas is coming up, and I've taken on extra staff. Sophie will also help out no doubt, and in the New Year when business slows down, I can make further decisions.'

The New Year? That's both of us then. 'Is there's anything I can do.'

'Could you help with the Christmas decorations? It's a big job making a country pub atmospheric. Garlands over the mantelpieces, lights, and holly and ivy. You know…what people expect.'

'I'd love to.'

'I'll pay you, of course.'

'No need, it's something I'll enjoy.'

'I insist.'

By the time I'm ready to leave I've arranged a day to install and explain her new bookkeeping system and help with the Christmas decorations. I mention Duchess and how I'm going to pick her up tomorrow.

'You did it then. That was quick. Do you have everything for her?'

'Don't have anything. I'm calling into the pet superstore tomorrow on the way out.'

'Oh, it's just that I still have Molly's car guard in the garage if you have need of one.'

'I do.' I happily reply. 'I was worried the superstore might not have one in stock. So it'd be brilliant if you think it'd fit.'

Stephanie looks at my car. 'It should do.'

We walk around to the garage and root out the guard. It's a simple one that slots over the back headrests and it fits perfectly when we try it.

'On me,' says Stephanie when I offer to pay her for it. 'Great to see it put to good use.'

On the drive back I'm happier than I've been for weeks or even months. Helping at the pub was a welcome distraction from my troubles. Jo was right.

After my lovely afternoon the thought of the lonely house and being stuck with columns of figures is horrifying me. The first lay-by I come across I pull in and phone Jo on the off chance she'll be at Hector's. She is and tells me she's in the process of moving in. Hector's away for the evening visiting his mother in hospital, so she says she'll be glad of the company. Although she feels weird inviting guests to Winterford House with Hector not there, he has insisted it's now her home and to treat it accordingly. Jo suggests I stay over, so I pop home to pack an overnight bag.

When I arrive at Winterford House an hour and a half later, Pamela, the housekeeper, shows me to my room, telling me to come down to the small sitting room on the first floor for tea when I'm ready and she gives me directions. In her forties, she has short dark hair and the air of someone who is totally in control. She oozes confidence.

My room is huge and gorgeous and on the top floor in the west wing. The walls are a relaxing mushroom shade with matching bed linen on the queen-sized bed. French doors lead out on to a balcony with wrought-iron railings, which looks over the grounds at the side of the house. The bathroom is beautiful with a marble floor, freestanding roll-top bath, and double shower.

After dumping my bag and freshening up, I head down to the first floor, getting lost on the way, but Pamela finds me wandering.

'Got lost,' I tell Jo, laughing, when Pamela directs me into the correct room.

'Oh that's all right. There are so many rooms I keep getting lost too.'

'Do you feel awkward without Hector here?' I ask, Pamela having left.

'What makes you say that?'

'You're whispering.'

'Keep forgetting this isn't a library. We hang out in this room most of the time. I expect I'll get used to it. If it had been a normal house, it would have been different. But it's the staff wandering about. Well, it's Pamela mainly this time of day, but she'll leave as soon as she's served dinner as it's her late shift. Not that I can't do it myself, and I would have been happy enough eating in the kitchen, but she insisted. Some of the staff live in the cottages on the estate. They take care of the house security too. One will stay over tonight while Hector's away.'

'So how do you like it so far?'

'Three days I've been here, but it's like being on honeymoon.' She opens her hands out to the ceiling. 'My fairy godmother came. Hector is so…' She leans forward and whispers conspiratorially, 'Today, he's telling his mother I've moved in. She knows about me already, and we'll meet once she's recovered from her op. Scary.'

'Can't tell you how happy I am for you.' Jo's about to embark on a new and exciting stage in her life. I hug her.

She pulls away from me and holding my arms stares earnestly at me, her blue eyes shining. 'Although you won't believe it now, you'll be happy again too, I promise.'

Pamela comes through the door with a tray of tea and puts it on the coffee table. 'Dinner will be at seven thirty, Miss Costelloe,' she says. 'I'll set the table in the morning room. I suspect you'll prefer it.'

'Lovely,' says Jo. 'Cosier.' Meanwhile, I've said thank you at least three times. As soon as Pamela has left the room and we hear her footsteps clatter down the stairs, Jo asks, 'So what does she think of me, would you guess? I can't make it out.'

'Hard to tell. Anyway, she'll have to get used to you being here, regardless.'

'I expect so. It's not as if I've been visiting here for a year or so before moving in. They probably think I'm a fortune hunter.' Jo makes a face.

'Gosh, I'm sure they don't.' But I don't envy her. The thought of starting again, getting used to another boyfriend, his habits, getting to the point of feeling comfortable around him, being able to trust him with your heart, is daunting. Better the devil you know maybe? But that can't possibly be true. The devil can only cause you misery.

Jo pours the tea. 'Shall I be Mother?' We both giggle like a couple of schoolgirls.

'So, what are we going to do with ourselves tonight?' I ask.

'Did you bring your swim stuff? The pool's lovely and warm, and the hot tub is prepared.'

'I did. How could I forget there's a pool?'

'So, swim, hot tub, champagne, but not necessarily in that order. Sounds like a plan.'

. . .

It's only later, dressed in a long white bathrobe, a towel around my hair and sitting by the pool, that the familiar ringtone of Skype reminds me I haven't spoken to Andrew since yesterday. I'm tempted not to pick up. The day has been lovely, spent with friends, and I don't want it spoilt, until I picture him at the Northwood Park Hotel and answer.

'Hi. Tried to call you earlier. Busy?'

'Er, well, not really. Just chilling.'

'Did the TV arrive okay?'

'Yes.'

'Great! Can't wait to set it up.' He frowns as he suddenly notices the white towel and bathrobe. 'Where are you?'

'Winterford House.' I leave it at that. Jumping up, I sashay over to the hot tub, pick up my flute of champagne and take it back to my lounger and start sipping.' Am I doing this deliberately? Yes.

'Treating yourself? Who's with you?'

'Jo's here, but she's just out the hot tub and having a shower before dinner.'

'She's not in Chester then, or are you up there?'

I raise my eyebrows at him. 'Er, no. Jo lives down here now at Winterford House with Hector from Langford gallery. He's her new boyfriend. She's just moved in.'

The surprise shows on his face. 'That's where you are now? You don't tell me anything these days.'

Cheek, I'm not the only one. 'Yes, Upper Winterford. Jo and I are having a girly night in.'

'You're getting in thick with that lot, aren't you?'

'Hi, Andrew.' Jo appears over my shoulder and waves her glass at him. She's gone before Andrew has time to answer, and plonks herself on the lounger opposite, grinning.

'Where are you then?' I ask Andrew nonchalantly. 'And how are the meetings going?'

'In Manchester, like I told you. Hannah's hard work. A perfectionist. Makes you slog. Not easy-going like Freddie.'

'When do you finish there?'

'Tomorrow, er I mean Saturday – evening. I'll be back late. A lot to do.'

How could he get mixed up between tomorrow and Saturday? 'Strange working Saturday. You'd think the clients would want to go back to their own homes for the weekend.'

'Well, not this week.'

Jo shakes her head and mouths, 'He's lying.'

As if I need to be told that. 'When I next speak to Freddie, I'll have to tell him it's not on making you constantly work weekends, and he should speak to Hannah.'

Jo stifles a giggle.

'No, look, this is my job, like it or lump it. Enjoy your day off by the pool. Some of us have to graft.'

'You may not have noticed, but it's six thirty. And it's not my fault you've chosen to work Saturday. Should I put my life on hold?'

Jo pours more champagne into my glass.

'No. And it's not my choice. Working hours are not

up to me. When did you say you were picking up the dog?'

'Tomorrow. Her name's Duchess.'

'Good. See you Saturday evening.' With a perfunctory 'love you,' he's ends the call.

Back to reality the next day, having had a lovely dinner, and a comfortable night's sleep, I rise early and drive home. As soon as I've made coffee, I take it upstairs and work non-stop for three hours at my desk until it's time to collect Duchess.

Netherbury Pet Centre is my first port of call.

I'm not sure what size bed Duchess will need so I ask the boy behind the counter, and he joins in with my enthusiasm when I tell him it's for a rescue dog. Soon goods are piled up in my trolley: bowls for water and food, dog food, treats, biscuits, collar and lead, identity tag, grooming brushes, bags for poop (large), and a few toys.

That should be everything. When the assistant asks if I have a dog guard for the car, I say yes.

'A good traveller?'

'I've no idea.'

'Oh, it's just that a customer once told me that she had a rescue dog that panicked in the car. Kicked up a right fuss. Jumped over the seat into the front.'

I refrain from thanking him for the reassurance and

begin to worry. Not knowing Duchess at all, I don't know if she will fret or even go crazy.

Time is getting on, and not knowing what to do I throw everything on the back seat of my car except for the pet blanket, which I stick in the boot, and instead of taking the route directly to Southampton I drive to Netherbury city centre.

Desperate circumstances call for desperate measures. My intention not to see Jack won't work if he's in the gallery, but I don't care. I need help. The important thing is to make sure I'm at the rescue centre by two thirty to collect Duchess.

I park up at the back of the gallery and hurry around to the front door, aware that I'm pushed for time. Jack is in and I run up to him. The panic must register on my face as I approach as he comes from behind the counter where he's doing some paper work.

'What's wrong?' he asks, concerned.

Quickly, I explain my predicament. 'Silly me. I could have asked Jo yesterday.'

'I'm sure Duchess will be fine, but don't worry, I'll drive you. I'll lock up for an hour or two. It won't be the first time.'

Glad to have everything taken out of my hands I wait for Jack to fetch his jacket.

He's back in a jiffy with a piece of paper in his hand. 'Right, all organised. I'll fix a note to the door. You go on out while I set the alarm.'

Outside a woman gazes into the window. I recognise her. She must feel me staring as she glances my way. It's that Velma girl again. 'Sorry,' I say. 'Did you want to go inside? Jack's closing for an hour or so.'

'No, no,' she says, and continues to examine a painting displayed in the window. 'I often stop on the way past in the hope of finding a little picture for my hallway. Just wondered if there was anything new, but nah, doesn't look like it.'

'I could ask Jack if you're quick.' But I lift my wrist to check the time on my watch, selfishly hoping to put her off.

'Oh no, better not, I'll be in there forever.' She giggles.

'Ah, I tend to do that too.'

'He's off the telly isn't he, the owner?' She looks directly at me, waiting for confirmation.

'Yes, he is.'

When Jack comes out to lock up, she eyes him appreciatively, leaving me to suspect she is indeed a one-person admiration society.

'Definitely a groupie there,' I say as I walk with him around to the car.

He grimaces and then smiles. 'If she is, it'll be a first.'

Jack opens the car door for me. Once in himself, he drives out of the side road. A few minutes later as soon as we're safely on the road to Southampton, he asks if Andrew is still away.

'Until tomorrow.'

He throws me a look of sympathy and I find myself telling him about Andrew's uncertainty to what day he is due back. Not wanting Jack to think I like being walked on, I mention I'm leaving all decisions until the New Year, hoping the truth will come out in the meantime so I don't have to do anything without knowing everything.

'I'm confused. Scared,' I explain, 'about the future. Uncharted waters. And if there is someone who's special to him, I don't know how I'll react to that either. He doesn't behave as if he's planning to leave me, but whatever's going on, it has been for a while.'

'Why don't you hire a private detective instead of putting yourself through this waiting and agony?'

'Everyone says that.'

Jack raises his eyebrows. 'I know, none of my business.'

I laugh. 'This may sound stupid, especially after I followed him, but apart from the cost I thought it a bit underhand.'

'Well, from my point of view, I'm glad you did choose to follow him.' The atmosphere is thick with the implications of his words. There's no point in hiding it anymore. We drive the rest of the way in comfortable silence.

When we arrive at the rescue centre, my excitement builds as we wait for Duchess. As expected, she reacts crazily when the girl brings her out and we make a big fuss of her. I pay my fee, sign the papers and Duchess is all mine. Outside, she happily jumps into the boot of the car and I make room on the back seat to be close to her.

On the drive back I'm more relaxed, knowing Jack is

with me. Duchess behaves well, and after a while she lies down, contented, car travel not being a problem for her. As soon as I can I'll get a bigger car; something more dog friendly.

'You two will be quite the pair,' Jack says, glancing at me in the rear-view mirror. 'You won't be sorry.'

'No. She's already lifted my spirits.'

We chat about Jack's TV work on the drive back. The series he's doing sounds big, and filming begins in earnest in January. I can't help noticing the lack of tension between us now as we chat. The trip is companionable.

Back at the gallery I'm confident Duchess will behave the rest of the way home. We both get out so I switch to the driver's seat.

Before getting in the car, I thank Jack again for coming to my rescue. During the return trip he was careful not to be in any way personal, probably not wanting a repeat of Wednesday, leaving me feeling we can do this – can just be friends.

The drive back to the cottage is uneventful, and I soon introduce Duchess to her new home, letting her wander as she pleases. After a good sniff around the cottage and then doing the same in the garden, she returns to me, wagging her tail approvingly. 'How about walkies before it gets too dark?' I say. This must be the magic word as she jumps around and almost trips me up. I fetch her lead and we head off for a walk by the river.

The river park is a popular beauty spot and I'm not

the only person with a dog on the path. When you have a dog, it suddenly makes you visible. People with and without dogs alike, stop to pet Duchess and chat. I never knew dog-walking could be so sociable. My conversation with each person is the same in that she's three years old, I only collected her today from the rescue centre and, yes, I am a good person (or something along those lines).

When we return, I light a fire in the snug and prepare dinner for myself and feed Duchess. Dishes stacked in the dishwasher I fetch my book from the bedroom, and make a mug of cocoa. Curled up in my favourite chair in the snug with Duchess doing her duty lying on the rug, content to watch me read, fulfilling one of my dreams, the evening passes perfectly. Suddenly I don't feel so lonely.

Before bed, I pick up my phone and send Jack a text. *'Thanks so much for coming with me. Hope I didn't put you out too much xxx.'*

A message comes back in seconds.

'You could never do that xxx.'

I delete them both.

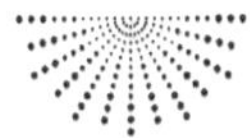

The following evening Andrew arrives home just as I reach the cottage, having walked Duchess down the lane. Both of us in our new reflective jackets. She's already making a difference to my life as normally I'd be waiting for him.

Andrew grins as he gets out of his car. Clad in jeans and a sweater he drops on to his haunches to pet Duchess, and makes a big fuss of her. 'Finished earlier than I thought. She's lovely. Good choice.' He stands and greets me with a kiss. 'How's she settling in?'

'Great. I love her. The previous owner must have been heartbroken that she could no longer care for her.'

'Could be cool having a dog.'

Why this remark would make me bristle, I don't know. I take her inside while Andrew fetches his suitcase from the boot.

I'm hardly in the door when my mobile rings. It's Jo.

'Randa, hope I'm not interrupting anything. I'm engaged! Yay!'

'Engaged as what?'

'Engaged to be married, twit, to Hector! How incredible is that?'

I almost drop my phone. 'Very incredible.'

Andrew stops in the hallway to listen in, intrigued by my surprised tone.

'As soon as Hector returned from visiting his mother, he proposed. I know it's impulsive –' she pauses – 'but I'm happy. I've wasted my twenties and I've no intention of wasting what remains of my thirties too.'

'Your decision,' I say.

'We're not exactly getting married tomorrow.'

I sigh. 'It's not that I don't approve. But it's so unexpected. First moving in together and now marriage – okay an engagement.'

'We're in love, no point in dilly dallying. Anyway, listen, a week Saturday we're having an engagement party. Seven thirty at Winterford House. Black tie.'

'Engagement party! It really is official.' Andrew stares at me and raises his eyebrows. 'Okay. Let me have the details again.'

I put the phone away and explain to Andrew. I'm flabbergasted as to what lengths Jo will go, to avoid paying for my pendant.

'Can't say I'm ecstatic about going,' Andrew groans, 'but will.' At least he's being honest for once. 'I suppose a party is something for you to look forward to though. Not much for you to do here, especially with the trips planned.' His frown of concern is almost genuine. 'We could move closer to Southampton. The commute would be easier for me and there'd be more for you to do.'

'Leave Holly Cottage after all the hard work?'

'We'd get a good price for it. You could take on another renovation project. You enjoyed this one.'

Of all the cheek. 'Spend another three years doing a house up, not bloody likely. Anyway, I thought you loved living here. We did choose Holly Cottage together.'

'I do, though Ashford's a bit quiet. A cottage in the country isn't what it's cracked up to be. Somewhere with more life would be better.'

My scowl tells him I don't agree with this sentiment.

He tries again. 'We could find a new house. Nothing to do on it.'

'Andrew, why all this now? It hardly matters to you. You're never here anyway.'

'Don't be like that. This is about you. You having a life and friends.'

'I'm fine, and I have friends close by. And I'll have Duchess too. Plenty to do. Plenty of people around.'

'You mean those people. The arty-farty lot.'

What does that mean? Andrew never used to be so petulant. 'If you mean Hector, yes, he's a new friend as he'll be my best friend's husband. Is that a problem?'

'No. Just consider moving, that's all I'm asking. Living near a bigger town will be more like before, in Chester. More places to hang out. Be in the thick of things. We're not old yet.'

This conversation is confusing me. We want entirely

different things. When did that happen? I bring the subject back to the party and describe Winterford House. The size of it, the grandeur, the staff, in detail.

He raises his eyebrows, pleasantly surprised. 'Really, that big? Won't harm going, I don't suppose. Will there be photos? That'll shut Matthew and Kate up. Why don't you ask Jo and Hector for a drink? Jo's your best friend and I hardly acknowledged Hector when I came to the gallery the other day. A good person to know maybe. Contacts and so forth.'

He is so predictable. Why haven't I noticed this before? I was so complacent living in my own perfect little world.

Andrew finds a photo of Winterford House online and texts it to his sister-in-law. 'Close – friends – of – ours – own – this – mansion,' he says aloud as he types. 'Having – a – party – in – a – couple – of – weeks. Black – tie. I'll – send – pics.' He examines the photo again. 'Ha. Beat that, Kate. Impressive isn't it?'

Suddenly I feel sorry for him. 'Come on, I'll make you a cup of tea. I ate early, but there's some carrot and coriander soup if you're hungry.'

'Great, thanks.'

While I make the tea and heat the soup, Andrew plays with Duchess. As I view the domestic scene, I recall that this is what I've been yearning for during the past three years. But domestic bliss lasts five minutes before Andrew goes to set up his TV, taking his soup with him.

'The snug, book, music, cocoa, and one doggy bickie for you, sound okay, Duchess?'

She barks me her answer.

Sunday afternoon we meet up with Jo and Hector for drinks at a country pub halfway between us both. Andrew was hoping, of course, to be invited to Winterford House. But Jo and I decided against it. He can wait until the party. Winterford House is the domain of my friends and Andrew can spend as little time there as possible.

Andrew is the soul of politeness once we find a cosy table by a roaring fire; you'd think he was always this way with Jo. With Andrew and Hector both designated drivers, Jo and I have a glass of wine. Strange, I almost feel as if I'm betraying Jack being out with Andrew and another couple, one of them his best friend.

'We'll be having the wedding at Winterford,' says Jo, date's not decide yet. 'So, Randa, will you be my matron of honour?'

Funny, could have sworn she said the wedding was a while away. 'Yes, of course, silly.'

'And Jack will be my best man,' says Hector.

My eyes widen as Andrew's narrow. I picture me on Jack's arm walking back up the aisle after the nuptials. My dress slinky and sexy, my bum looking as good as Pippa Middleton's.

'Jack,' says Andrew, letting the name hang in the air. 'From the gallery?'

'That's the very one,' says Hector, and he realises he

has hit on a sticky subject and throws me a quick apologetic glance.

'Anyway,' says Jo, quickly changing the subject, 'the party is going to be fabulous. Black tie. Did I tell you that?'

'Yes, twice already,' I quip.

'With you looking like a film star in black tie, Andrew,' Jo says, patting his arm, 'the other men will be sooo jealous.'

Andrew laughs. 'Don't be daft, Jo.' But, all the same, the flattery has worked.

'So, everything arranged already?' I ask.

'Yep, the caterer's sorted and extra staff hired. Invitations have gone out and we've had a good response already for all the short notice.' Jo takes an iPad from her huge handbag. 'Most of the list is ticked off.'

'You should have asked Miranda to help you,' Andrew states. 'She's going into event organising, aren't you, darling?'

Jo winces. 'Ooh. Completely forgot about that.' Needless to say, she knows that my business idea was, and still is, only a possibility.

'There's so much to think about, regarding extending the business,' I quickly say, making a mental note not to make up stories as they tend to catch you out. 'Maybe in the New Year…'

'How about some practice? Hands on stuff,' suggests Hector. 'We could do with help organising the garden, especially in regard to the lighting and Jo's told me about your skills.'

'Happy to,' I reply.

Hector checks the list on the iPad over Jo's shoulder. 'So, only the photographer to arrange and the band. Such awfully short notice. But with Christmas coming up…'

'A photographer?' asks Andrew. 'Hey, I can help there. I know a great one. My company uses her.' My heart skips a beat.

Jo stares at me, the shock reflected in her eyes. 'No, don't worry,' she says hurriedly. 'Wouldn't want to put you to any trouble. There's bound to be someone free.'

Andrew takes his phone from his inside pocket. 'No trouble at all, I'll call her now. Wait until you see her work, you'll be impressed. Very professional. Does magazine shoots. *Women in the Know* on occasions. And I'm sure you can come to a decent arrangement with the fees with me knowing her.'

Women in the Know is no longer my favourite mag, I decide.

Jo nudges Hector. 'Well, very good of you,' says Hector innocently, completely getting the wrong idea. 'Sounds perfect.'

The expression on Jo's face matches mine – horrified.

'My round, I believe,' says Andrew. 'I'll fetch the drinks while I'm there.' And phone in hand, he's gone, leaving me speechless. My hands go to my face. Jo winces.

'What?' says Hector, noticing our joint expressions. 'Have I put my foot in it?'

'You've just given Andrew permission to phone his

lover,' groans Jo. 'The photographer he mentioned is most likely the same one Miranda believes he's having an affair with.'

'Oh, goodness me. I'm so frightfully sorry. I'll try to put him off when he comes back. Say I've had a call and we already have one.'

'Did you see his enthusiasm,' I cry indignantly. 'He couldn't wait to phone her.' A blush grows in my cheeks.

Jo shrugs. 'Well, she's possibly booked up. It is short notice. And if she isn't, at least you'll see how they interact with one another. Might give you an opportunity to discover the truth and get the grief over with.'

Perhaps Jo's right. 'And she'll see that I'm a sensible, elegant, and intelligent woman.'

'Yeah,' says Jo. 'At least one of those.'

I pull tongues at her. 'All and more.' I imagine the scene unfolding. Leticia takes one look at happy and vivacious me and cries in horror realising immediately that Andrew has lied to her. A massive scene ensues. At Jo and Hector's engagement! 'We have to put him off. Your party could be ruined.'

Jo dismisses this worry with a wave of a hand. 'Unlikely. They'll probably keep their distance from each other. It's the little things you need to watch for, sneaky glances and so on.'

Hector agrees. 'And if they are having an affair she may well be reluctant to come.'

'Yes. And if she's happy to come along, perhaps I'm wrong about it. Either that or she knows I'll be there and won't care, like that Maxwell woman, thinking I'm an idiot. Oh God.'

'Well, she'll discover you're not,' Hector says kindly. 'But we'll weather this, so don't worry.'

Jo smiles lovingly at him.

With one eye on the bar, I whisper, 'Of course, this could be another photographer and we're on the wrong track.'

Andrew arrives back with the drinks and puts them on the table. 'All arranged,' he says, beaming, obviously pleased with himself, and I could cheerfully kill him. 'Do phone her to sort out the details. Her name's Leticia Fuentes.' He takes a card from his wallet and hands it to Hector.

Andrew carries her cards! What an absolute louse.

Jo audibly gulps and grabs her glass of wine.

***

The following Monday I have another stroke of good luck, mine not Andrew's. He's ill, a lifesaver. Even better, he has a throat infection and a fever. With any luck he won't be well enough to attend the party and I can stop fretting. Okay, I don't want him to die or anything, but still, if I can get Leticia on her own, I might be able to discover the truth. Just because Andrew won't be honest, it doesn't mean she won't. This could be the best solution.

Chicken soup is on the menu in between catching up on work, apart from one day when I slip over to The

Three Horseshoes to help Stephanie with her accounts and Christmas decorations. Andrew spends a lot of time holed up in the sitting room with his home cinema or on his iPad, keeping it in his sight at all times, along with his phone.

When I call Jo, to find out what she intends to wear, I take myself for a walk with Duchess and out of Andrew's earshot. Jo tells me Hector has spoken to Leticia Fuentes and had tried to put her off, saying she must be so busy this time of year, and he wouldn't want to put her out, but it hadn't worked.

'With any luck Andrew won't be well enough to go, anyway,' I say. 'And this time it's not man flu. I even felt sorry for him once or twice. I'm feeding him honey and lemon and the odd hot toddy.'

'Ooh, sounds nasty. Have you tried echinacea?'

'Euthanasia did you say?' I imagine me at Andrew's bedside with his family, looking sad.

Jo laughs.

'Joking aside, it is bad enough for antibiotics. Anyway, I really don't want him to go to the party. And it's not just Leticia, Jack'll be there too.'

'Ahh. Don't want to mix your men.'

'What! No, of course not. Nothing like that. But it's bound to be awkward. You know how Andrew is if anyone pays me attention. And Jack and I are trying to keep our distance as much as possible.'

'Why?'

'Because—'

'Because you're getting attached to him?'

'Because…because nothing. Jack knows Andrew's cheating, that's all. Saw him at the hotel. Then on their first meeting he was bristly. He might…'

'Be hostile to Andrew?'

'Possibly. And Andrew hasn't exactly taken to him either.'

'Perhaps he senses you fancy Jack?'

'Don't be silly.'

'I bet you dream about him every night.'

'I don't. In fact, I'm more likely to have a nightmare, like the one last night. Horrible.'

'Tell me.'

'Okay. I was on a wheel.'

'A big wheel like in a fairground, or the London Eye?'

'Neither. More like one of those wheels where someone throws knives at you. Anyway, I was sitting on a spoke enjoying the sensation of going around and around, my stomach doing a free fall, you know when you want to shout "wheeeeeeee". Jack was on the wheel too but on the other side, minding his own business. Then the wheel started to spin faster, and I clung on for dear life.'

'And you fell off and woke up,' Jo suggests.

'No, I slipped down but managed to grab another spoke, and with every bit of strength I could muster, I pulled myself up. Finding my balance so I could be comfortable again was impossible. I was wobbling, really insecure. Then I woke up.'

'The Wheel of Fortune.'

'What do you mean?'

'One minute we go with the flow, happily letting life take us where it wishes. Then suddenly it shakes us up and forces us to move along. Causes insecurity. It happened with me, you know, and Phil – threw me onto another path.'

'A better path then?'

'Erm, well, a different one. No one knows.'

'Love you, Jo, you're so wise. Any path has to be better than this one.'

I close the call and still don't have a clue what Jo is planning to wear.

What do you buy a wealthy couple as an engagement present? An antique perhaps if it wasn't for the fact that Winterford House has the look of carefully selected pieces. Something for the garden, except it's winter and there's not enough time to put thought into buying an unusual garden ornament.

Andrew comes up with a suggestion of 'his and hers' monogrammed bathrobes. He even orders them himself from his sick bed. With mounting horror, I realise there is no way he intends to miss the party. This is confirmed by him phoning Matthew and telling him how friends of his are getting engaged, and how the party is at their mansion house, even though Kate would have told him already.

The cosmos is now taking events in hand. This is meant to be. Saturday will be *detecting-if-one's-husband-is-*

closet-binge-eating-cake day. How horrible. If only he were choosing a healthier option. Carrot cake? Nope, that would be me and he hates carrot cake. Ginger cake then? That would be spicy Maxwell, not something he'd often want. But Leticia Fuentes is like a big, multi-layered chocolate gateau with lashings of cream and sprinkles, and Andrew has a sweet tooth. My stomach somersaults.

***

Amazonian woman kicks in by Wednesday and I go to help Jo and Hector with the garden lights, taking Duchess with me.

Winterford House is a hive of activity. The weather is chilly and I'm glad I've dressed for warmth with thick jacket, woolly hat and boots. Fully expecting to be hands-on, I find I'm just the project manager as there is a small team of men and women assigned to help me with the task.

The project management is something I find I enjoy, and I should seriously consider adding it to my business. But with all the insecurity surrounding my marriage it would be hard to let go of my bread-and-butter work. Little by little I might manage it.

A good few hours later and the work is complete and we retreat to the kitchen for soup. I'm glad I don't have to return to untangle the lights from the trees. What a nightmare.

Wednesday evening I have to do accounts to keep on schedule with my work, so by Thursday morning I'm tired, but have to go shopping for my gown. Andrew is improving and promises to keep an eye on Duchess. He's enjoying having a few enforced days off and is intent on making the most of them.

In Southampton, finding a glamorous but sexy dress is a nightmare. Thankfully, because we're approaching December, there's plenty of glitzy choice. My feet are soon killing me going from shop to shop then back again to try on gowns if only to rule them out one by one. Eventually I enter a more expensive shop and find one that costs far too much for the fact I might only get to wear it once.

Wine coloured, it suits my complexion. The dress has a ruched, fitted crossover top and a long, flowing skirt with a thigh high split, thankfully falling short of being a gynaecological asset. The straps fall off my shoulders, draping over my arms. The gown is glamorous with an understated sexiness. At least I'll feel confident in front of Leticia, and Jack will be there too. My heart leaps on both counts.

I take a selfie in the mirror and text it to Jo who answers immediately with *Buy it!*

Without questioning the cost further, I pay. There's no question about it – my gown must be perfect. And this will my last chance to dress up and feel attractive for some time to come.

Although on the surface the party presents in my head as being glitzy and glamorous, a dark shadow of impending doom is lurking.

I send another text to Jo. *Please cancel the photographer. Your party – it'll ruin it.*

No chance, she replies. *Too late now anyway.*

She follows that text up with, *Trust me, it'll work out fine. Just buy the dress.*

I wish I had her certainty. Dark clouds are looming, and just like in a cartoon, one is hanging directly over my head, waiting to rain on me.

CHAPTER TWENTY

On Saturday evening I'm so apprehensive about the party I have a glass of wine while I finish dressing. The only jewellery items I'm wearing are gold drop-earrings with diamonds, a gift from Andrew on our wedding day. With my glamorous gown and my thick, wavy hair styled loose over my shoulders, they are all the decoration I need.

When I glide into the kitchen, Andrew says, 'Just in time. Taxi should be on its way. Wow, you look stunning.' As he runs a critical eye over me, he nods. 'Freddie's right – you could be a great asset to me, especially if you dress like that more often.'

'Thanks,' I say sharply.

'Not wearing your antique necklace tonight?'

'What? No, it doesn't go with the dress colour.' I should add a 'duh' to that.

'Just thought with Jo buying it, you'd like her to see you wearing it.' There's an emphasis on 'Jo'.

'Jo will be far too busy to notice. That photographer friend of yours all set up is she?'

'Wouldn't know. Hector handled the arrangements.' His expression is deadpan but he fidgets with his lapels then brushes imaginary specs from his sleeve.

The pet sitter duly arrives followed shortly by the taxi and my stomach churns in anticipation of what's ahead.

We arrive at Winterford House at the same time as several other guests and wait our turn to congratulate the happy couple.

Standing to the edge of the line with a large camera is Leticia. Hard to miss, she's wearing a gold, calf-length strappy dress, the skirt of which, ballooning and fully ruched, wouldn't look amiss on a Ferrero Rocher. Still there's something wild and confident about her and the pressure builds in my chest.

Andrew is standing slightly in front of me as Jo's mum, who has been hovering in the background, spots me and comes over to say hello. When I turn back, Andrew is waving to Leticia, barely lifting his hand. Strange he should act so furtively when she works for his company. Surely, when someone meets a colleague they greet them properly. Meanwhile, Leticia has no problem waving, and smiles hugely at him before holding up the camera and clicking away. I cringe as I picture her poring over them later. Andrew quickly turns his attention back to Hector who is holding out a hand to shake.

Jo gestures in Leticia's direction with a nod of her

head, and kissing me on the cheek whispers, 'What does she look like? We should stick baubles on her and a bit of tinsel.'

I laugh nervously.

Jo's royal-blue gown with beaded appliqué on the bodice complements her fabulous curly, red hair, which is hanging loose past her shoulders. 'Gosh, you look beautiful and positively pre-Raphaelite. Love the dress.'

'So, do you, a real Lauren Bacall. Sultry and sexy.'

The mutual admiration society of two restores my confidence and I sneak another glance at Leticia's gaudy get-up and feel even better. Jo shows me her engagement ring, a huge ruby surrounded by diamonds that surely must be a family heirloom.

'It's gorgeous,' I say. 'Congratulations.

As I kiss Hector's cheek, he grabs my hand and squeezes it reassuringly.

With as much poise as I can muster, I take Andrew's arm and we move further into the room. As we pass Leticia, my breath quickens and I can't keep my gaze from drifting towards her. She's staring at him and can't hide her surprise as if only now comprehending I'm with him. Hurt registers in her eyes, causing me inner turmoil but confirming my suspicions. How can Andrew do this to us both?

Curiosity causes me to glance back over my shoulder to find Leticia is staring at me too and has caught my anguished expression, her eyes growing wide as she suspects I might know. Smiling as if just noticing her, I turn my attention elsewhere, frowning off into the distance as if searching for someone and hopefully putting her off the scent.

One of the hired staff directs us to the saloon, and a waitress standing near the door offers us a flute of champagne. I take one and survey the crowded room. At the other end a swing band plays, 'I've Got You Under My Skin'.

'Impressive place,' Andrew says. 'Introduce me to people. I need to network.'

'I don't know that many people myself,' I protest, 'apart from Jo's parents and one or two friends of hers, but they're not in the room.'

Andrew glances at me in disgust. 'Yes, you do. Over there, look. That client of yours, Jack Langford, the art dealer, has people with him. Didn't you say he was well known?'

Jack is standing near the French windows with Sophie and talking to Stephanie of all people. She must also be a friend of Hector, so why wouldn't he invite her. Jack's shoulders are impressive in his dinner jacket. And although Andrew could pass as James Bond in black tie, Jack looks hunkier, his cummerbund somehow sexier on him.

Without waiting, and a little annoyed at me for dithering, Andrew marches over and shakes Jack's hand, and I bet he's using his bone-crusher grip. I'm dying. Jack looks stern and the rest of my champagne disappears down my throat.

Hoping for the best, I saunter over, dropping my empty glass on a passing waiter's tray en route. Sophie greets me first, telling me I look hot, which astounds me, but also makes me happy in equal amounts. She wearing a scarlet, full-skirted dress and Stephanie looks sleek in black and gold.

Jack kisses me on both cheeks, barely touching them. Stephanie gives me a gentle hug as if not wanting to upset my makeup and hair. 'Thanks for your help recently,' she says. 'I'd have gone crazy trying to handle everything on my own. The bookkeeping is much easier now too. You're a treasure.'

'This is Sophie, my daughter,' Jack says to Andrew. 'And her mother, Stephanie. This is Miranda's husband, Andrew,' he adds, turning to Stephanie. Do I detect a note of churlishness in his voice?

Andrew shakes Stephanie's hand vigorously and gives her a winning smile. Is he presuming Stephanie is Jack's wife?

Leticia heads our way, so I put my arm through Andrew's. We dutifully pose for photos. I encourage her to take a separate photo of the two of us, leaning right into him, tempted to wrap a leg around his. Her face gives nothing away as she snaps us and immediately moves on to another group. Andrew's expression gives nothing away either. Hmm, Plan B is necessary. Showing her my marriage is in good order even though it isn't and therefore prompting a reaction from her, didn't work that well. Instead I should try to get into a conversation with her, but it won't be easy while she's working.

Andrew spots someone he knows, a Chris something-or-other, he probably has a bare acquaintance with. He excuses himself, obviously feeling safe to leave me with Jack and his family.

'Handsome husband you have there,' Stephanie says, and laughs.

'Sophie, come on, I'll show you how charming the garden looks.' Jack's voice is tight. He strolls away. Sophie grimaces at me and follows him. She reminds me of her mother.

'Well, excuuuse me. What did I say?' Stephanie shakes her head from side to side. 'Ignore him, tetchy bugger. Come on, let's get you a drink.'

Did I deserve such a rebuff? Jack is the limit. Doesn't he understand my false enthusiasm and vivacity is part of the ploy to bring Andrew's affair out into the open? Surely Hector told him about Leticia.

Stephanie spots a waiter with more champagne and we find a seat. The next thing I'm spilling all to her and she lends a sympathetic ear.

'What really. She's here. The photographer? Gosh.' We scan the room until we find Leticia and watch her for a minute or two while she does her job like any professional, going from couple to couple and groups of people taking photos. 'Doubt there's anything to worry about. Surely they're not idiotic enough to betray themselves at a party held by your friends.'

'But I want them to.'

'There's no chance you could be wrong? She looks relaxed.'

'No, that's an act,' I reply. 'She's not happy I'm here. You should have seen her expression when she saw me.

Later will be the danger time when everyone's had a lot to drink and are no longer photogenic. She might try to speak with Andrew.'

'Ah, now that sounds familiar.'

'You've had a similar experience? Surely, it wouldn't be with Jack.'

'My first boyfriend. And it was at a party.' She laughs when my hand goes to my chest in relief. 'Jack's not the type. He's straight-up. You like him a lot, don't you?'

'What? No, no, I mean yes, I do, but not in the way you mean.'

'You're fooling no one, Miranda. Neither is Jack. Watch yourself. You're vulnerable with your husband's antics and it's natural to turn to someone for support, especially someone of Jack's heroic capabilities. Give yourself breathing space.'

Does she have regrets about Jack?

'Definitely not,' she says, reading my mind again.

I laugh. I'm quite obviously an open book. No one has any problem getting into my head. 'Okay, I am attracted to him,' I admit, 'but I'm doing my best to keep it professional.' My mind flashes back to when I pretended to be his wife, and when we went to choose a dog together. 'I'm not always making a very good job of it. But be reassured, sorting out my marriage is the only thing I'm intent on.'

'Does Jack know you have feelings for him?'

'No. Yes.' Blood rushes into my cheeks. 'I'm not sure. He's admitted he has feelings for me.'

Stephanie pats my hand. 'The atmosphere says a lot.

Be strong, it'll all come good in time. You'll eventually find your way through the fog and out into the sunshine. That's what I'd hang on to.'

How hard it must be for Stephanie losing her husband. Her fog must still be dense. Whatever happened to me it could never be as bad. 'I hope so. Have you decided what you're going to do with the pub?'

'I'm stopping in the spring. Handing over the reins to a manager and employing an assistant. Then I'll take a long holiday – three months or so. Visit a few countries I'm fond of. Nothing too far away, but maybe starting with Ireland, then France and if there's time, Italy.' She shrugs as if not convinced.

'Sounds like heaven. I wish I could go off to some far-flung land out of this mess.' I wave my hand towards Leticia.

'Perhaps you might work through it with Andrew. Find something to rescue and build on.'

'Erm, it's a big perhaps.'

'Do I detect an "And pigs might fly" in that answer?'

'Yes,' I reply sadly. 'He can't undo what's done. This was such a bad idea and I regret it so much. Leticia obviously had no idea I was coming and I'm not out to hurt others, even her. He's probably told her a pack of lies. He told her I was having counselling for depression or something.'

'Does Jack know Leticia is…you know?'

'The other woman? I presume Hector told him. He disapproves, no doubt, that she's here, and with good reason.'

'I'd tell him anyway. Men don't swap info like we women.'

I grimace. 'Good point.'

'As for Leticia, surely if Andrew has told her you have mental health problems, she knows now you don't or will do by the end of the evening. Keep cheerful, show her you're far from depressed. In fact, just have a good time.'

'Will do. Come on, let's get another drink and mingle.'

We join Jo and Hector who have moved away from the door. 'You look wonderful,' I tell Jo again. Hector slips his arm around her waist. 'I'm a lucky man.'

'We're both lucky,' responds Jo, her eyes brimming with love.

Thinking about love and luck, I glance around to where Andrew is, and spot him still chewing the ear off some poor bloke and his wife on the other side of the room, the wife mesmerised by Andrew, gazing adoringly at him. But it's hardly his fault he's so good-looking. Meanwhile, Leticia is still wandering around like a shiny gold Christmas gift, smiling and chatting to guests, putting them at ease before getting them to pose. She eventually drifts over towards Andrew's group, takes a photo and then whispers something to Andrew. He replies to her and she spins away frowning. What was that about?

Jo follows my gaze. Suddenly, Leticia spots us and walks determinedly our way. She lifts her camera up and we scramble to line up.

'Your party is very wonderful,' she says to Hector and

Jo. She clicks and checks the photo in her screen. 'Beautiful house. Many handsome people.' Her voice is husky and sexy. When she puts the camera to her eye, again, I have a distinct feeling she's using it as an excuse to peer more closely at me.

Leticia, for all the poor taste in evening wear, is vivacious, voluptuous and exotic, but what oozes from her most is her super fertile vibe. My competitive streak rises and with an Oscar-winning smile, I say, 'Wait a minute, I'll fetch my husband. He should be in this too.'

Leticia pretends she didn't hear and, tight-lipped, swiftly snaps another photo. When she lowers the camera, I spot tears in her eyes and I'm overcome with guilt. I'm so stupid to feel guilty. This woman is blatantly having an affair with Andrew, sending him provocative messages when she knows he's home, and phoning him behind my back. I must not lose my nerve.

'OMG,' says Jo when Leticia slips away, clearly uncomfortable. 'Did you see those eyes spout water when you mentioned Andrew? She must know now.'

'Knows what though? The enormous lie that my marriage is strong and she's the bit on the side? She'll dump him and then I'll be none the wiser. Where will that leave me?'

'Hard one,' says Stephanie.

'Yes,' agrees Jo. 'But don't be a doormat, Randa. In the end, Andrew's controlling you both to his own advantage.'

That's so true. Somehow I must find a way to remove that control. But I can't let this overshadow the party, so change the subject to how lovely everything is, and Jo tells me the garden is enchanting, and that I must go and walk in it, especially as I had a hand in it. 'You'll find shawls on a stand in the hallway. But first let me introduce you to Hector's mother.'

Alice Thackeray is a tiny, but formidable, woman. The direct type. However, she seems genuinely happy with her son's choice and glances over to Jo as if proud.

'I haven't seen you for an age, dear,' Alice says, turning her attention to Stephanie. 'Sorry to hear about your husband. What rotten luck.'

'Yes, it was.'

'And Jack hasn't settled down yet?'

'No, not yet.'

'Well, there's no rush, I suppose. He already has a grown child. She smiles at Jo.'

I suddenly realise why she's so happy Hector has found someone. She wants to be a grandmother.

Jo and Hector move away with Hector's mother to mingle with their guests. Stephanie says she'll seek Sophie out as she's determined to make the most of her couple of nights off. Jack is nowhere in sight and I hate it that he might be avoiding me until I persuade myself how unfair I'm being. Who could blame him? Best to find him as soon as possible and explain what's going on, in case he really doesn't know.

Meanwhile, I rejoin Andrew as he has left his friends. The band starts to play, 'I Get a Kick Out of You' and Andrew's arm goes around my waist and he says, 'I could get used to all this.' And I wonder what it would be like now if he had remained faithful. Loving it too, most probably. But now I only find it annoying and make an excuse that I have to freshen up.

As the evening progresses there's still no opportunity to speak to Jack and I give up for now and allow myself to be herded with Andrew into the dining room where a number of delicious dishes are displayed on the long, dining table. Most people have already eaten. I nibble smoked salmon but have no appetite. Leaving Andrew to it, I continue my search for Jack who, let's face it, must be bloody well hiding behind a bush, a big one, or tree in the gardens as he's not exactly that hard to spot.

As I enter the saloon, Jack is there, standing near the French windows, staring out onto the terrace, tall and commanding. He adjusts his cuff thoughtfully before looking up, his gaze immediately alighting on me. My heart flutters. The few couples dancing fade into oblivion. Jack bows in acknowledgement before picking up a whisky glass from a side table and raising it in salute. With a side smile, he steps out of the doors and disappears into the gardens. What does he expect me to do, follow like a little lamb? Play hide and seek. He makes me so angry. Andrew makes me angry. Men are shitbags. I'll find another drink instead. There's champagne back in the dining room.

As I turn the corner Leticia bumps into me, having been reading something on her phone. At first we're both shocked and stare at each other, but I quickly come to my senses, remembering Plan B, and block her way as she tries to walk past. 'Enjoying the evening?' I ask.

She looks disconcerted but answers, 'Yes, very much so. Beautiful people. And Jo and Hector are very nice.'

'Yes. Salt of the earth. Trustworthy.'

She frowns. 'And you are enjoying the party also? Such a surprise this house. So big.'

'Yes, well, Jo's my best friend so I've been here before.'

'You and Jo are best friends? Oh, I thought these people were Andrew's friends.'

'Really? Ha. He hardly knows Hector and never really liked Jo. You work with him much?'

She's taken aback. 'Erm, yes, sometimes. Sometimes I work for the same company.'

'And attend events together?'

She has the grace to blush a deep fuchsia and shifts her gaze downwards. 'Not really. I do not know him so well. He seems a nice man though, kind.'

Anger soars through me at her nerve. When she tentatively glances up again, I smile as it's time to reveal I'm not mad, and that Andrew lied about me and has no intention of leaving our marriage. 'Yes, he is kind, loves animals and children. We've just adopted a rescue dog and now we've been married seven years are planning to start a family. After our holiday that is. Second honeymoon. Greece. He surprised me with it.' It's my turn to blush as I rattle on without a pause, fearful she'll walk away before I get it all out. I must take Stephanie's advice and mention my business to show I'm a capable woman and not depressed. 'Have you walked in the garden? I designed the lighting. It's the new part of my business, organising events. Concentrating on the creative aspects. Andrew is so supportive. My job is so interesting and fun right now. Much to look forward to with my expansion.'

For some reason she stares at my stomach. 'Very nice for you. The garden is very nice too.'

'Are you married or have a partner?'

'No, not right now. Sorry, but I have to go and do the job they hire me for. Enjoy the evening.' And with that, like a will-o'-the-wisp, she whips past me and darts around the corner, leaving me standing shaking.

My job is completed. I need a drink.

In the almost empty dining room Andrew tucks into yet another plate of food surrounded by a group of three adoring females. He's easily the best-looking man at the party: great body, stylish hair, and leading-man poise. But totally oblivious of the turmoil he's causing everyone right now.

I pick at the food. More people come in and join the group, including the man and his wife Andrew was chatting to earlier. Andrew waves me over.

He introduces me to Chris, mumbling 'the wife' at the end. The women stare at me.

'Yes, Miranda, Andrew's wife,' I add loudly, and lean into him. 'How do you do?' I could kill myself for acting so obviously insecure. This must stop. But I can't bear him adding more women to his already overfilled harem.

Andrew though responds, slipping his arm around my waist proudly. His expression suddenly changes. He drops his arm and I follow his gaze, and there is Leticia standing at the door, frozen. She must have been seeking Andrew out to talk to him, my words having got through. When I look again, she's gone.

Andrew loses interest in the group and, pulling away, excuses himself, saying he should talk to Hector. He's gone to find Leticia. Typical, now I have to stay to be polite. Chris asks me what connection we have with Hector and his fiancé and I'm eaten up with frustration over what Andrew could be doing.

Five minutes later I excuse myself and go back into the saloon. I can see Leticia talking to a woman on the other side of the room, and Andrew is not with her. I spend time speaking to Jo's parents and her other friends until eventually running out of people to talk to, I decide to find Stephanie. Jack is still hiding somewhere and there's no sign of Andrew.

I go to freshen up first, and the bathroom mirror tells me I look a little haggard. I brush on some lipstick and tidy my hair. Time to enjoy myself.

Stephanie appears with more champagne like my fairy godmother as I enter the saloon. 'This is the first time I've enjoyed myself in absolutely ages,' she says. 'Come into the garden. You helped with it, I'm told. Knowing what you did with my Christmas decorations, I'm not surprised. Looks bloody fantastic.'

'No, haven't seen it yet, but I will now.'

The garden is a fairyland. The steps down to the lawn have a lantern on each end, my own idea. The lawn itself is encircled with solar lights. Strings of fairy lights and more lanterns dangle from trees. There are tables on the terrace with candles lanterns too. The night is clear with a full moon, and there isn't a breath of wind.

We do a tour of the gardens and I'm vaguely aware of being chilly, but the alcohol dulls it. We duly arrive back at the terrace.

Hector and Jo join us and we find a table so Jo can rest her feet. My own are killing me and I drop into a chair with more force than I intended. 'Oops.'

'You're pissed' Jo says.

'You're sober,' I say, and laughing raise my glass, making Jo shake her head.

'Anything happen yet with…?'

'Not that I know of, but I spoke to her briefly and I may well have put the cat among the pigeons by indicating we're a happily married couple.'

I shiver. Blankets are piled on a chair, another of my ideas, and I take a few and pass them around before wrapping one around my own shoulders. We chat for a while about the success of the party and the wonderful food. And Stephanie tells us funny pub stories. The champagne flows freely.

When Jo and Hector leave, as it's late and guests are preparing to go, Stephanie and I stay a while. A bottle of champagne sits half-full on the table. With my glass having disappeared, and with no one else around, I pick it up and take a few swigs. Cold with sitting, we rise and spot another group of people meandering along the path chattering.

'Shall we?' asks Stephanie.

I laugh and we follow – me with the bottle, and Stephanie with her glass of champagne. The path leads down to the riverbank, and we giggle when we step onto the grass, trying to keep our balance on the uneven surface, our high heels sinking into the soft ground.

When we reach the water's edge, we spot a rowing boat tied to a tree, sitting there invitingly. Stephanie giggles and says, 'Shall we go for a midnight row?' The group of people join us, laughing and egging us on.

Stephanie, high heels, clutch bag, and her drink in her hand, climbs into the boat. The people gasp as the boat sways and rocks and she totters. One man shouts, 'Sit down, you're going to tip it up.' Taking dainty steps, Stephanie attempts to turn around.

'Sit!' more male voices echo.

A woman remarks, 'Look at her in her high heels. She's going to go in.'

'What's this? The Health and Safety Executive training day?' I say. 'Let me help you, Steph.'

I hand my bottle to someone, drop my bag on the grass, and kick off my shoes. Hoisting up my skirts, I clamber into the boat, hanging onto Stephanie as we try to sit.

'Sit down,' the same man shouts as the boat rocks violently. We both move at once and the boat tips.

We giggle, both balancing remarkably well and righting the boat. Stephanie at last sits, still daintily holding her drink.

'Sit, Miranda.'

Oh God, great, that's Jack's voice. Deciding I'd better

do as I'm told, I try to turn but Stephanie is in the way as she's sitting in the middle of the bench. There's another seat behind, so facing outwards, I put one foot over the front bench.

The boat suddenly lurches and tilts. I grab an overhanging tree branch with both hands, but my feet push the boat away, leaving me stretched between it and the branch, the river beneath me.

'Let go, you idiot.' The voice jumps out at me – it's Andrew's. Hell, is everyone here? I ignore him as letting go means I'll fall in the river. Instead I pull on the branch, at the same time using my feet to haul back the boat. Once I've lifted my foot back over the bench I let go of the tree feeling pleased with myself.

'Now sit down or get out of the boat,' Jack orders. Facing Stephanie, I attempt to manoeuvre myself past her again, managing to get both feet over the bench while holding onto her head. Lots of laughter comes from the riverbank each time I teeter while I screech. I slowly begin to turn to position myself ready to sit.

'It's going well,' a man says. 'She's going to sit down.'

'I am,' I shout, and screech again as I wobble.

As I complete my turn, I'm too near the edge and my weight causes the boat to pitch. Hard as I try to keep my balance, and in what feels like slow motion, I fall backwards through mid-air.

CHAPTER TWENTY-ONE

The last thing I hear is a collective intake of breath as the freezing water closes over my head.

Struggling in the blackness, unable to breathe, I splash around, desperately trying to resurface, the skirt of my dress weighing me down. My first thought is that I'll drown, and even worse, that someone will jump in to save me. Suddenly my knees and one hand touch the bottom of the riverbed and I'm aware the water is shallow and propelling myself up, I struggle to my feet gasping. Only a few seconds have passed, but it feels like minutes. As I try to move forwards, coughing and shivering, a man in the boat reaches down and tries to pull me out, but the boat rocks and he lets go. I fall backwards landing with a huge splash, throwing out my hands behind me, one touching the riverbed, water up to my neck. As I struggle to my feet once more, he shouts, 'Sorry, love, you were going to tip us in.'

Jack, standing on the edge of the bank, holds out a

hand to Stephanie and she steps out of the boat in a lady-like manner, totally unscathed, clutch bag tucked under her arm, followed by the man who's now given up trying to help but has taken Stephanie's glass off her. Having no choice as my sodden dress is hampering me, I grip the material and haul it up to my thighs and manage at last to reach the bank. Jack hauls me out to cheers from the crowd. I'm just in time to spot Andrew's back as he leaves the scene and marches up the hill. Leticia lowers her camera and follows him probably having filmed it all. Unbelievable, the pair of them.

Someone sniggers. Suddenly the whole incident tickles me too and I roar with laughter, bordering on hysterical. The small crowd joins in.

Between giggles I say, 'It's like *Titanic* all over again. Thanks, Jack, for saving me,' which results in more peals of laughter from the crowd. Then there's a collective whoop as I trip over the front of my trailing dress and a woman points at my chest.

Jack, still gripping my hand, moves his imposing frame in front of me, blocking out everyone else, and pulls up my dress to cover one exposed nipple, his expression thunderous.

'Rescuing me twice in one night?' I declare, ignoring his serious demeanour, wondering why he can't see the funny side like everyone else. Abruptly, he lets go of my hand and I stumble backwards, balancing precariously on the edge of the bank, only just managing to steady myself. 'Well, really.' Blood rushes into my indignant face, laughter abating.

Stephanie grabs my arm and yanks me forward, away from the water's edge. 'That went well. Eek, you're drenched, what a shame, and such a gorgeous gown. Here.' She hands me her clutch bag. She yanks the straps up my arms one by one and pulls on the front of the bodice which results in a loud tearing noise as the delicate material gives way. 'Oops, sorry. You're standing on the hem, but it's only the seam. On the good side, your boobs are covered properly now.' She removes a couple of twigs and leaves from my hair.

The reality of how I must appear finally hits me.

Surprisingly, Jack is still standing there. He scowls at us both before rolling his eyes, and whipping off his jacket, gently drapes it around my shoulders. This time I'm more gracious and mumble a quick thanks. I can't find my shoes, they're at the bottom of the river no doubt, and the grass is icy under my feet. I keep it to myself. The last thing I need is Jack carrying me into the house.

'As much as you might think is the case, I don't have ulterior motives when I try to help you,' Jack says on the way back up the slope. 'I'm not following you around, hoping to rescue you. That is entirely a coincidence.' He throws a stern glance at Stephanie who grimaces guiltily on my other side. With his tight grip on my arm I feel like a naughty schoolgirl being marched to the head teacher's office.

None too soon, we reach the terrace and Stephanie holds my dress up for me as we climb the steps. 'You go inside and wait. I'll find Jo.' She disappears inside.

'I'm fine,' I retort, lying. 'Not cold at all.'

'That's because you're pissed,' Jack replies, matter-of-factly. 'And it's all the more reason to go and get warm.' My stomach flutters at his look of genuine concern. I touch his arm, and he says, 'You need to decide what you want. You can't go on like this.' He tries to usher me through the doors, but I'm reluctant to let people see me looking like a drowned rat.

I stand my ground and say to him, 'It's Leticia, the photographer, she's Andrew's—'

A loud voice interrupts me. 'For crying out loud. What are you like? Just heard.' Jo is hurrying across the terrace.

'With the horrible goings on here with Andrew and that woman I was just trying to have some fun. Not that some people care when they're supposed to be your friend.' This is aimed at Jack and his eyebrows knit into a frown.

'I care,' says Jo. 'Come on. You're shivering. Come and get a warm shower, and I'll find you some dry clothes. We'll use the back stairs.'

Jack raises his eyebrows, an I-told-you-so expression written on his face. Oh, he's so infuriating.

Upstairs, Jo takes me to the master bedroom on the second floor, complete with four-poster bed. Reluctantly, I take off the jacket and hang it over a chair, asking Jo to make sure Jack gets it back. The wet dress sticks to my body like cling film and she helps me peel it off. I'm surprised both my earrings are still in place. In the bathroom I can't get into the shower quickly enough and eye the lovely thick white towels piled on a chair, awaiting me when I get out.

'I've left a sweatshirt and joggers on the bed,' Jo calls from the bedroom. 'They were too long for me so shouldn't come too far up your legs. Party's almost over anyway, the last of the people are leaving. I'll be back in a sec. Just going to arrange a hot drink for you.'

'Thanks,' I shout back.

The water soon washes away the river but not the mortification. Jack's already iffy opinion of me must have sunk completely now. All is lost – Andrew as my husband, Jack as my friend.

By the time Jo comes hurrying in, I'm dried and in the grey jogging gear and thick pink socks. Warm and comfortable the jogging bottoms come just above my ankles. I'm definitely in hiding now until it's time to leave.

'Cocoa's on its way,' Jo says breathlessly, and throws my clutch bag and shoes on the bed. 'Someone found them on the grass.' When I move towards them, she grabs my arm. 'No, leave them. Come with me.'

I grab a towel, intending to finish drying my hair.

'No. Now, quickly.'

I drop the towel and follow her down two flights of stairs to a hallway at the back of the house. She drags me by the sleeve into a room and over to a window. 'Spotted them on the way back up from the kitchen,' she says. 'I went out and heard Leticia confronting Andrew, demanding he tells her what his game is, or something to that effect. I didn't wait to hear any more.' She flattens her face on the glass, trying to see along to the side. 'They're still there.' She carefully slides the window open, grimacing as it scrapes. 'I hope we can hear them from here. If not we'll go out.'

We put our ears to the gap. Andrew's raised irritated voice is just about audible below. 'I'm sorry, haven't I said already. Seemed a good idea. I wanted to help you make new contacts, and then perhaps you won't need Freddie's work anymore.'

'A party where you are here with your wife?' Leticia's voice sounds anguished, but I have to strain to hear it. 'Why should I give up the work of Freddie?'

'I thought it would be better for you. If you don't, you'll have to get used to us being together. Freddie likes Miranda and is insisting she comes to social events. And he almost offered her a job, imagine that. Be grateful I managed to stop it.'

There's a cry of protest.

Both voices are louder now, so they must have moved closer to the window. I take a chance and move a curtain, peering out, anger bubbling up. They're standing facing each other directly below. Not touching. Whatever was between them, it's over now, and Andrew wants to carry on as if nothing has happened. Typical.

Leticia wipes away tears and shakes her head disbelievingly, saying calmly, 'That is so selfish, Andrew Stone. Did you not think how hard it would be for me to see you with your – your wife?' She sniffs loudly and her voice breaks. 'I did not know she would be here. I thought you wanted to see me. Hoped… Instead you break my heart.'

'Sorry but I—' When he moves closer, she moves back. 'Look, I can't leave her, I told you that, and surely you understand. It may not seem so but Miranda has lots of issues.'

By now I'm shaking so much with sheer anger that Jo grabs my hand.

Leticia pushes Andrew in the chest with one finger. 'Okay, she has problems. At first, I say to myself, no, she is not so crazy, and then I talk with her and she is a little crazy. Talks, yap, yap, yap. Drinks much also and straight from the bottle.' She acts this out. 'She almost drowns herself in the river. But still, it hurts to see her. She is beautiful – like a model – when she is dry. When you are together, it makes me small, tiny. You understand? How cruel, Andrew. I did not think you so cruel.'

Cheeky mare, but she's right, he is cruel. Someone I don't know anymore. A complete stranger.

Andrew raises his eyebrows. 'Miranda looks like a model? Really? Freddie said that too, funnily.'

'Andrew! Are you listening? God, I cannot do this. You kill me inside. I love you too much.' She stabs at his chest again, this time with the fingers of both hands. 'You said you love me too. Was I just a nobody? Someone who gives you good sex?'

Andrew throws out his arms, spins around and walks down the terrace before spinning back. 'No, not a nobody, a somebody, but I can't handle this. Freddie suspects something. Keeps pointing out how he hates office gossip. How I'm married and have a nice home – and a pretty good life. Says I mustn't lose focus because there's a future with the company, further promotion.' He hits his hand on his forehead.

Leticia shakes her head. 'Andrew. Please don't. You hurt me with the things you say. What am I to you? Tell me. Fun? That is all?'

'Look, yes, it was always fun, and exciting. Fun for you too, I believe, but it got out of hand. That's dangerous, and I could lose everything.'

I step backwards in alarm. *He* could lose everything? Didn't either of them consider my feelings when they were having their fun? It wasn't fun for me when I read those texts and heard their conversation. And it's hardly fun now with him only staying because of Freddie. Tears trickle down my cheeks and with a groan of anguish I turn, intending to go out onto the terrace. Jo puts a restraining hand on my arm and a finger to her lips. She's right. I should hear the rest.

When I turn back and peer out the window, Leticia has sunk to the ground onto her knees, her hands covering her face. She flings them out dramatically and says, 'Fun? No, never for me. Not even at the start. I am flesh and blood, not a toy. This love I have is real, and you said you loved me also. Do you not want to be with me…ever?' She places her clenched fists by her sides.

My heart beats frantically as I await his answer.

Andrew checks to see no one is watching before bending and grabbing Leticia's upper arms, pulling her to her feet. She bows her head, resting it on his chest. 'Oh, darling, yes, I mean no, I – I don't know.'

'You love your wife?'

'You wouldn't understand. It's complicated. Anyway, Miranda's not that innocent. And be honest – you knew I was married from the start. Knew the stakes. Not much use complaining now.'

Gosh, Andrew is lying to her to excuse himself, blaming us both and taking no responsibility.

Leticia agrees as she pulls completely away. 'What is this "complicated" business? The facts are clear. You love her – you do not injure her. You love me – you do not injure me.' With that and with a swish of her skirt, she retrieves the camera bag from the ground behind her. 'I am leaving, Andrew Stone, this is too, too much. Freddie can find someone else. Do not worry, you will never see me again.'

Andrew runs both hands through his hair. 'No! No! Don't go, Tish. I'm confused. You confuse me. I do love you, but—'

I begin to shake and Jo's arm goes around me.

Leticia stares at him. 'No, Andrew, no. You get unconfused, then maybe we can talk.' She hurries off into the house and Andrew strides down the steps into the gardens. A breeze has got up and some of the lanterns have faded out and the fairy lights sway on the trees giving the garden an eerie glow. There's no one else in sight. Andrew stops at a fork in the path and without hesitation takes the right-hand one and disappears into dark woodland.

When I spin around, Jo grips my shoulders. 'Don't do this, Randa. Wait until tomorrow when you're sober and calmer. Daytime is better and you'll have recovered from your dip. The plan worked. The affair is literally out in the open. That's good, isn't it?' She looks earnestly at me.

I blink slowly. Yes, the plan worked. Three months it's taken me to discover the whole truth. Shouldn't I be relieved now I've been proved right instead of feeling this growing emptiness? There's nothing left to do. The talk with Andrew can indeed wait. 'Yes, it's good it's out in the open. Sorry, Jo, for ruining your party.'

'Don't be daft. Nothing's ruined. Been the best party ever. Everyone had a fantastic time. No one knows about this business –' she waves her hand – 'but your swim in the river will be remembered by the few people that saw it as the funniest moment of any party. They found it hugely entertaining. Not least that you showed them your boobs from all accounts. Don't be surprised if you're invited to more parties now.'

Remembering my dip in the river, I can't help but give a wry laugh. 'One boob.'

'I'm proud of you. You've seen off two women and now you're seeing yourself off. What was it we were saying that time in the pub, a bird in hand is worth two in the bush. And Andrew will end up with no one. I think I have it right this time. '

'Yes, you do.'

'Or should I say a steak in hand is worth two chipolatas in the bush?'

I can't help laughing.

Jo continues, 'And should you need us tomorrow, we're only half an hour away. There's plenty of space at Winterford. Come here.' She throws open her arms and we hug the kind of hug that only good friends can give. The sort that leave you feeling comforted and that you're not alone in the world.

———

Late Sunday morning, I lie in bed with a hangover coupled with shock, too dizzy and sick to start the most important conversation with Andrew I'll ever have.

Once, when I was sixteen, I was involved in a head-on car crash. Not injured apart from a jarred neck and bruising from the seatbelt, but the impact traumatised me, stunned me to silence, and it took days to recover. The impact now is similar but ten times fold, and the temptation to stay under the duvet and hibernate for the next few weeks is hard to fight.

In the taxi home last night we barely spoke. Andrew was lost in his own thoughts and didn't mention my dip in the river. At one point I could feel him staring at me intently when he thought I wasn't looking, but I closed my eyes and pretended to fall asleep. Once home I saw the pet sitter off in the taxi and by the time I got to bed, Andrew was snoring. He was still asleep when I slipped downstairs to let Duchess out in the garden for a wee at six thirty and returned to bed.

With Andrew up, showered and out of the room,

Duchess climbs into bed with me. We have a cuddle before I drag myself out. Dogs sense distress and Duchess doesn't leave my side, waiting patiently while I shower and dress, mentally preparing for my confrontation with Andrew.

When I venture downstairs to find painkillers, Andrew is nowhere in the cottage and his car has gone. A note on the kitchen worktop says he didn't want to wake me but won't be back until later and not to worry about dinner as he needs to discuss with Freddie the possible new business that he drummed up last night. Code for he's gone to see Leticia. Lies fall so easily from his fingers as well as his tongue, but it hardly matters now. Anyway, it gives me time to think. Perhaps when he returns he'll have made a decision and will talk to me without prompting.

As I inspect the kitchen, taking in each carefully thought-out detail of it, the lighting, the tiles, the cupboard arrangements, the flooring, and the artwork, I wonder what it's all been for. All the years I've spent lovingly restoring Holly Cottage ready for a family have been wasted. I threw myself into my marriage thinking everything would be perfect, then when it wasn't, I tried to be the perfect wife. Along the way, I forgot to be real. To think of my own wants and desires. Didn't see that I also lost sight of what Andrew desired. That we wanted different things.

Now if I move out of Holly Cottage, I won't be able to bear it that he might bring another woman into what was once our home. If I stay, it will be a constant reminder of him and the grief and pain that he caused. Moving in with Mum and Steve might be awkward, but I might have to. If it wasn't for the party last night, I'd phone Jo for support, but she'll be resting after her hard work and organising the clearing up. Anyway, she'll be giving me a chance to talk to Andrew first, expecting a call afterwards.

And Jack. What about him? Last night I'd stayed in Jo's bedroom until the pre-arranged taxi arrived. But at one point I'd picked up his jacket and smelled his aftershave on the material, holding it to me for comfort before telling myself not to be stupid. He can't keep rescuing me. Still, I should at least tell him what happened. Explain my actions. Especially if I'm forced to go to Mum's house, perhaps even staying in Chester, and missing the chance to talk to him in person while it's all fresh.

Too scared to phone him and dreading him not answering, I text instead and ask if he can please meet me this afternoon as I'd like to speak to him. When a text comes back saying both Sophie and Stephanie are staying at his house in Lower Winterford, but he would like the chance to speak to me too, I cry out with relief. We arrange to meet at the gallery instead as it's closed for the day.

As I root out my coat and Duchess's lead, I know that this will be the last chance to vindicate myself, so Jack at least respects me. And missing that chance, my instincts tell me, would be something I might regret.

On the way to Netherbury, Duchess in the back of

the car, I'm curious about what Andrew will do when I confront him. If the affair is truly over because he's decided to – as Leticia put it – 'unconfuse' himself, he's living in cloud cuckoo land if he believes that I'm that in love with him I'll stay.

Still, my ego will take a huge bashing when we part. People will talk. 'I told you so,' they'll say. 'We always knew it wouldn't last.' Or they'll pity me, all of which I'm dreading. I'll have to 'get on with it' as Mum is wont to say. And that's something else I should do, phone Mum. Tell her before someone else does. Jo's mum is still at Winterford House and could hear about last night and get to her before I do.

Five minutes later I pull into a side road and dial her number, my hand shaking with emotion.

'Mum,' I say when she answers. 'Mum.'

'Oh God, darling, what's happened?'

Through my sobs I tell her everything that occurred last night and add in the other suspicions about Jane Maxwell.

She commiserates, saying her intuition hadn't failed her. 'Look, dear, you need to talk to him as soon as he gets back. Don't put it off. Stick with what you know. Tell him you saw him kiss that woman, what's her name?'

'Jane Maxwell.' I weep for a moment, trying to gain control until Duchess whines and I grab a tissue from the glove compartment, wipe away the tears, and blow my nose. 'Sorry, I'm okay.' An involuntary hiccup of emotion wracks my chest.

'I'm coming down there.'

'No, Mum, I must talk to Andrew first.'

'Well, if you insist. Be sure to tell him everything you and Jo overheard when he spoke with…?'

'Leticia.'

'Indeed. With witnesses he can hardly deny the fact. And while this is getting sorted avoid that lovely man from the gallery, Jack. It'll only complicate matters.'

'Why?' I say aloud, sniffing. 'There's nothing going on between us.'

'If you say so.'

Gosh, she sounds like Stephanie. 'Mum! I'm not becoming involved with Jack, so don't worry on that score. We're not like Andrew and Leticia, unable to control ourselves.'

'Okay. I'll take your word for it. But come back home for a while.'

'I'll think about it. Love you, Mum.'

CHAPTER TWENTY-TWO

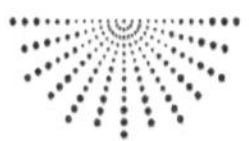

Not heeding Mum's advice, I drive on to Netherbury, park at the back of the gallery, and walk Duchess around to the front. Jack appears and turns the key in the lock before I have time to tap on the glass. He's smart and sexy in jeans, white shirt and a navy jacket. My eyes are drawn to his strong hands and then his chest where his top buttons are undone. When he opens the door, shyness grips me.

Concern reflects in his eyes when they meet mine, a small frown etching between his eyebrows. I must look wrecked. 'Saw you park though the flat window. Come on up, I've put the heating on.' He pets Duchess who greets him like an old friend, jumping up, wagging her tail, and running around in circles.

Upstairs, Jack takes my coat and leads me through to the small kitchen while he makes tea. 'Only the basics with no one living here, but a cuppa I can do. I expect Hector will rent the place out shortly.'

'Shame not to,' I reply, glad of the small talk, and take a seat at the small wooden table.

The hiss of the kettle as the water comes to the boil fills the awkward silence. How do I explain about last night? How do I tell Jack that when Andrew put Leticia forward to take the official photographs, I selfishly went along with it, not only placing her in an awkward position and causing her hurt, but chancing ruining the party, and, not least, confusing Jack by my odd and contradictory behaviour?

When he passes me a mug of tea, he sees my worried expression and smiles gently. 'Don't worry, Hector updated me. Actually, it was a relief to hear. Last night was confusing until your remarks about the photographer and nasty goings on with Andrew. So, once you'd gone safely upstairs, I immediately sought out Hector. Made sense then your manner and subsequent antics. Hector told me how he and Jo thought it impossible for you to continue living in such a terrible position and the opportunity to accelerate events was too good to miss.' Jack attempts to imitate Hector's voice, but fails somewhat. 'Then Jo rang and told me this morning about what transpired on the terrace.'

'I'm glad you know. You must have thought me awful. Sorry, in my determination to find out exactly what was going on, I was thoughtless.'

'Understandable. So, what happened last night when you arrived home? I've been rather anxious wanting to know. I presume you're saying goodbye. Chester?'

'I am saying goodbye and, yes, Chester is a possibility. But I've yet to speak to Andrew. Being a little the worse for wear –' I grimace – 'I thought it better to leave discussions until today. By the time I rose this morning, Andrew had left for the day. On business, according to his note.'

'He went to see her?'

'I think so.' Admitting this aloud causes my eyes to sting and I attempt to swallow the lump forming in my throat.

'So, there's much to face still.'

'Yes. Oh God, it's all such a mess.' A sob escapes. Jack places a hand on my arm while I compose myself, taking deep breaths. I wipe away the tears with my fingertips not worrying about my appearance. I point to my red and swollen eyes, laughing wryly. 'On the way here, I stopped to phone Mum. Sparked me off. Hence the—'

'No need to explain. This is how we started, with you crying. And we're now saying goodbye with you crying. And with Andrew having caused it both times.'

'Yes, full circle. Thanks for coming to my rescue. Though it might not appear that way, I do appreciate it. You were my knight in shining armour, truly. Without you…'

'For purely selfish reasons.' Jack looks reflective. 'Rescuing you has been the highlight of my life in recent months.'

'Not getting your own TV series?' I give a little laugh.

'Okay, that was second. Sorry for being touchy yesterday when you fell in the river. You looked beautiful by the way, I mean before you fell in. I mean…never mind.' His lips twitch with amusement and I laugh again. 'I assumed you'd forgiven Andrew again when he far from deserved it. And on top of that, Stephanie found it fun to torment me about rescuing you. Thinks I've lined you up to be my next wife.' I expect Jack to laugh, but he doesn't. 'She only means it in jest, but for some reason, where you're concerned, I don't find it the least bit funny. Last night there seemed no hope of keeping you, even as a friend.'

'But nice you have that jokey rapport with her.' I wrinkle my nose. An image comes to mind of a future friendly relationship with Andrew once the worst is over. Impossible. Sighing deeply, I say, 'I doubt I'll remain bosom pals with Andrew, once he's an ex.'

'Do you have to? There's no child to consider.'

'Ouch.'

'Damn it. Sorry.'

'Well, it's true.' But my voice breaks. 'The future is stretching out into emptiness before me. Everything I hold dear is disintegrating – marriage, home, the opportunity to have children. My work will suffer, already is suffering. Perhaps, having to move away from…friends.' A sob bursts from me, followed by another being too difficult to prevent.

Jack gently pulls me to my feet and briefly hugs me, then letting go so he's just holding the tops of my arms, he looks down into my face. 'You're tired. Wrecked. A lot's happened. Lie down for a while and I'll walk Duchess. Have you eaten?'

'No, not since a few nibbles last night. Not that hungry.'

'You should eat, or at least try.' Jack guides me through into the sparsely furnished bedroom and fetches bedding from a cupboard in the hall.

Not knowing what to do with myself, and glad to have the decision taken out of my hands, once Jack has made up the bed, I remove my shoes and climb in.

'Now try to rest. I'll take Duchess for a walk and I'll order some food when we get back.'

Hearing her name, Duchess trots over and, disconcerted, climbs onto the bed.

Jack gently takes her by the collar. 'No you don't, girl. We're going walkies.' She doesn't need asking twice and jumps off again, running around excitedly.

'Thank you.'

Jack pulls the duvet up to cover my shoulders. 'No problem. You will get over this in time, I promise. Meanwhile, you're not alone. Okay?'

'Okay.' When Jack leaves, I silently weep into the pillow, comforted at being in the bed he once slept in. Feeling safe. He's so different from Andrew. The perfect husband, the perfect home, the perfect life. What an idiot I am, thinking that's what I had.

What seems like a few minutes later, Jack gently wakes me. He's holding a mug of tea and places it on the bedside table. 'You've been asleep for an hour and a half. Thought I'd better wake you. I've ordered Thai. Don't worry about Duchess, I remembered her dog-food brand.'

I sit up. 'Thank you.' Suddenly I feel awkward sitting in bed, knowing Jack watched me sleeping. He senses it so leaves me with the tea.

I find the bathroom and freshen up, then take my mug into the kitchen to find Jack has already left to pick up the food.

When he returns, eating is difficult, and I have to force down every mouthful. Conversation is non-existent. There's Andrew to face and in the next hour or so my life will change drastically. Tomorrow, who knows where my home will be. Probably a small flat in the Outer Hebrides.

Jack scoops more noodles onto his plate. He shakes his head before putting his fork down, staring at me accusingly. 'Do you know how frustrating it is that I can do nothing to help you today?'

'You've helped already, more than you know.'

Jack's hand covers one of my own. 'There's no point in holding back. You know what my feelings are towards you.' His grip tightens.

My skin tingles at his words and at his touch. Shy again I cast my eyes down as his gaze is disquieting, but nod in acknowledgement.

'If you can let me know sometime how you are, I'd appreciate it.' Jacks rises and clears his plate away, emptying his food into the bin.

Abandoning any more pretence at eating too, my

brief respite over, I say, 'Time to go. Andrew will be back shortly.'

'Jacks nods. I'll fetch your coat.'

When he returns he also has Duchess's lead and fastens it to her collar. After helping me into my coat he walks with me downstairs.

'Will you be all right?' he asks.

'I'll have to be. No one can do this for me.'

When we reach the front door, he unlocks and opens it and we turn to face each other, standing close together on the doorstep. I slip my hand and wrist through Duchess's lead to pull it short as she's on the pavement.

Jack touches my arm. 'Can I phone someone for you – Jo?'

'I'll be okay.' To walk away is difficult, as is saying good-bye. Knowing I can't delay any longer and overcome with emotion, my hands flutter to his chest, my face turning up to him. Then I'm up on my toes, my lips spontaneously moving towards his. With a swift movement his arms come around me, and after a short pause when his smouldering eyes as deep green as a stormy sea, look deep into mine, our lips meet, briefly, gently, my stomach somersaulting.

'Sorry,' we both say simultaneously when we part.

'Caught up in the moment?' Jack asks.

'Yes, caught up in the moment.' It's not quite the truth and I don't move away. Instead we continue gazing into each other's eyes.

'Miranda—'

A motorbike roars up the road, revving as it passes,

cutting Jack off mid-speech and breaking the spell. Good sense returns with a jerk. This is supposed to be a goodbye visit, a chance to tie up loose ends. Nothing else. 'I have to go.'

'Yes. Good luck. And remember, I'm here should you need me.'

'I know,' I reply. 'I know.' With Jack reluctant to move I slip Duchess's lead back down my arm and shake it into my hand. Stepping away, I walk briskly around to the side lane, tugging Duchess along, wanting to show Jack I'm perfectly in control. Trying to be fair to him.

When I reach the car, I'm aware of the lingering pressure of his lips on mine. Not only did I allow the kiss to happen, I instigated it. When Jack held me in his arms, I wanted to stay in them. But this can't happen, everything must be done in the correct order. I'm still reeling from the hurt of a broken marriage. A marriage my husband doesn't yet know is over. A relationship now with Jack would be sure to come to nothing. The rebound effect. And I like him too much to chance it. No, first I must speak to Andrew, then there will be the divorce to organise, finances to sort, not least, having to find a new home. Once I'm accustomed to a new independent life, the recovery process can begin. That's a while away yet.

When I drive out of the side road, Jack is still standing by the door, so I wave and turn directly onto High Street, grateful there's little traffic and that I live in the other direction.

Mum and Stephanie were right. One step at a time is

best. If only I'd met Jack somewhere in the future when all this was over.

Meanwhile, I'll have to be honest with Andrew. Tell him I like Jack and kissed him. I can hardly expect him to be truthful if I'm not.

Andrew's car is already on the driveway as I pull in. Suddenly I'm hesitant. Before today, I only wanted to know the truth. But now, I tremble uncontrollably, my heart pounding and stomach churning with the rising nausea, reminiscent of when I read his texts to Leticia and saw him with Jane Maxwell. I get out of the car with dread. When I let Duchess out, I question whether it would be better if I spoke to Andrew first before bringing her in. The impending conflict might be upsetting.

Before I have the chance to decide, the front door flies opens with force. Andrew is standing there with a furious expression on his face. 'I knew it,' he shouts vehemently, 'you two-faced hussy. You're having an affair. Seen with your lover today. Jack Langford. Look, proof!' He thrusts out his phone revealing a photo of me in Jack's arms, kissing him. 'Did you really believe you could get away with this and I'd not find out? I'm not an idiot.'

Staring at the photo in disbelief, I want to smack the phone out of his hand. 'How?'

'A private detective. How d'you think?' His voice is so filled with aggression Duchess gives a little growl.

'I – I…' A number of replies run through my head:

'It's not what you think', 'It didn't mean anything', 'It was an accident', 'He kissed me,' until the ludicrousness of this hits me. Lying is not okay for me, any more than it is for Andrew. But anger rises at his nerve, standing there, pretending he is innocent. The hurt party. Without further ado, I push past him into the hallway, Duchess at my heel. This conversation should be private, not held outdoors.

Once, inside he says, 'And? Nothing to say?' He doesn't wait for me to answer, which is just as well as how to broach his infidelity while explaining my own actions is challenging. 'You're unbelievable. Making a show of me last night while fooling around with him and then straight into his arms today as soon as I'm out of sight working,' he adds. 'Weeks ago, I was suspicious. Weeks ago. That day you blacked out and I couldn't get hold of you, that's when it began. You never do that.'

'What? I've never fainted in my life.'

'A phone black out. A whole day of it. You were with him, not having lunch with friends. And don't lie, someone saw you alone together. Jack Langford gave you that bloody necklace you said Jo bought. He put it around your neck himself.'

The Jane Maxwell weekend. I was alone with Jack for part of that lunch. I blink rapidly. 'I—'

'Don't deny it,' Andrew spits at me. 'Sheena said he was a big man and she recognised him from the TV, and that he runs a gallery in Netherbury. She presumed we'd split up – imagine that. How mortifying. Only one man fitted that description. Ha, the perfect excuse – working. How many times have you used that one?'

I exclaim aloud in horror and outrage. Sheena? The only Sheena I know lives in the village. Yes, I thought I saw her in the pub that day, I remember now. I shake my head at the absurdity of it.

But Andrew doesn't let up. His voice rising with every syllable, he cries, 'At first I thought, no. I couldn't comprehend it. Was convinced there was some mistake. But you became distant, avoided me, avoided sex. Made excuses.' He shakes with rage and anguish. 'The bag of sexy underwear I found behind the cushion in the snug, you never wore it. Not for me anyway. And then it was gone. Disappeared. Don't lie, I've searched and it's not anywhere in this house. It's at his place, no doubt.'

Andrew, rooting through my belongings, invading my privacy, thinking such things? 'That was—'

'And,' he continues, 'there was the red wig in your car. What's that about? Bloody role-play? You disgust me.' By now he's bawling so much Duchess growls again and I take a step back, but Andrew follows my movements, continuing to spit words into my face. 'Do you know the stupid thing? Even then I gave you the benefit of the doubt. Until this.' He stabs at the phone again. 'And Karen tells me that Langford isn't married but divorced.'

'Karen?' I question.

'The pri-vate de-tec-tive.' He sounds out each syllable slowly as if I'm thick.

That wasn't a joke then. He paid someone to follow

me. What a horrible thing to do. Oh God, I did that – followed Andrew. But a private detective? How did I miss him – or her? A vision of Velma the Scooby-Doo woman springs into my mind, nosing through Jack's window. 'Well of all the—'

'Please leave this house. I can't bear to see your lying face any longer. I've packed you a bag. Go to your mother's and I'll let you know what I've decided to do once I've spoken to a few people. You're having an affair, God damn it. Get out and take that bloody dog with you.' At last, spent, his hand drops to his side.

Get out? The shock of his accusation wears off and my anger grows. Aware of Duchess, I keep my voice low but fire out with venom, 'That's what you would believe. Takes one to know one. Don't worry, I'm happy to go and I'll pack my own bag, thank you.' Pushing past him, I drag the suitcase that's standing in the hallway back up the stairs. How much satisfaction did he get from packing it? Standing there, self-righteous on his moral high ground, clutching the photo, the so-called proof. How ridiculous.

In the bedroom, I repack my case, enough for a few days. Then continue up to the attic to pack my laptop and a few other items I'll need for work before hauling the lot back downstairs bit by bit, Duchess with me at every step.

Andrew still stands in the hallway like a vengeful god, arms folded, cold and resentful. He's the one having an affair but he's throwing me out? No discussion? In all the time I suspected him and he denied everything, never did it cross my mind to ask him to leave. There's zero tolerance when the situation is reversed, in his mind anyway. Not that I intend to stay.

After flinging open the door, I take everything to the car and return for Duchess's gear, putting it on the back seat. Finally, I open the boot to let Duchess safely into the back so she isn't temped to eat Andrew. Only then, having assured a quick getaway, do I stomp back to the house.

I step right up to him. 'You have a nerve accusing me. You're a sleazebag, a liar, and a cheat. For your information, I know about your women. Your affairs. Jane Maxwell and Leticia Fuentes.' His mouth drops open. 'Don't look so shocked. No, it wasn't a private detective. You wined, dined, and kissed Maxwell at the Northwood Park Hotel in Bath after telling me a pack of lies. I was suspicious so followed you.' I pause before adding, 'And what made me suspicious in the first place was reading your love texts from Leticia Fuentes when you left your phone in the bathroom back in September.'

'Most people stick to reading magazines in the bathroom,' he snaps, on the defensive now he knows I've found him out. His expression has changed from indignant to derisory.

Ignoring his snide remark, I continue, 'Later, I overheard you on the phone talking to your precious Tish in the kitchen – our kitchen. You didn't hear me come home. Until then, I was willing to forgive you for that first indiscretion. Wanting to save our marriage. Wanting you to talk to me. Open up. I'd have listened and not made rash judgements. But you wouldn't talk to me even though I prompted you often enough. And last night, you and she, Leticia, discussed your affair on Hector and Jo's terrace in public. How you love her. How she loves you. How you have a mad wife. And don't bother denying it, there's a witness.'

'I didn't—'

'Shall we phone Leticia to hear what she has to say, I know her number? Or Maxwell?'

His brain is working overtime: eyes darting, jaw clenched, lips twitching with surprise at having his accusations thrown back. Too much information fired at him to engineer a believable excuse.

But I don't let up and declare, 'And for your information, I am not having, nor ever have had, an affair. Not everyone sinks as low as you. Trying to deflect from what you're doing to make this my fault is despicable! That way I suppose you could get rid of me and look the innocent party, and can go your merry way with your women without fear of consequence.'

'It wasn't like that. It's not like that.'

'It was though. It is. What I've been finding out about you and your not-so-secret life has injured me far beyond anything you could possibly feel in that ice block of a heart. As for Jack, yes, I do like him. I admit it. Today happened because I turned to him, a friend, for comfort, because of what I overheard. Though, yes, we kissed briefly, caught up in an emotional moment while saying goodbye. Because yes, I was leaving you. Am leaving you. And if you were hurt by that kiss, I'm heartily sorry. But you have hurt me far more, and for longer.' I spin around and march towards the car. 'Phone me when you're ready to talk seriously, but we're over, Andrew,' I say over of my shoulder. 'Our marriage is over. It was over last night when I heard you tell Leticia you loved her.'

As I shut my car door, I glance back. Andrew is standing in the doorway staring in disbelief, trying to take in all that happened. What a sham our marriage turned out to be.

Still fuming and shaking from the confrontation, I drive a good way along the road before pulling into what's becoming my favourite lay-by. Not wanting to face the long drive to Chester, I phone Jo, who tells me to come straight over.

Duchess starts whimpering, so I get out and walk to the boot, slipping her lead on to bring her out for a cuddle, bending down to pat her head and tickle her ears to reassure her all is okay. She gives me a big lick. 'Thanks, girl, we're in this together. You'll be fine. We'll be fine.'

CHAPTER TWENTY-THREE

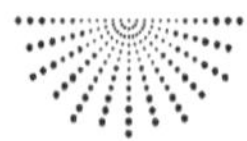

It's Christmas week and I'm dressing the small but lovely tree Jo and Hector brought me in to brighten up the staff flat. Winterford House looks fabulous with garlands draping fireplaces and the staircase, and tradiional holly and ivy. In the entrance hall stands an enormous tree, and with Jo's mum visiting, we all drank mulled wine while we helped dress it.

Duchess loves Winterford with all the space. Two of the staff have dogs, so she has friends to play with. Just outside the door we can walk for as long as we want along pathways, through woods and over fields, without having to step onto a road. Jack lives only a short distance away, but we've stayed away from his part of the village. He knows I've chosen not to go to Chester now as Hector and Jo have let him know my current position. But he has thoughtfully stayed away from Winterford House to give me space.

Christmas will be a trial. Last year when I'd suggested

to Andrew that as the worst of the building disruptions were over we could host Christmas at Holly Cottage, he had protested that Fliss would have a fit as it was her turn and we had spent the previous year at my mother's. He promised that this year we could invite everyone. Although disappointed, I took heart that perhaps we would have good news to share or celebrate too. Now, instead, I'm spending the few days over Christmas and New Year with Mum and Steve, and Andrew most certainly with his parents or Leticia, who knows, I haven't spoken to him.

For the next few weeks I'll be here at the flat, a suite of rooms on the top floor at Winterford, formerly the accommodation of Pamela the housekeeper. Hector was so kind to agree to me staying here when I suggested it, having remembered Pamela had recently moved into a cottage. And it meant I could keep the inconvenience caused to a minimum. Hector and Jo have insisted I stay as long as I want to, but in the New Year I'll start divorce proceedings, citing Andrew's adultery, and Holly Cottage can be valued and put up for sale.

Rifling through a box, I pull out a pretty bauble. The very first one Andrew and I bought from an antique fair. A week ago, I returned to Holly Cottage to fetch a few belongings, and while there, picked up the decorations, knowing Andrew wouldn't bother with them. Jo had accompanied me. Even though I knew Andrew was away, I preferred not to take chances as until he was truthful, I refused to speak to him.

Several times over the past three weeks, he tried to

phone. His subsequent messages always following the same theme: he strayed because I ignored him and lost interest, or stopped having sex. Then there was that incriminating photo. According to his private investigator I was also photographed getting into a car twice with Jack. Initially I messaged back saying that when he was ready to speak the truth, we could talk. But the messages kept coming. So, not rising to the bait, I refused to reply anymore. As Jo would say, Andrew needs to own it.

For now, the flat with its four rooms, kitchen, living room, bedroom and bathroom, is ample enough space for one woman and her dog. The furnishings are lovely but basic, so Jo brought me in a few extra items such as cushions and ornaments. Living with friends is comforting and the future less daunting.

A knock on the door interrupts my reverie and when I open it, Pamela is standing there. 'Madam, there are two people downstairs who purport to be your mother- and sister-in-law. As instructed by Miss Costelloe, I've shown them into the saloon while you change.'

The drawing room is usually where guests are greeted, not the saloon. Why there? And what's wrong with the way I'm dressed? Pamela's eyes twinkle and she raises her eyebrows. Glancing over my clothes – jeans and a sloppy jumper – I smile and say, 'Ah. Thank you, Pamela. Please tell them I'll be down directly.'

'I'll be hovering on the landing for when you wish to order tea.'

I'm beginning to like Pamela more and more.

Once Pamela leaves, I quickly change into a grey sweater dress and red shoes. Even putting earrings in. To finish off I run the brush through my hair. Then thinking that will have to do, I hurry downstairs.

Pamela is indeed waiting by the saloon door and gives me an encouraging smile as I enter. Why Fliss and Kate are here I can easily guess at, and I'm ready for them.

With confidence I stroll in to greet them. 'Felicity – Kate, how lovely to see you,' I gush, and they both jump up from the sofa where they were sitting awkwardly, overawed by their surroundings.

After air kisses all around, I choose the sofa opposite them. 'Do sit down. Oh wait a minute, you've travelled so far, let me order some tea.' More like they travelled half an hour from Holly Cottage. Strolling to the door I go through onto the landing and call, 'Pamela!'

Pamela, who is sitting at the top of the stairs, answers loudly, 'Yes, madam.'

'Oh, there you are. Would you bring us some tea, please?'

'Right away, madam.'

Like the lady of the house, I trip back into the saloon and elegantly perch on the edge of the sofa.

The usually vocal Kate is stuck for words, but clearing her voice, Fliss says, 'Well, yes, we're here on behalf of Andrew. He didn't ask us to come…' Her hesitation gives her away. 'Nevertheless, we thought we should. We're staying at Holly Cottage overnight. Obviously, the cottage is still Andrew's home.'

'Of course. As it is mine. But you're most welcome to visit.'

Fliss blinks then purses her lips. She has come armed in a smart suit and a full face of makeup. She's still a beautiful woman even though close to seventy. 'Why won't you speak to him?' she states. 'Be civil. He's most distraught and all because of a silly misunderstanding. Not that we know the finer details.'

I bet they don't. Andrew won't have admitted to more than one affair and probably played it down as a slip up or minor dalliance. But mentioning the others will only confirm to Fliss that Andrew was married to the wrong woman. But then, she might have a point. Still he should not get away scot free. 'Having an affair is hardly a misunderstanding.'

Fliss regards me sternly. 'But you're not so innocent from what we hear. Andrew had to hire a private detective, and they don't come cheap.'

'That's because those who have affairs, judge everyone by their own behaviour. And the money was ours and a waste too. But, anyway, I'm quite willing to speak to Andrew and he knows under what terms. What happens after that is our business and ours only.'

Pamela enters with the tray of tea which she places on an occasional table. That was quick. I'd lay a bet Jo had already started making it. I get up to help her pour.

In the awkward silence, once I've handed out cups of tea and Pamela has left again, Kate finally speaks. 'We're moving soon, you know, to the house in Alderley Edge, I told you about. Mixing with the famous.'

'How nice,' I reply in the most condescending voice I can muster. 'Much acreage?'

'A large garden but—'

'Lovely. And how's your health, Felicity? Keeping well?'

'Can't complain, but the stress and anxiety you're causing with this silliness is quite impossible to endure. The tension, the headaches, I really—'

'Fruit cake?' I ask, rising from my seat.

Fliss's eyes widen.

'Not for me,' says Kate. 'Trying to shift the baby weight still.' Her eyes rake over me, taking in my recent weight loss. 'Of course, you don't have to worry—'

'And the baby is what? Three now,' I say, interrupting. 'Time flies so.' Kate and her snide remarks on my childless state are not something to which I have to listen anymore.

Pamela knocks at the door lightly and walks in. 'Excuse me, madam, just to confirm. Drinks at seven thirty and dinner at eight?'

'Yes, thank you, Pamela.'

Pamela is enjoying this. In all likelihood, Jo put her up to it. Tonight, Jo and Hector are out and I'm having dinner I've made myself.

Fliss leans back in her chair to watch Pamela go out of the door before speaking. 'Going back to Andrew,' she says, pursing her lips, 'I really don't—'

'Dahling!' Jo strides into the saloon followed by Hector. 'Thank you for keeping Winterford going in our absence.'

I rise and greet them both, even though I saw them an hour ago. 'Yes, dinner is organised.'

'Fabulous, dahling. How are you, Felicity, Kate? So lovely of you to visit us, and so unannounced.' Jo has suddenly developed a plummy accent, dropping her usual Cheshire twang.

Fliss colours, but Kate smiles, not getting the implication.

Jo introduces Hector, who turns to me. 'Don't you have the appointment with your solicitor at three thirty, my dear? You have ordered the Bentley to be brought around? James will happily drive you.'

'The chauffeur,' explains Jo to Kate even though there isn't a chauffeur and isn't a Bentley.

Jo kisses my cheek. 'We'll leave you to drink your tea. We'll be in the library.' She nods. 'Felicity, Kate.' They sweep out of the room.

I check my watch. 'Gosh, almost three. Sorry, the solicitor's appointment. Shouldn't be late. Still have to change and the Rolls will be here shortly.

'Didn't they say the car was a Bentley?' asks Fliss.

Oops. 'Oh, that's right, the Bentley. The Rolls is in the garage for repairs.'

Fliss rises and puts her cup on the table. 'You will speak to Andrew. This is all so silly. No need for solicitors yet, surely?'

'Perhaps you should speak to Andrew as there's every need to consult a solicitor. Please do inform him that when he's ready to take responsibility, I shall talk to him. Until then, I shall carry on the way I am.'

Fliss bristles. 'Really. This is not the way…'

Pamela promptly arrives and shows them out.

The next morning, I receive a text from Andrew simply saying, '*Sorry, about everything. All my fault. Please call,*' which is the briefest and most sincere message I've had from him.

When I phone, he suggests I come over to the cottage after lunch for a chat. I agree once he assures me Fliss and Kate are leaving before noon.

At one o'clock, I drive the half hour to Holly Cottage.

Andrew opens the door before I have time to use my key. 'Hi,' he says. He unshaven and wearing sport's gear. We go into the kitchen and he puts the kettle on. He takes the cafetière out of the cupboard then stares at it. 'Sorry, coffee or tea?'

'Coffee's fine.' Weird, but suddenly I'm a stranger in my own home. When we speak, our voices seem to echo even though nothing has changed apart from the obvious lack of dusting.

Andrew makes the coffee while we talk about mundane subjects like work and then take it through to the snug.

'Where do we start?' He says, settling into an armchair while I perch on the sofa.

'Are you prepared to be honest? And to answer my questions?' I ask, and he rolls his eyes. 'Please don't spare my feelings by leaving anything out. Equally I don't want you leaving anything out to make yourself look better. You can't look any worse – believe me. But before you start, it's only fair to say I'm not coming back. So if you don't want to go any further, I'll go.' It all comes out in a rush.

'God, Miranda.' Andrew brushes a hand through his hair and sighs. 'What do you want to know?'

'That's exactly what I mean. Why can't you just volunteer the truth?'

'Sorry, you did ask me to answer your questions.' He rests his elbows on his knees and clasps his hands.

He's exasperating. 'Jane Maxwell. We'll start with her. What made you do it?'

'The contract. As much as my mother thinks I can, I can't live off my looks.'

'It hasn't stopped you from using them for other reasons.'

'We both know I've had an affair, so let's keep this civil.' I purse my lips and he continues. 'Getting the contract with Jane Maxwell was important to me to get that promotion. And then, when Freddie told me to do whatever I had to do to get it, I took him literally.'

'I thought Freddie liked it you were married?'

'Am married. He did. Does. I got it wrong. Later, he guessed something had gone on, as Maxwell wouldn't leave me alone, and he started lecturing me about keeping a decent personal distance from the clients, saying my good looks tended to attract women and I should bring you to more events and trips.'

'Too late by then, wasn't it?'

Silence.

I jump to my feet. 'Didn't you consider me even for a moment when you were in bed with her?'

'No, I mean, it wasn't like that. I just wanted the contract and Maxwell was making it clear what she expected of me to achieve that. I regretted it so much afterwards, you have to believe me.' He pauses. 'She's still pestering me. Worse, I have to be nice to her without being encouraging, and that's bloody hard.'

'Worse? Okay. So, you don't regret cheating because you love me? And risked losing me and ending our marriage without a thought?'

'You know I didn't mean it like that.'

I sit again and sip my coffee. As there's nothing left to say on the subject of Maxwell, I move on to Leticia. 'And Leticia Fuentes. The affair began a while back, didn't it?' I ask.

'Not that long. A few months. Easter perhaps.'

My chest tightens, my heart beating wildly. 'Not that long! You started the affair with her in the spring?' I grit my teeth. 'I want to know everything. What was so bloody special about her you chose her over me?'

'I didn't choose her over you. It just started. She was doing a shoot at work and the whole team stayed to watch. She was so vivacious, vibrant – sexy, I suppose.' Andrew eyes light up at the memory, turning my insides to jelly. 'Time ran on and, afterwards, we all went out for a bite to eat. She came too. Later, I drove her back to her car…'

'This is killing me, Andrew? What were you thinking?'

He drops his head again. 'She was so different from any other woman I'd ever met. Passionate, feisty, outrageous even. So much talent. Headed for the big time. She liked me a lot. Wanted to photograph me. Half the team were seething with jealousy. They all fancied her.'

His words stab at my heart, destroying my self-esteem. Perhaps I was none of those things, but I was his wife. 'Didn't you question what you were doing? How much it would hurt me if I found out?'

'Excitement took over. I was hoping you wouldn't find out.'

Silence follows.

Eventually I ask, 'Do you love her? You told her you did at Jo and Hector's engagement party.'

'I don't know.' He casts his eyes down.

'She knew you were married all along?'

He squeezes his eyes shut and throws his head back. 'Yes, but she's a good person.'

'You lied to her about me? About our marriage?'

'Yes, I didn't want her to stop seeing me.'

This makes me fume and blood rushes into my neck and face. 'For pity's sake, Andrew. While you were having an affair, stupid me was hoping we'd start a family.'

Andrew bites his lip.

'You never wanted to try again for a baby, did you?'

He ponders on this. 'It hurt, you know, the miscarriage. I was excited at the prospect of being a dad. But as years went on and money became tight, and with my new job, I couldn't be up all night with a crying baby.'

The one up with a crying baby I am sure would have been me. 'Why didn't you tell me how you felt? Ignoring the issue wouldn't make it go away.'

'Don't I bloody well know that? I can't even change my mind. You'll probably have one with someone else now.'

I scowl at him for wanting me to feel sorry for him. 'Did you ever bring her here? Leticia?'

Silence again.

'You lowlife. Our home. Oh my God.' I jump to my feet again and march away from him into the kitchen, only to turn and march back as I don't know what to do in there. 'When?'

'Can't remember. Summer sometime when you were at your mum's.'

'In our bed?'

He closes his eye briefly and shakes his head. 'No, nothing like that. I thought I'd show her the cottage as I had to pick up my suit. She didn't want to come in, but I persuaded her. Showing off, I suppose. Tish took one look around and demanded I tell you about our affair. That brought home the enormity of what I was doing. Of the affair and the consequences. So, I ended it.'

'How long did that last?'

'Not long, but I ended it a few times. She was putting pressure on me. Then when I found the underwear in the snug, and you started going out more, I was more interested in finding out what you were doing.'

'For crying out loud. I bought the lingerie to wear for you as a surprise. When I got home from the shops, I hid it behind a cushion. Then I overheard you whispering sweet nothings to Leticia. When I eventually found the bag slipped down the back of the sofa, I threw it in the bin.'

'Oh.' He shakes his head. 'Well, finding the underwear, red too, which you normally never wear, made me get Karen in to investigate. Along with you having stopped wanting sex and the comments from Sheena.'

'You wanted to believe I'd been unfaithful because blaming me justified your own behaviour. Did you really think I'd want you touching me when you were having sex with other women?'

He squeezes his eyes shut and then opens them. 'But still, you did kiss Langford. When did you really meet him?'

'When I told you I did, the weekend I followed you to the hotel because of the texts from Leticia and instead found you with Jane Maxwell. That's also why I wore the wig not to "role play" but to disguise myself.'

'Oh.' He grimaces.

'When I saw you all over Maxwell, I was distraught, crying, and Jack was at the hotel and drove me home. We became friendly and he asked me to do his accounts. Jo and I had lunch with him that weekend too and it was Jo who bought me the necklace on the same day. Sheena saw what she wanted to see.'

'Sounds so innocent.' The inflection in his voice tells me different. 'Until you kissed him.'

'Yes, I did, but once only. I was going to confront you after the engagement party, was planning to leave, but you were gone when I got up. You went to see her.' I raise my eyebrows but Andrew doesn't react. 'I wanted to say goodbye to Jack as I thought I'd be going back to Chester. And yes, we kissed briefly. I can't explain it. It had never happened before.'

'You like him a lot if you felt the need to say goodbye. Chester is hardly Outer Mongolia.'

'Yes, I admit I do, and became closer to him than I should have. But Jack's never behaved in any way except in a –' I channel my inner Elizabeth Bennet – 'most gentlemanlike manner.'

Andrew abruptly stands, thrusts his hands in his pockets and strolls around the room.

'Andrew, I adored and worshipped you and as a reward you trampled all over me and our marriage.'

He stops. 'I know what I did. I do love you even if it doesn't seem that way.'

'Well, not enough, and not as much as I loved you, obviously.'

'God, I've been an idiot and now I've lost you.' He pauses then frowns and comes to stand in front of me, arms folded. 'Hang on, you said, "loved" that's past tense.'

I stare up at him. 'Did I? To be honest, I don't know what I feel, but you must realise we can never move on from this, so what does it matter?'

'Never? I read an article the other day in that magazine of yours, *Women in the Know*, that affairs can make you stronger and even improve your sex life.'

'Written by someone who was justifying having an affair, no doubt. Rubbish magazine.'

'We could sell the cottage, begin again? Go on a second honeymoon. Try—'

'No, Andrew. I might, in time, forgive you, but I can never trust you again. We're separated and I want a divorce.'

'God, I'm not ready for that.'

'Perhaps you should have considered that earlier before making a conscious choice to cheat.' I instantly regret saying it. 'Sorry.'

'For crying out loud.' His walks away, his hands covering his face. He wipes his eyes and turns back. 'What do we do now? Do you want to move back in? I can leave.'

Holly Cottage is no longer my home. 'To be honest, it's tarnished. I'm comfortable where I am, thanks. You may as well stay. Please don't bring any women here, no matter what. This is still our joint house.'

'Of course not.' He follows me into the kitchen.

What will you do about Leticia?'

He shrugs. 'No idea. She won't accept my apology. What will you do about him – Jack?'

'Although I do like him a lot, believe it or not I'm still reeling from all of this. With my life in tatters I'm hardly ready to embark on another relationship. You'll move on before I ever will.' I scoop up my coat and bag.

'We'll need to discuss selling the cottage and…and other stuff in the New Year.'

Andrew shakes his head. 'If I could turn the clock back…'

'Do your next love-interest a favour, Andrew, either you're in the relationship or you're not. You can't be married and single at the same time. Maxwell while you were seeing Leticia? Really? You couldn't even be faithful to your mistress.' His mouth opens as if to protest, but he closes it again and his feet become interesting. 'And I think Leticia means more to you than you're ready to admit. I don't think you want to let her go.'

Without kissing him, even for old times' sake, I leave and go to my car.

As I drive away, I know he'll probably be straight on the phone to Leticia. It's over. Time to make my own plans. Begin again.

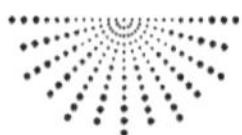

CHAPTER TWENTY-FOUR

The next day, as it's Sunday, and having had breakfast with Jo and Hector on their insistence, I decide to take Duchess for her long walk. The weather is frosty and cold but the sun is shining as it has done the last few days. Wearing thick boots, long thick cardigan, parka, bobble hat, gloves and scarf, I might not look the height of fashion, but I won't freeze.

As I'm leaving, Jo runs along the hall, catching me by the side door, and says breathlessly, 'Caught you. Gosh, you walk fast. Wanted to let you know, I have it on good authority Jack's at home…all day.'

Shaking my head, I laugh and reply, 'Thanks. I'll call on him in that case.' Hector had mentioned Jack at breakfast and I'd remarked that I should speak to him as he shouldn't feel he must stay away from Winterford House on my behalf. Jo or Hector phoned him no doubt to ensure I wouldn't change my mind. Remembering my less than groovy attire, I think what the hell, this is me. From now on what you see is what you get.

'You have a life, Randa,' Jo says. 'Start living it. It's been on hold for months.'

In other words, move on. I don't want to contradict her when she's been so supportive by replying it must be in my own time. So, I give her a kiss and slip out the door.

Not wishing to seem too eager and as the hoar frost is glistening on the shrubs and trees, turning the garden into virtual fairyland, Duchess and I stroll around the grounds first.

Duchess is well behaved, so I let her off her lead and let her roam at will, and she takes me down narrow paths, through woods, along by the river and back up to the walled garden. Pushing open the stiff door, I venture in. The garden hasn't escaped the fierce cold and has a coating of silver-white. A splash of red in the corner, close to the wall, attracts my eye, and I stroll over to find a single red rose, tired but alive, free of the sparkling frost, gladdening my heart, and I fix it back closer to the wall to further protect it.

When we eventually come back to the estate gate, we exit and saunter towards Lower Winterford. The tarmaced surface is slippery and I tread carefully. Several people are out walking and greet us as we pass.

The Winterfords are a friendly group of villages and I hope my new house, when I find one, will be in such a place. Holly Cottage is in a lovely setting, but is outside Ashford. Perhaps Andrew was right about the isolation.

All too quickly we arrive outside Jack's house. At first, I hesitate, but Duchess barks at a cat further up the road and Jack must hear her as he glances out of the window before disappearing. Either that or Jo phoned him and he's expecting me. My stomach turns over. It's strange how one man can cause my stomach to churn with hurt and fear while another causes it to churn with shyness and anticipation.

The door opens, but as I am about to step onto the path, my feet slip from under me and I land hard on my bum. The extra padding I'm wearing helps cushion the fall, but how embarrassing. Jack hurries down the path, but just as he reaches down to me, he slips and lands partly on top of me, his hands ending up on my boobs.

'Feeling me up again?' I say.

'I go to great pains when you fall to do just that,' he replies, removing his hands. 'Anyway, it's hard to feel anything through all your armour.' Duchess circles Jack in excitement as he sits up, wagging her tail. He tries to catch her lead. 'Are you all right?'

'In one piece though a trifle cold and a little bruised here and there. And you?'

'Same. I must put more salt down here.' He struggles to his feet and steps sideways onto the grass, holding out his hand to pull me up. We both brush ourselves down, laughing. 'Come on in,' he says matter-of-factly. 'You can help me with this damned tree. Usually, I leave it to Sophie but she's helping her mum in the pub.'

As we walk along the hallway, I glance into rooms and

see the house looks great and smells of fresh paint, but there's a lot to work to do to get it completely finished and furnished. He explains he'll do it gradually when I praise it, then adds, 'Glad you approve.' Once he helps divest me of all my outdoor gear, he offers me a cocoa.

While we're waiting for the milk to warm, Jack puts a bowl of water down for Duchess and gestures to me to take a seat at the table. 'Hot drink first, then the tree,' he says. 'How are you settling in at Winterford house? Jo says you're bearing up well.'

'Feeling a bit lost. And, yes, Hector and Jo couldn't be more welcoming. Still, I do feel I'm intruding on the lovers, so in the New Year, once the cottage goes up for sale, I'll find a place of my own.'

'Chester?'

'I decided not to as all my clients are here and I need to earn a living. Andrew expected me to go to Chester, but why should I? My best friend, my work, my home, they're all here. Though my home will be sold. Yes, there's Mum, but she has Steve now.'

Jack pours the steaming milk into two mugs and gives them a good stir before bringing them over to the table and sitting opposite me. I tell him most of what transpired at Holly Cottage yesterday. Missing out the part about the lingerie and admitting liking Jack.

I finish with saying Andrew has accepted the separation and coming divorce. 'So I'll go my way,' I add, 'and Andrew, will go his.' I gulp.

'A difficult time ahead. I haven't forgotten how

stressful and upsetting that is. Acceptance is the first step.'

'I'm there already. Andrew might take a little longer.'

'That helps. Took me a long time, I'll admit. But then it all happened out the blue. On my part, anyway.'

'While I saw it coming months ago and was just delaying the inevitable, hoping he would tell the truth.'

'And all the time he—'

'Was investigating me. It's so ridiculous, it's hysterical.' I laugh heartily and Jack joins in.

'Come and help me. Sophie is very critical, just like her mother. The tree has to be perfect even though she's likely to spend five minutes here now there's a boyfriend on the scene. Stephanie is dropping her off later. By the way, Stephanie said to tell you to call in on her soon. She's sure you could do with a chat as could she.'

'Yes, I will in the New Year when it's quieter.'

In the sitting room the tree sits half bare and a bit of a mess. 'Let's start again,' I suggest.

Once stripped and only the lights remain, I take over, making suggestions over the placement of baubles and ribbon. It's fun and soon the tree looks fabulous.

'Are you spending Christmas at Winterford House,' asks Jack.

'With Mum and Steve, but I'll be relieved when it's all over. I've no idea how Andrew intends spending Christmas.'

'May I ask what you told him about our kiss when he confronted you?'

'I told him it was our first kiss. And…I admitted I like you.'

'Our first kiss, hmm.' Not reacting in the slightest, Jack climbs onto a stool, and as he puts the star on top of the tree, he says, 'Holding you in my arms that day at the gallery, that first kiss, do you know how that affected me?' He straightens the star, then jumping down, turns to me. Here…' He points to his stomach. 'And here…' He points to his head. 'And here…' He points to his heart. 'My own feelings are deeper than mere like, but I've told you already. What about you? Is it like-like, or plain…like?'

I smile shyly. 'Yes, it's like-like. But I must be honest, I can't embark on a new relationship right now. I need to sort my head out. Heal. There's still the divorce, the cottage to sell, and a new home to find.' Duchess nuzzles my hand. 'But on the good side, at least I get custody of Duchess. That's not in question.'

Jack steps closer to me and holds my arms, staring earnestly into my face. 'I understand. But did you know I'm the most patient person on earth? If you want me to wait that is.'

Having resigned myself to the prospect that Jack and I could never be, this takes me by surprise. How long would he wait? Long enough for me to establish I'm not, in my desperation, heading to any port in a storm? Seeking refuge in Jack to lessen the ache? And say I am doing those things?

He reads my mind. 'For however long. And even if in

the meantime you change your mind, I'll happily take that risk.'

'I think I'd like that. If you're sure.'

He takes my hand and kisses the inside of my wrist, sending flutters into the depth of my belly. Spontaneously, my hands sweep up to him, pulling on his neck, bringing his face closer to mine. His arms come around me and he kisses me gently but deeply, and it reaches to my core, shaking me. And I respond and sink into him as our kiss deepens into a hot passion. I breathe in the scent of him, his aftershave. Savour the sensation of his lips, soft and warm on mine. Enjoy the shivers running through my body, making me feel alive again. My hands are in his hair, his are kneading my back, my spine sensitive to his touch, and I want to climb inside him.

We let go, breathless, Duchess separating us by wriggling in between. I step away, knowing that the future no longer stretches out so emptily before me.

'Jealous boots,' I say. We make a fuss of Duchess, both feeling self-conscious.

Jack at last steals a glance at me, and I touch his arm and smile sadly, letting him know that this kiss, regrettably, must last us for some time. His returning smile is gentle and reassuring, but also happy. We've sealed our intentions. That's enough for us both for now.

For now.

Thank you for reading. If you enjoyed *The Trouble with Cake*, please consider leaving a review on your favourite online store.

COMING SOON IN 2019 FROM MAJELLA JAMES

Don't miss the second book in the Cake trilogy
Another Slice of Cake

Majella James was born in Liverpool and has additionally lived in the Netherlands, Belgium and Ireland, eventually settling on the edge of the Cotswolds UK with her husband and their three cats. She loves writing, nature, and walking in the countryside.

Having had an interest in writing since she was a child, Majella went on to study English and Writing to post graduate level in Liverpool and Bath. For the past eleven years, she has worked for a mid-list publishing company. She is the author of several Mind Body Spirit books and a children's novel under different pen names and has written for national and international magazines.

Now that she has taken a step back from publishing, Majella has returned to her first love, writing fiction. *The Trouble with Cake* is the first book in the *Cake* trilogy.

ACKNOWLEDGEMENTS

I have so many people to thank. Family and friends first for being there for me and for various contributions to the story: A big thanks to Rick, my ever-patient husband and knight in shining armour. To my son Mikey (and partner John) and sister Diane (and husband Brian) for their contributions and humour, and also the children and their partners Glenn and Nancy, Owen, Rosemarie and Anthony, James and Hollie, and Tanya, for various helpful input and encouragement. Not forgetting sister Francesca, Beryl and Kerrie. And a special thanks goes to my dear friend Krystina. Love you all.

Others to thank for their encouragement are my friend Darcie and friend and neighbour Ann and husband 'PITA' Chris. So much encouragement came from 20BooksTo50k® and The Writing Gals that they deserve a massive thank you. There are many other people who have helped, often without even realising it. Too many to mention here. Thank you all.